'After reading this first novel I believe that Anthony Heal has laid claim to being admitted to that small band of accomplished British thriller writers. His approach is fresh, his characters realistic and his dialogue alive ... compelling'
Police Review

'Mr Heal has worked for nine years with the Metropolitan C.I.D. and his experience has given stark realism to his novel about a crime fighter hired to infiltrate rival gangs and set them against each other. Exciting first novel.'
Yorkshire Evening Post

'Some marvellously atmospheric reading ... guaranteed to hold interest'
Paperback & Popular Hardback Buyer

The Decimate Decision

ANTHONY HEAL

SPHERE BOOKS LIMITED
30/32 Gray's Inn Road, London WC1X 8JL

First published in Great Britain by
W. H. Allen & Company Limited 1979
Copyright © 1979 by Anthony Heal
Published by Sphere Books Ltd 1982

Printed and bound in Great Britain by
Cox & Wyman Ltd, Reading

Chapter One

The awakening was like most others – neutral light gradually strengthening to colour, within a narrow spectrum. Grey dominated. The only brighter intrusion came from a small window. Even that was muted, dingy, a view through a dirty kaleidoscope.

Bellman coughed and tasted the previous night's drink. Nothing unique. He fumbled for cigarettes and lit one, automatically grimacing at its foulness. A scattering of coins lay on the unpainted bedside locker. Thirty-two pence. He knew that was all he had. Blind drunk, habit still safely conveyed his total finances from pocket to bedside.

Pushing himself into a sitting position he caught his own smell. Everything was right. Perhaps today would be the day. Only the courage was missing.

'A bottle of courage, chemist, to go with the pills.'

'Sorry, sir, we don't stock it.'

'Then you're a prat. You'd make a fortune.'

He had not heard the door open but suddenly she was beside the bed, glaring down at him.

'Don't you ever knock?' he asked.

She ignored the question, replacing it with her own. 'Talking to yourself, were you?'

Bellman groaned and closed his sleep-crusted eyes. 'No there's a big-titted blonde in here with me. What do you want? It's not rent day.' He opened his eyes quickly, 'Is it?'

'You know very well it's not,' she said angrily.

He groaned again, the day already complete. Another hassle with the revolting Mrs Clarke.

'It's the last time,' she said, arms folded, large breasts squeezing between chunky wrists.

'What is?' He was forced to play the game.

'Last night.'

'What about it?'

'You were drunk again.'

He risked the light and opened his eyes. 'But I'm always drunk.'

'Yes and last night was the last time.'

'It wasn't, I promise,' he said.

'The last time you come in *here* drunk, I mean.'

Bellman stubbed out the cigarette and made to fling back the sheets. She usually fled at this juncture, but this time she stood her ground.

'I mean it. If you're not out of here by four, I'll call the police.' She turned and flounced to the door. 'Out by four o'clock.' The door slammed.

Bellman yelled, 'I've paid for the bloody week!'

The door opened a crack and three pound notes fluttered to the floor. Savage old bitch. She would not have refunded anything unless he had reminded her.

He lit another cigarette. It tasted as bad as the first. The pound notes lay on the floor where they had fallen. Like everything else, they were creased and dirty.

The interlude with Mrs Clarke had occupied him for a time. Now he felt sick and hopeless again.

Getting out of bed caused the usual upheaval in head and stomach. The trip to the bathroom was perilous, but he made it in time to vomit into the bowl. He did not bother to shave, sluicing his face with cold water instead. The half-hearted action with the tooth-brush seemed pointless. His gums were numb.

He was at the front door, suitcase in hand, when Mrs Clarke opened the door of her own flat. 'I've got others to consider,' she said.

Bellman said, 'Bollocks,' and walked down the steps to the street.

It cost thirty pence to lodge the suitcase. He always used the left-luggage office at Victoria coach station. It was cheaper.

The walk to the pub only took a few minutes. In the lounge the barman looked pointedly at his creased clothes and stubbled chin, but he served the whisky Bellman ordered without comment.

Only a pound note and some odd coins remained before the merest hint of a glow warmed him. His brain began to function. He looked at his watch. Past midday. Fowley would be expecting him in an hour. Three quid for the afternoon. An afternoon of watching layabout bastards coming and going from the scrap-yard, making sure they did not nick anything on the way out.

After an hour he did not know if he had enough money left to pay for another drink, but he was not particularly worried. The fresh intake had finally joined hands with the previous day's and his senses were thickening. If necessary he would see Fowley and sub from him. Stuff the work.

The barman slid a whisky to him reluctantly, eyes flickering to the man beside Bellman in explanation. Bellman turned jerkily to look at his benefactor. The man raised his glass in a small salute.

'Fellow travellers.'

Bellman left the drink untouched. 'I'm not going anywhere.'

The man was tall. His grey suit, flecked with a darker mixture, was immaculate. The hair was fair, almost white, trimmed close to the sides of his head. He waited to see if Bellman changed his mind then shrugged and reached for the glass.

Bellman's hand easily out-distanced the other's long, searching fingers. 'Don't be hasty,' he drained the glass. 'Do I know you?'

'Does it matter?'

Bellman said, 'Not if you're paying.'

The stranger motioned to the barman and indicated the glasses. 'Doubles.'

'I may have something for you,' the man said quietly, glancing along the counter. 'Would you like to move to somewhere less public?'

Bellman struggled upright. 'Don't mind. Somewhere with drink?' He sagged against the grey suit as he finished the whisky.

'Of course,' the man said. Though obviously embarrassed by Bellman's leaning he made no reproaches as he steered a course for the door.

Bellman registered the car ride only because he hated such journeys when he was drunk. Seasoned as he was, the jolting always threatened to unleash his stomach. He half-registered being helped from the car and the upward surge of a silent elevator, then further helping hands. He had no difficulty in recognising the familiar feel of a glass when it was pressed into his palm. The chair he was guided to was exceptionally comfortable.

The room seemed very high-ceilinged and the furniture was two miles away on the other side of the floor. Everything looked old, antique.

Bellman drank deeply and attempted to focus on the man who had invited him there. He failed but he heard him say, 'Drink up, Bellman.'

Bellman tilted his glass obediently, then said, 'There, I was sure you knew me.' A bottle gurgled in the background and his glass grew heavier. A hand encircled his own, lifting the drink up until the rim of the glass touched his lips. He sucked for a time then stopped. The whisky dribbled over his chin, forming a river which ran down his neck before soaking into the collar of his shirt. When Bellman slumped sideways he was only dimly aware of a blow to the side of his head as it met the edge of a table.

A voice said, 'Bellman!' with studied contempt.

4

Another voice said, 'Yes.' The tone was neutral, disinterested.

The man with the fair hair said, 'Delivered as requested.'

Bellman heard none of the remarks. His body was jerking spasmodically, its safety system attempting to eject the excess alcohol. Bile streamed from his mouth, descending the inch or so to the carpet where his head rested. The front of his trousers darkened slowly as urine escaped in a restricted flow.

Chapter Two

Something was different. Everything was different. The light was bright – no greys.

Bellman closed his eyes. Even then the glare penetrated his eyelids. He ran a dry tongue over his lips. The dryness was normal. But the taste? There was no whisky aftermath, no vomit echo. He tasted ... hygienic.

His brain struggled. Thoughts tumbled, collided. There was a rushing sound in his ears. Even the noise was clean. No muzziness.

An accident. This was a hospital. He tentatively opened his eyes and tried to focus. After several attempts he achieved a degree of success.

The bed he lay in was narrow, the linen stretched tight across his chest, hospital fashion. The coverlet was patterned, no hospital uniformity here. Above, the ceiling was white, supported by walls patterned in green and gold. There was no equipment; no terrible metal stands or clamps; no saline drips.

A gentle experiment of movement failed to produce the tearing agony he half-expected, but the small effort tired him. He closed his eyes and slept.

When he woke again the light was fiercer and he realised he was staring at a neon strip. He turned his head but kept his eyes open, content to take in the immediate view: a chair and a small cabinet, and further back the double doors of a built-in wardrobe.

A voice said, 'You're back with us then?'

Bellman stayed motionless, attempting to identify the voice before turning. Nothing.

A white coat appeared, obscuring the wardrobe. Bellman turned his eyes upwards. The wearer of the coat was stocky, dark, pleasant-looking. There was no stethoscope badge.

An ancient sense of politeness made Bellman struggle to sit up.

Without fuss the white-coated man assisted him.

Bellman tried a smile. 'I've got to say it. What happened?'

The smile in response was an appreciation, tinged with relief. 'It *is* traditional.' The speaker moved towards the door. 'I'll bring some tea and a little food. See if you can manage it.'

'You haven't answered my question,' Bellman said.

'Eat first. Gather your senses. It will take time to acclimatise. It's a whole new world for you.' The words were kindly with no hint of sarcasm.

'It is the same world?'

'Yes. It's just a few days older than when you last knew it.'

The man disappeared and Bellman surveyed the room again. This time it seemed warmer. He decided it was because the curtains were drawn; heavy, green drapes which matched the wall covering.

In front of the curtains there was a small desk with a modern steel-frame chair tucked into the leg recess. A chair identical to the one near the small cabinet stood on the other side of the bed. There was nothing else.

The door opened and the man in the white coat backed into the room, holding the door with one foot to prevent it sweeping away the bridge-tray he carried. He smiled at Bellman as he placed the tray across the bed. 'Manage?'

Bellman looked at the tray and nodded. His intention to ask some direct questions dissolved at the sight of the tea and food. He could not recall the last time he had felt hungry. Thirsty – yes. And why did he not need a drink? A proper drink?

The man stood at the half-opened door. 'Sure you'll be all right?'

Bellman said, 'Yes, thanks,' and reached for the mug of tea. There was a bowl of soup and a non-invalid gammon rasher, thick-cut, covering most of the plate. A smaller plate held a pile of buttered toast. He ignored the soup and attacked the meat, pausing only to drink from the mug, or take occasional bites from the toast which was still warm. Half-way through the gammon his hunger faded, disappearing altogether before he had finished it. He left what remained and drained the mug.

Habit, as much as need, made him search for cigarettes. He found a new packet in the drawer of the bedside cabinet. His own lighter lay beside it. He lit up and drew tentatively, remembering his new, hygiene-infested body. The taste brought back a memory, an almost forgotten, sharp flavour, unimpaired by continuous abuse. He even felt slightly light-headed.

The combination of food, warmth and the comforting presence of a cigarette had a soporific effect. His eyelids drooped before the cigarette was completely used up. He stubbed it out and was asleep before the last strand of smoke reached the ceiling.

Within seconds he was awake again, roused by the revolt of some unconscious mechanism. What the hell was happening? Why was he eating? How had he arrived in this sterile, comfortable place?

He looked around for a means of summoning someone who could answer the questions crowding in on him, but there was nothing. No bell. No dangling cord to relay flashing lights. With a hint of desperation he grabbed the metal ash tray and banged it violently against the cabinet. His raised hand was halted in mid-air by the opening of the door.

The one who had brought his food looked in and said, 'What is it?'

'Who are you?' Bellman asked.

'Me, sir? Why do you want to know that?'

Bellman's temper rose. 'I don't really give a shit who you are but I want to know what's going on.'

The man nodded understandingly. 'If you'll just wait for a while, sir, someone will come to see you.'

'Who?'

'Please,' the other held up his hand. 'Be patient, it won't be long.'

Bellman subsided. 'Tell whoever it is that it had better be soon.'

The door closed quietly. Bellman put the ash tray down and closed his eyes.

'I'm told you're making your presence felt,' the voice said.

Bellman surfaced slowly. He did not immediately recognise the voice but his senses flashed a warning, a transmission of aggression, controlled but definite. He opened his eyes and saw a pair of well-pressed trousers. Upwards there was an equally smart jacket, with pallid hands hanging from the cuffs.

Then the face. Kitholm's face.

But that could not be. He hated Kitholm. The last person he was likely to see again was Kitholm. Yet there he was beside the bed. It was like awakening from a nightmare to find the dream was fact.

Kitholm had not changed. His face was still as rounded and white as ever. And it still contained the incredible eyes; dark sloes of vision which could sneer without assistance from curled lips. The podgy nose and small, petulant mouth were no different. Even the neatly trimmed hair was exactly as Bellman remembered it. The inevitable brief-case dangled from one hand.

'What in the name of fuck are you doing here?' Bellman snarled.

Kitholm's face relaxed into a mirthless smile. He lifted the chair from beside the cabinet, swinging it to face the bed before sitting down in a smooth, controlled movement. The brief-case he lodged beside his feet.

'I'm glad you're the same,' he said. 'I was worried.'

9

'You'll be a bloody sight more worried in a moment if you don't tell me what's going on.'

'That is why I'm here.'

Bellman remained silent and waited. Infuriatingly he wanted to urinate. A natural function, but one that Kitholm, without word or movement, was capable of deriding if he became aware of it.

'Well, how do you feel?' Kitholm said, accompanying the question with a light slap on his knee.

'Weak. Otherwise – all right.'

'That's hardly surprising, you've been without food for some time.'

'How long?'

'Two days,' Kitholm said, watching to see what effect the answer would have. Bellman's face was a study of unsurprised interest.

Kitholm shifted his position gently and said, 'Or drink.'

'What?'

'Drink. You've had no drink for two days either. Alcohol, I mean.'

Bellman felt his blood quicken and knew Kitholm was getting to him. 'Then you'd better hurry up and get me one,' he said.

Kitholm's smile was superior. 'You wouldn't want it.'

'So what's happened? Some sort of treatment?'

'Yes.'

Bellman thrust his face towards Kitholm. 'Whatever's been done to me, Kitholm, had better be of short duration.'

'It won't last,' Kitholm promised, fluttering a hand in a well-remembered gesture.

Bellman's patience evaporated rapidly. 'Then WHY?' he shouted.

Kitholm leaned back and made a bridge with his hands. 'Ah! Now that's the question.' He appeared reluctant to continue. After savouring the tense bond for a further few seconds, he said, 'Do you remember where I went when I left the Yard?'

Bellman shrugged. 'No. As far as I know you were seconded to some government department – Home Office or something similar. Kicked upstairs, were you?' When Kitholm did not answer, he said, 'Still Detective Chief Inspector? That must hurt.'

Kitholm sighed. 'Bellman, just for once couldn't you forget the past? Forget your dislike of me?'

'Hatred.'

'All right – hatred. I assure you, I have to control my feelings where you're concerned.'

Bellman managed a laugh. 'Come on now, Kitholm, you're slipping. Admitting that you hate someone. That's not in the book of rules, surely.' He jerked his head in simulated surprise. 'Don't tell me you no longer follow the rulebook.'

Kitholm shook his head sadly. 'Time certainly hasn't changed your opinion of those who favour a conventional line. I thought that your ... unfortunate tragedy would have given you more to think about than remembering old dislikes. The accident was no fault of yours. It's a pity that the aftermath has been your complete disintegration.'

Bellman struggled with the bedclothes, attempting to swing his feet clear of the bed. 'Listen to me you ...'

Kitholm jerked his head. 'No, Bellman, you've had your turn, now listen to me.'

Bellman drew back, surprised by the violence of Kitholm's reaction.

'You lost your wife in a terrible accident,' Kitholm said. 'I'm sorry. Obviously you thought a lot of her. Anyone in your position would be upset – distraught, in fact, but you cannot go on blaming the world for ever. Sometime you have to accept that what happened was an accident – a tragic one admittedly, but purely one of life's injustices. Not you, though. Oh no. Public breast-beating was the order of the day and everyone suffered. In the last year of your service you had more help than even you know about.' He paused to glare defiantly at Bellman. 'Yes, from me too. You were given more cover-ups than I care to remember.' His voice dropped slightly. 'Finally it was impossible. No-one wanted to see you go, but there was no way you could be kept on. If you had not resigned there would have been a charge. The ultimatum didn't have to be spelled out.'

Bellman was still in the position he had adopted at the beginning of Kitholm's tirade: legs half-out of the bed-covers, knees drawn up to his chest, one hand poised in mid-air.

Kitholm and the trappings of the room disappeared and once again he was in the mortuary, looking down at Sandy his wife. Sandy the vibrant. The laughing girl. His love. Beautiful. Except she was no longer beautiful. This Sandy had the same dark hair which belied her name, but the roots were caked with blood. And one side of her face was missing. Not actually missing, but compacted into a shapeless mass. On the untouched side of her face the remaining eye was dull as though coated with dust. It looked at him. And he had gone crazy.

A hit-and-run. Some bastard had transformed his wife into a statistic – and stayed free.

Bellman's body shook with the frenzy that often overcame him when he thought of Sandy. When the spasm was over he focused his eyes on Kitholm who was watching him curiously. The possibility of Kitholm being prey to the emotion of sympathy was beyond Bellman's comprehension, but at that moment he could almost believe it to be true.

Kitholm shook his head wearily. 'It's partly because of your attitude that you have been chosen, but that doesn't make it easier to explain.'

'Chosen?'

'Yes,' Kitholm said. 'Before continuing, however, I should tell you that in here,' he tapped the brief-case by his feet, 'I have a file devoted to you. Properly I should read directly from it. In deference to your aversion to listening to formal words, I propose giving you a résumé.' He leaned back and closed his eyes.

12

Knowing that Kitholm would enjoy demonstrating his retentive memory, Bellman was tempted to demand that the file should be read out in full, but he resisted the thought, realising that a summary would take less time.

'Michael Bellman, aged thirty-six, born Nottingham, no surviving parents,' Kitholm began. 'Received secondary education in home town to the age of fifteen years, took up employment in an engineering factory immediately after leaving school and stayed there until joining the army at the age of eighteen years. Trained with an infantry regiment in England before being posted to the Far East where he volunteered for the Special Air Service. Came through the stringent training of that particular outfit with flying colours. Served total of six years in the army, the early ones in the Orient. Involved in several engagements with terrorists in eastern trouble-spots, acquitting himself well.'

He opened his eyes a fraction. 'The SAS appear reluctant to hand out plaudits, but a confidential note records that you were responsible for the deaths of a considerable number of bandits.' He closed his eyes again and said musingly, 'In areas that were supposedly free of the problem too.'

Bellman lit a cigarette and expelled smoke in a violent gust. 'I killed several raggy-arsed little yellow men who were fighting for something they believed in; tough little sods who lived off the land – something we found hard to do – but don't be kidded by the facts you've picked up. Mainly we killed from ambush. Slaughtered.'

'But you killed efficiently,' Kitholm murmured.

'Anyone who takes another's life kills efficiently.'

Kitholm's eyelids flickered briefly, then he nodded and went on, 'When you left the army you returned to your home town and worked for some months as a builder's labourer. In nineteen sixty-seven you joined the Metropolitan Police, served two years as a uniformed officer before appointment as a trainee detective. You were confirmed a CID officer in nineteen seventy.'

He paused and coughed. When he continued his voice

was lower. 'You married in May nineteen seventy-one and were promoted to sergeant in nineteen seventy-two. Immediately after promotion you were taken off divisional work and sent to the Yard where you achieved considerable success in an undercover capacity with certain specialist teams ...'

'Why the recital?' Bellman interrupted. 'I didn't know you knew the details of my army service, but the rest, if not exactly public knowledge, is certainly ...'

Kitholm held up a hand. 'I have to go through everything – confirm. Those are my instructions.'

Bellman turned his head away in disgust and drew on the cigarette.

'In September nineteen seventy-five,' Kitholm ploughed on, 'your wife was killed in a motor accident. Thereafter you deteriorated rapidly. All aspects of your work suffered. After frequent warnings about your insobriety you resigned from the police in August nineteen seventy-six. Since then you have been irregularly employed as a barman, labourer, watchman, and work of a like nature.' He straightened his back and stared fixedly at Bellman. 'There is a notation at the bottom of the report. I can give it verbatim. Would you like to hear it?'

'If it helps you get your rocks off.'

'Subject affected by wife's death to such an extent that previous life-mode impossible to regain. Probable suicidal tendencies.'

Bellman looked at him with something near amusement. 'Am I supposed to be impressed?'

'You agree it's an accurate description of your life to date?'

Bellman was tired of the whole business, but too lethargic to be agressive. 'Accurate, inaccurate. Who cares?'

Kitholm's mouth puckered and he regarded Bellman closely. 'Are you up-to-date with news in general?' He paused. 'What I mean is, have you kept up with events during your retreat?'

'Retreat? What bloody retreat? I'm no monk. No, I haven't "kept up with things" as you put it. The world's full of crap and there's no justice, sense or God. That I know without reading the newspapers. As for my so-called retreat – that's my business. If I want to get pissed – I get pissed.'

'Every day?'

'As it happens – yes. What's to stop me?'

Kitholm blew out his cheeks. 'Under the circumstances I suppose you have been reasonably patient. Now we come to the point of all this.'

'Thank Christ for that,' Bellman said, 'but you'll have to hold on a minute. Where's the bathroom?'

'Out the door, first on the right.'

Bellman made it to the door without buckling on his rubbery legs. In the corridor outside, the white-coated individual was examining a picture on the wall. He turned and smiled as Bellman entered the bathroom. Bellman nodded as he closed the door.

The bathroom was small. No window. He used the lavatory then examined himself in the long mirror on the wall. The first thing that struck him was that he was wearing pyjamas, something he had not found unusual earlier. Now he recalled that it was a long time since he had troubled with sleeping-wear.

The mirror was long enough to reflect all of his five feet ten inches. His brown hair was tousled, but it appeared to be finer, cleaner than normal. Heavy drinking had failed to fatten his face, but the skin usually carried a degree of puffiness which was now missing. His eyes still retained the deadness of apathy, but the whites no longer had the delta-land of bloodshot veins running through them. He ran his fingers down the line of his straight nose, finishing the journey with a scrub over the bristle of his chin. Finally he opened his mouth and examined his teeth. They were all there.

He let himself out and returned to where Kitholm waited.

Chapter Three

'So you're not in touch with the local situation?' Kitholm said as Bellman settled himself into the bed.

'Where is local? That's another thing ...'

'Wait,' Kitholm said, getting to his feet and pacing the room. 'A little more patience, Bellman, please. You will understand everything shortly. By local situation I mean the criminal goings-on in London.'

Bellman laughed cynically. 'I'm not really up-to-date, no. I haven't been interested, but I suppose the usual things are happening – thieves are thieving, murderers are killing, and toe-rags with connections are getting away with whatever they're doing.'

Kitholm nodded. 'It doesn't change.' He made a tour of the room before speaking again. 'Before you ... left you must have formed an opinion of how things were going – from the police point of view.'

'Yeah. Badly.'

'Well,' Kitholm's lips tightened. 'Not exactly badly – but with difficulty.'

'Was it ever simple?'

'No, but for a time it became a little easier as far as big-time crime was concerned. After the gang-busting operations.'

'Maybe,' Bellman said uninterestedly.

Kitholm dropped heavily into his chair. 'There was a lull after the big firms took their heavy knocks – the Twins, Richardsons and so on. With no aspirants for the vacant leaderships organised crime was virtually non-existent. Occasionally, of course, a decent-sized blag or high-jacking

16

made the headlines, but no single organisation was responsible for the many diverse crimes. The clear-up rate proved that. In fact, success from the police viewpoint came on an unprecedented scale. I'm only speaking of the big stuff, I remind you. The overall crime figures climbed as steadily as ever.' He fell silent.

Bellman said nothing; he did not wish to do anything which might delay Kitholm's explanation. In the last few minutes he had been experiencing a strange feeling. His body was troubling him, but he could not identify what was wrong. He had a craving. Normally a drink would have been the answer but, incredibly, the well-known urge for one was absent. Instead, the need for *something* consumed his whole frame. Small pin-pricks stabbed at the veins in his arms and legs and his head felt heavy. But the main problem was centred in his stomach. A continuous straining of internal muscles begged for relief. When Kitholm showed no inclination to continue, Bellman tried to restart the conversation by saying, 'As I remember it there were rumbles of large-scale dark doings just before I resigned.'

Kitholm's head pecked in agreement. 'Yes, and "rumbles" is an appropriate word. No one *knew*. It was only when the complete picture was viewed that it became obvious that *something* had happened – was happening.'

'The view coincided with a fall-off in the clear-up rate, I suppose?' Bellman said caustically.

'Of course,' Kitholm said unperturbed. 'Things became difficult. The presence of organised crime was a fact once again, and we were ill-equipped to deal with it. As you well know, the clean-up campaign under Robert Mark was something much needed by the Metropolitan force, but it did a lot of damage too. Detectives who had previously lived for their work found themselves tight-bound with rules. Morale sank so low it was almost non-existent. All in all the campaign salvaged public trust ...' he held up his hand as Bellman made to interrupt, '... it also effectively sapped the strength of the CID. Men who had never considered a crooked deal were looked upon with suspicion. Of course, the move was a necessary one, but finally it defeated its own object by its thoroughness and lack of compromise. A snow-white force ensured that thieves were dealt with to the letter of the law – it also meant that information dried up. Officers refused to take chances, the rule-book became king, and the villains thought it was Christmas every day.'

Kitholm tapped his own chest. 'That's me talking, Bellman. The man who welcomed the new order. It failed.' He got to his feet again and resumed his restless pacing. 'It was soon obvious that the new criminal management was something entirely different. Crimes were being committed by the usual criminal types, naturally, and the operational side retained its old image, but the method of financing each caper was hidden – as was the eventual destination of the major share of the loot.'

'You must have had some success in finding out who was responsible,' Bellman said, 'otherwise you wouldn't even know that much.'

'Oh, indeed we did,' Kitholm said, coming to a halt and raising a finger. 'But not by the usual methods. When the conventional lines of communication proved ineffective, and the new criminal order, if allowed to go unchecked, showed every sign of eventually threatening the very economy of the country, it was decided that a specialist department was needed to combat the menace.'

'Tell me something new,' Bellman sneered. 'Encounter a different kind of problem – form a squad, create a new department, another little empire for someone to lord it over. That answer is as old as ...'

'Not this time,' Kitholm broke in. 'No, this time it was recognised that drastic counter-measures were of prime importance, not just an efficient investigation.' He returned to the chair, plumping down heavily again, stretching his legs before him when he was seated. 'It was decided by a very high authority,' his eyes flickered briefly over Bellman, 'a *very* high authority,' he repeated emphatically, 'to con-duct, in the first place, an investigation that would not be hampered by procedural strictures.' He moved his shoulders slightly and a touch of colour invaded his neck. 'As an experienced detective, I was chosen to participate. There is a staff – not police officers, apart from myself – and considerable back-up assistance available. I am second-in-command. My immediate superior is answerable only to a Government Minister.' He paused and waited for Bellman to comment.

'Big deal,' was all that Bellman offered. The stomach cramps were intensifying, creasing his gut so that he was forced to bend to ease the pain.

Kitholm's eyes flared briefly, then he continued in the same level tone. 'I was not exaggerating when I said that the economy of the country could be affected by the new menace. Normally only a massive fraud directed at the Bank of England or against government bonds would have that kind of effect, but general crime, if centrally controlled, could also be a serious problem. Think about it.'

Bellman had closed his eyes. 'I don't want to,' he said.

'The powers invested in us,' Kitholm said, a catch of ex-citement in his voice, 'are absolutely unprecedented. Every kind of surveillance technique is ours for the asking. More importantly, facilities which an ordinary investigative team would never dare to ask for are readily available: in-depth run-downs on any individual we care to name; unlimited access to company dealings; immediate permission to place an intercept on any telephone we wish ...'

'Hello, Big Brother,' Bellman murmured.

Kitholm responded with a vigorous shake of his head. 'Not at all. The department only employs those with a high security clearance, and once the emergency is over all the usual restrictions will once again apply. In any case, it is justifiable. With the freedom granted us we know practi-cally all there is to know about the new crime lords. I should warn you, though, Bellman, I have told you a good deal about how the evidence has been assembled, but do not press for more information. You won't be given it.'

'Kitholm,' Bellman said wearily, 'I don't know why you're telling me all this. As a matter of fact I find it very hard to believe – coming from you. No matter, it sounds as though you and your boys have done a grand job discovering who the bad guys are. Now go out and bring them in.'

'Ah!' Kitholm said. 'If only it were that easy. Some of the names that have come up are extremely well-known.'

'That doesn't mean they're immune from prosecution.'

'True, but knowing they are guilty is one thing; producing *admissible* evidence is something else.'

'Then you're in the crap house,' Bellman said with satisfaction.

'No, we're not ... beaten,' Kitholm said. 'The answer to the problem was devised at the outset. It would take years of formal investigations and drawn-out prosecutions before all the ends were tied up – an expensive method. Apart from that, the time factor prohibits such action. Long before a successful conclusion was reached, the situation would be out of hand. No, the time is now ripe to take action – the unorthodox solution originally planned. *You* are a major part of the solution.'

Bellman never knew if it was the devious manner of Kitholm's explanation, or the result of his body finally submitting to the pressure caused by the treatment – whatever the treatment was – but he launched himself from the bed and attempted to lay hands on Kitholm. As soon as his feet met the floor, his knees buckled and his clawing fingers could only reach Kitholm's trousers at the knee. It was an embarrassing wrestle with Kitholm on his feet, trying to shake his leg free like a postman with a determined terrier.

From a distance Bellman heard Kitholm shout, 'Jenkins! Jenkins!' He was still scrabbling desperately at the immaculate trousers when the stocky man bent over him.

'Now, sir. Calm down. We'll have you okay in a jiffy.'

It was the exasperating plural language of the trained nurse, but the hands that lifted him and placed him on the bed were far from soft. He recognised the touch of linen as it closed around his body. His mental processes disintegrated. In split vision he saw a miniaturised Kitholm looking down at him with a flushed and angry face. That much pleased him: the imperturbable perturbed.

Later there was a long white coat with no one inside it. But the others deferred to it and a voice emerged from where the head should have been. 'I did warn against a protracted session.' There was a murmured question and the voice replied, 'Tomorrow, but don't expect him to be as placid for as long as he was today.'

Then Bellman felt a pressure on his arm and a sharper pain overlapped the million pin-pricks he had nearly learned to live with. The light went out very suddenly.

This time there was no period of adjustment. Bellman felt himself being firmly shaken. The light, previously a gauge of his condition, appeared in splintered fractions as his eyelids fluttered spasmodically.

'Come on, sir, shake it about.' The voice, like the hand on his shoulder, was firm if not urgent. Bellman sat up.

The stocky man was at the bedside, looking at him with pleasure as though the awakening was a work of art. He placed a tray over Bellman's knees. 'It's just tea for now.'

'Jenkins, isn't it?'

'That's right, sir,' he said, surprised.

Bellman sipped the tea, watching Jenkins over the rim of the mug.

'The gentleman who was here yesterday will be with you shortly,' Jenkins said.

'Will he,' Bellman said non-committally. When the other man made no move to leave, he said, 'It's all right, you can leave me now.'

Jenkins coughed apologetically. 'I'll be staying until the gentleman arrives, sir.'

'All right,' Bellman said resignedly, 'but get one thing straight – that man is no gentleman.'

The smallest quiver at the corner of his mouth was the only indication that Jenkins had heard what he said.

Kitholm appeared before Bellman had finished the tea. He was carrying a parcel in place of the brief-case. Jenkins left.

Kitholm approached the bed cautiously. 'How are you?'

Bellman said nothing, following Kitholm's every move with watchful eyes.

'Try to be ...' Kitholm began.

'Listen,' Bellman said. 'Finish. Tell me the rest as quickly as possible. I don't want to hear it, but I realise I won't be able to leave until you've got it off your chest.'

'At least that's sensible,' Kitholm said silkily. He moved to the chair he had occupied the day before and sat down, placing the parcel on the floor. 'Do you remember all that was said yesterday?'

Bellman found a cigarette and lit it. 'Yes. It seems to be an unfortunate part of the present situation that I have total recall.'

'Good,' Kitholm said, still eyeing Bellman carefully as though fearing a repetition of the previous day's outburst. 'I believe the last thing we spoke of was the answer to the present level of criminal activities. Instead of constantly referring to it as "the answer", I will give it its official designation – "Decimate L". The L,' he said pedantically, 'stands for London. Later it may be necessary to take similar action in other cities. "Decimate" is self-explanatory – pare down – kill a portion of. A very appropriate word as it so happens ... Decimate L ...' He tested the phrase with half-closed eyes.

'You always did love melodrama,' Bellman taunted.

'Not at all,' Kitholm snapped. 'Now ... to explain what Decimate L entails. The intention is simple. By a process of what is known as disinformation, and the maiming or killing of certain criminal figureheads, Decimate L will effectively cripple the system of organised crime.' The statement, deadly, cold, was uttered with complete sincerity in a perfectly normal voice.

'What the hell are you talking about?' Bellman said.

'It will be exactly as I say.'

'You're a joke.'

'No. Neither is what I'm saying meant to be a joke.'

Bellman stubbed out his cigarette. 'Someone's gone off his head. Oh, I know it's not a unique solution. If I remember correctly, one of the South American countries had a team of police executioners running around doing the same thing.'

'They were unofficial, badly paid, frustrated men who took the law into their own hands,' Kitholm said disdainfully.

'And this is official?'

'That's what I'm saying.'

Bellman laughed and made a negative movement with his hands.

'It is the only way,' Kitholm insisted.

'No government would ...' Bellman began.

'No?' Kitholm barked. 'You would be surprised at some of the things that governments decide to do.'

'Ah, but we're one of the bastions of civilisation.'

'Indeed we are, but when the occasion arises ...' Kitholm's voice faded, then began again like a revitalised engine. 'Which nation would you say is the most ruthless in war or times of national crisis? Exclude the insane actions of the Gestapo and the like.'

'I've had this before. You're going to say the English with their innocent faces and old school ties.'

'Yes I am,' Kitholm said. 'Because it's true. In the past I only heard the legends – like anyone else. Now, though I am by no means privy to many secrets, I believe we are probably the most ruthless race that has ever existed. Many other nations think so too.'

'You sound proud of it.'

23

'I think there is a lot to be said for men who have the courage to decide on a course of action as desperate as Decimate L. Every possible alternative was considered before the decision was made – that is why the action I have outlined to you will be pursued to a successful conclusion.'

Bellman's head was moving slowly from side to side in disbelief. 'I still don't believe that ...'

'Of course,' Kitholm ploughed on, 'it would never be given open status – or anything like. The fact remains that the decision has been taken, that is all you need to concern yourself with.'

'I'm not in the least concerned.'

'But you are,' Kitholm said quietly. 'I told you yesterday. You are very much concerned. You see – you are the man who will do the killing.'

There was a long silence. Then Bellman began to laugh. At first it was the purely ridiculous notion which amused him, then the incongruity of the situation struck him. Himself being named as a future killer by of all people Kitholm, a man whose every move was governed by correct procedure.

Kitholm waited patiently until Bellman quietened. 'It takes getting used to,' he said. 'I am sure you can appreciate how difficult it was for me to assimilate the order.'

'Order?'

'Yes. It must be obvious that I haven't sufficient authority to devise something of this magnitude.' He waited before continuing. 'Look at the position, if you can, from a detached point of view. The decision has been taken. Whether you agree or disagree with it is immaterial. Certain men will be dealt with – that is a fact. The next step is to find someone to conduct the executions. Now consider yourself. You are perfect for the job. A policeman who has left the emotional rails. A man with no close, living relatives. A man who would hardly cause a ripple if he disappeared – and no surprise if named as a murderer.'

Bellman stared straight ahead. Very quietly, he said, 'I

don't know what's going on, Kitholm, this is way beyond my understanding, but if you're only half serious – then you're mad.'

'I am fully serious and quite sane. Apart from the advantage of your present ... uninvolved life, you have other qualifications.' He averted his eyes from Bellman for a few moments. 'You may not believe this but I always agreed with the generally held opinion that you were an exceptional detective. Your methods were hardly what I would recommend, but you got results. You were devious – an essential requirement in your new role. You possess an encyclopaedic knowledge of London and there is no doubt that you have an instinctive feel for off-beat situations which assists your anonymity. Further back, you have killed your fellow man, and that is something that cannot easily be taught. You can either do it or you cannot.'

Kitholm got to his feet and began to pace beside the bed as he had done the day before. 'You have been selected, Bellman. It sounds shocking to you right now, but you will be surprised how easily you can get used to the idea.'

'Okay, let's pretend. Why me?'

'For exactly the reasons I have been outlining. A ... professional agent could accomplish the work – particularly the killing – but it would take a long time to train someone for the necessary job of blending into murky backgrounds. In fact, I don't think it would be possible to train anyone for that part. It would seem it's a gift. Most villains are very astute, they have an uncanny nose for infiltration. You have fooled them in the past and you can do it again.'

'Shit, Kitholm, those days are long gone.'

'You are in work, Bellman, and so far you've only been told the bad side. The job also has its compensations.' Kitholm's tone became almost jovial as he warmed to pleasanter topics. 'Your instructions will be kept simple. Accept them, do as you're told, and enjoy the rewards.'

'Go on,' Bellman said, determined to give no assistance.

'It's very simple. You will be given a sum of money when you leave here – five hundred pounds. After that you will be paid one hundred pounds a week.'

'Great,' Bellman said. 'I can get pissed for months on that sort of money.'

'We know.'

'And?'

'And nothing. We expect it. We also expect you to do the work. Even if you are drunk.'

'You *must* be mad.'

'And you repeat yourself. We're not mad. Think, Bellman. With the initial payment you will be given a task. Fail to do it and what has the country lost? – five hundred pounds. No more. And someone else will be found to take your place. We are prepared to gamble that you will find the money a greater attraction than your conscience. If you are caught or prevented from doing the job because you are drunk – we won't mind. Any story you put out about being officially employed is hardly likely to be believed, but we think your natural talents will eliminate that chance. If they don't – you're a drunk.'

'I might change.'

'You won't.'

'Supposing I agreed, took the money, and then did nothing to earn it?'

'We won't talk about that.'

'Why not?'

Kitholm sighed. 'You still don't seem to appreciate that you're in, Bellman. *In!* You were in from the moment you accepted that first drink in Victoria. You cannot refuse.'

'That doesn't tell me what would happen to me.'

Kitholm shrugged. 'You are one of the few people to know of Decimate L. You are a poor security risk, but it was necessary to give you an outline of the operation, consequently, if you made no attempt to do the task allotted you, well, you would be eliminated.'

Bellman threw his arms wide, laughing. 'Kitholm, we are

in the nineteen seventies; London – I think. Things like that don't ...'

'There's no arguing, Bellman.' Kitholm's reply was flat, sobering. He picked up the parcel and threw it on the bed. 'This establishment is a treatment centre. Normally it is used to cure men who have had a bad time while ... employed ... by a certain government department.'

'These places really do exist then?' Bellman said, feeling obliged to make some comment to show he was not completely overwhelmed by Kitholm's mundane treatment of the outrageous.

Kitholm nodded sharply. 'It would be impossible to use open hospitals. The treatment you received is advanced in its field. You feel no craving for drink, right? The treatment will be tailed off during the next twenty-four hours, and you will suffer for a time, but then you will be as you were before – with all your old urges.'

'Then why bother to dry me out?'

'You haven't been dried out. Temporarily suspended is a better term. It was essential to embed instructions in your mind while you were sober. In that parcel you will find your clothes. They've been cleaned,' he added, his nose wrinkling with distaste. He reached in to an inside pocket. 'Here is the five hundred pounds.' The bundle of centre-bound notes bounced on the bed-cover, landing beside the parcel. He reached into another pocket and produced a small book.

'Proper bloody magician, aren't you?' Bellman said.

'This contains details of your first assignment,' Kitholm said, opening the book.

Suddenly Bellman felt beaten. Kitholm was treating everything so matter-of-factly that the very things which previously had appeared ridiculous, now seemed credible.

'You will need to make notes,' Kitholm continued. 'Open the parcel. You will find your papers and pen in the jacket.'

Bellman obediently extricated the clothes from the parcel and found his tattered note-book and ball-point pen. 'You must have been watching me for some time,' he said as he flicked through the book to find an empty page.

'A few weeks,' Kitholm agreed. 'You have been under observation since your name was put forward. You weren't the only candidate.'

'I just proved to be the unluckiest.'

'We're beginning with comparatively small-fry,' Kitholm said evenly. 'Heard of Ronald Toper?'

Bellman shook his head.

'I'm not surprised,' Kitholm said. 'He's pretty un-remarkable – neither villainous nor straight. One of those in-betweeners who haven't the brains to be anything to a significant degree. He's being used. At the present time he is fronting a fair-sized cash-and-carry outfit, dealing almost exclusively in straight merchandise. It may transpire to be a "long-firmer" but I doubt it. He's useful because of the hounds he mixes with.'

He looked up quickly. 'He's not for the chop, by the way.'

'He'd be pleased to hear that.'

'At the moment he's being directed by a pretty big wheel. We want Toper maimed – gangland fashion. The idea is to cause friction – give the impression that competition from similar outfits is getting fierce.'

'I'm sure he'll believe it,' Bellman grunted.

'Shoot him in the legs.' Kitholm issued the terrible in-structions in a purely conversational manner.

'Shoot him?'

'Yes. How you get hold of the gun is your affair. Steal it – buy it, it doesn't matter. When you do the job it would be helpful if you could somehow convey that Datchett's mob is responsible.'

'Vic Datchett?'

'Yes. At least that *is* someone you've heard of.' Kitholm held out his book to Bellman. 'There's Toper's home address and the location of the warehouse. Copy them down.'

Incredibly Bellman found himself recording the details.

Kitholm was on his feet and moving towards the door. 'Good luck, Bellman.'

'That's all?' Bellman said in astonishment.

Kitholm stopped with his hand on the door. 'So? A while ago you were urging me to finish.'

'Yes, but ...'

'Five days. We want the job done within five days of your departure from here. You will be leaving tomorrow.'

The door closed behind him.

Chapter Four

When Kitholm had gone Jenkins appeared carrying a tray loaded with food. Bellman ate most of what was put before him, deliberately blanking out the conversation with Kitholm.

Immediately after the meal the prickling sensation and stomach contractions returned. Jenkins re-entered just as Bellman had decided to call for something to relieve the agony. He placed a glass of water on the small cabinet and held out his hand, palm up. Two tablets nestled on a small square of paper.

'Take these, sir. No more needles for you.'

Bellman took the tablets from the paper and looked at them suspiciously. 'Will these do the same job as the needle?'

'Not quite. The injection is part of the treatment but it also contains a sedative. These will merely ensure that you sleep.'

Bellman put the tablets in his mouth and washed them down with water.

Jenkins watched approvingly.

Bellman did not remember going to sleep.

He was awakened by pain. Pain in his head. Stomach pain. And the flying needles were attacking his arms and legs. He staggered to the bathroom and squatted on the lavatory, groaning.

He returned to the bed and lay down thankfully, attempting to drift back into the darkness of sleep. He was only partially successful. The realisation struck him that he could manage to drink something alcoholic. There was no desperate urge, merely an awareness.

He was dozing and waking with machine-like regularity. But the waking moments gradually lengthened until he hardly slept at all. The pain in his head seemed to be receding but now he *needed* a drink. He began to thrash beneath the covers.'

'Suffering, Bellman?'

Bellman attempted to sit up but only managed to raise himself on a supporting elbow. He had heard no one enter the room but through poorly focused eyes he could see the figure of the speaker standing at the end of the bed – a tall shadow without detail.

'Who the fuck are you?' Bellman croaked, straining his eyes until he realised that the light was out and the curtains nearly fully drawn.

The figure appeared to bend slightly. 'Good, good. You seem to be aggressive enough.' The articulation was precise but the timbre held no dialect or educational influence. 'Me?' the voice went on. 'I am directing this operation, Decimate L. My name is of no consequence to you but when we do have occasion to speak you can refer to me as Praeger. It's not my real name of course, but it will suffice.'

Bellman groped beside the bed.

'There's no switch there, Bellman, you should know that by now.' The voice hardened. 'I will waste very little time with you. You have been told what to do. Personally I have my doubts about your capability but ... we shall see.'

Bellman felt something land on his feet. 'That is a cheque book,' Praeger said. 'The account is in your name. You will have no problems. On the back of the cheque book you will find a telephone number. It is allocated to a respectable business.' There was a small sound which could have been a laugh. 'At least, ostensibly so. Having done that you will ring that number and give details of your new address. You must also inform the office when an assignment is completed and give an account of what happened. Further orders will be relayed to you by telephone – or personally from Mr Kitholm. Your weekly money will be paid into your account in cash. There is already one hundred pounds deposited there.' He paused then said, 'Makes you quite the little rich man doesn't it, Bellman? Compared to your recent position, that it.'

Bellman said, 'Bollocks,' and tried to control the shakes that ran through his body.

'There would be no point in ringing that number and asking for help,' Praeger said, ignoring Bellman's oath. 'You are on your own.'

The figure loomed over Bellman for an instant, then receded. A shaft of light appeared as the door opened and a shadow blotted it out but Bellman only saw Praeger's departure as a fleeting impression of black on white.

Then Bellman's nightmare began. There were moments when his head was clear but they only served to accentuate the pain that racked him. The stomach spasms increased, threatening to push his bowels from his body. In desperation he left the bed and went to the window, throwing back the heavy curtains. His view was restricted by the branches of a tall tree, the only area visible being a corner of well-tended lawn with a border of stunted flowers.

Bellman turned and crossed the room to the door. In the corridor Jenkins waited like an affable sentry. 'Would you mind popping back inside, sir, we're just coming to attend to you.'

The words had an ominous ring despite the pleasant way they were uttered.

Bellman retreated and perched himself on the edge of the bed. He was slumped with bowed head when the man who had picked him up in Victoria entered the room. He was accompanied by a shorter, wide-shouldered companion. Jenkins hovered in the rear.

'All right, Bellman. Get dressed.' The voice was the same but lacked the persuasive tone of days earlier.

Bellman did not move. Despite his protestations to Kitholm he was now reluctant to leave. The room represented security and somewhere nearby was the treatment which would relieve his agony. The menace in the words finally filtered through and he fumbled for his clothes.

When he had finished dressing the shorter man motioned towards the door.

'Where are we going?' Bellman asked mechanically.

'You're finished here – free,' the taller man said.

As they moved out Jenkins murmured, 'Goodbye, sir.' Bellman thought he detected a note of pity.

He was led down a flight of stairs. The house was old, the bruised panelling of the stairway testifying to its age.

At the bottom he was ushered through a small door and down a flight of stone steps to a cellar. He squinted at the glare of electric lights. When his eyes adjusted he saw that the cellar had been converted into a garage, a spacious, modern affair with the accoutrements of a motor engineer scattered about. At the rear there was a car of some kind but he was pushed towards a van which waited by the large, double doors, with a man already at the wheel.

The taller man opened the rear doors of the van and motioned Bellman inside. He got in and sat on a narrow bench which ran down one side of the vehicle. A plywood partition separated the compartment from the driving cab. There were no windows. The men who had collected him climbed up and the doors closed. A small, overhead light seeped a yellow glow into the interior.

The van jerked into motion and Bellman's agony was complete, his already tortured muscles screaming at the extra movement as he tensed them to counteract the vehicle's swaying passage.

'The big drinker doesn't look so good this evening,' the well-remembered voice said.

Bellman stared silently back at the speaker.

'Nothing to say, Bellman?'

'No,' Bellman said. 'Nothing to say. I just want to look at you – and remember.'

The other gave a disparaging lift of the chin. 'Remember away. You're a fore-and-aft punk. You worry no-one.'

Bellman leaned back and closed his eyes, attempting to ease the pain in his head.

The journey was punctuated with varying pressures as the van twisted and turned. Bellman made no effort to identify street sounds, satisfied by the volume of traffic noise that he was still in London.

When the van stopped there was a tap on the wooden partition and a muffled voice said, 'Arrived.'

'Where are we?' Bellman asked.

'Get out and see,' Bellman's tormentor said.

Bellman turned the handle of the door and edged it open. Before he could lower himself to the road he felt the pressure of a hand on his back, then he was sprawling to the ground in an untidy heap. He could hear the bastard laughing.

He picked himself up, smiling as though his own clumsiness had caused the fall. 'Just a minute,' he said, 'there's something I forgot to tell Kitholm.'

The van doors paused in the action of closing then opened again. 'What is it?' The hated face looked down at Bellman. Ignoring the tearing pain, Bellman lifted a foot and kicked the wavering door.

The fair head jerked quickly aside as Bellman's foot contacted the metal, but the movement was too late. The edge of the door struck the narrow skull and slammed it against the rigid frame of the other door. There was a short scream of agony and the door rebounded. Bellman lifted his foot again but the stocky man appeared in the opening and deterred him with a shake of the head, motioning him to move away. It seemed to Bellman as though there was the ghost of a smile tugging at the man's mouth. Bellman turned and walked away. He heard the van move off but did not look round.

He was in a narrow street lined with small, flat-topped terraced houses. It was a run-down locality. The short flights of steps leading to the door of each dwelling and the iron railing which fronted the basement areas were typical of many of London's crumbling districts. He could be in Notting Hill, Brixton, the East End or any of a dozen different places.

Bellman walked to the end of the street. From the corner he could see heavy traffic on a main thoroughfare and stumbled towards it. It did not surprise him when he emerged into Clapham Road with the signs of Stockwell tube station on his left.

He stopped and debated his next move. A drink was what he desperately needed and there was a pub only yards away, but something made him cross the road and enter the station. Without questioning the decision he bought a ticket to Victoria, riding the train in a strange dream-like state.

When the train stopped at Victoria he got out and merged with the hordes of travellers heading for the main-line station. He realised he had come full circle being only a stone's throw from where he had been picked up.

In the station bar he made a conscious effort to resist the urge for powerful drink, knowing he should consider his position soberly; but before the beer he ordered was finished he added a whisky, and then another. Within minutes he felt better. The stomach spasms receded and the needling pains in his arms and legs disappeared altogether. Only the ache of his throbbing head remained unaltered.

Half a dozen drinks later his body was at ease. Alcoholic warmth engulfed him; the sort that accompanies apprentice drinking and is the prelude to drunkenness proper. Then memory struck home and he experienced a shaft of real fear. For the moment he was in possession of his faculties, but he knew it was a short step to oblivion, and he had not yet analysed recent events or made a decision about his future intentions.

The thought of being directed by Kitholm or the shadowy Praeger was abhorrent to him, but their total indifference to the prospect of his possible failure sparked off an urge to succeed. Or at least the intention to stay alive. Mulling it over he found no strangeness in the most powerful instinct of all taking over – that of the will to survive. He laughed into his glass. It was a strange paradox nevertheless; days before he had been telling himself that he wished for death.

He patted the wad of money in his pocket, then took out the note-book and read the details he had copied from Kitholm. The writing brought back the memory of Kitholm and Praeger and a wave of anger possessed him when he remembered what he had been ordered to do to the man whose name was recorded there. His own life hung on his ability to maim a man he had never seen. He ordered a double and downed it quickly. After two more he was beginning to lurch.

The bar was crowded and as he grew progressively unsteadier a space appeared around him as it always does near one verging on drunkenness and a possible source of trouble.

Bellman studied the ring of empty faces with their stares of bovine interest, ghoulishly waiting for an eruption, but anxious to avoid contact.

'What's the matter with you lot?' he shouted, confirming the mass anticipation.

'Now, now, love what's the trouble?' The elderly woman behind the bar was experienced enough to make a placatory first approach but her voice carried an undertone of firmness which Bellman heeded.

'Nothing,' he muttered, 'don't worry.'

'Why don't you go home, love. You've had a good drink.' The words spelt out a kindly order.

Home!

Bellman left the bar and walked on to the concourse. In the past he had taken far more drink than he had in the last hour and remained comparatively sober. Now he felt ill. The pain in his body had been replaced by an overwhelming feeling of sickness.

He felt a desperate need for cover. Refuge.

He saw it was nine-thirty. Where to go? Despite his

depression he smiled when he thought that it was one of the few occasions he could stay almost anywhere he pleased. He had the money, so where should it be? The Hilton? Savoy?

His eye was attracted by the word 'Hotels'. The sign was above a small kiosk. The man behind the counter watched his swaying approach with doubt and trepidation.

'You'll have difficulty in finding a single room. Everywhere's booked up,' he answered to Bellman's slurred enquiry.

'Nothing at all?' Bellman asked.

'I can find you a double room but it would cost twelve pounds.'

'S'okay,' Bellman said belligerently.

While the agent was filling in his particulars on a duplicate sheet, Bellman searched for his left-luggage ticket, finding it between the pages of his note-book.

When the booking details were complete he walked to the front of the station. Taxis were swooping to a stop at the entrance, gradually swallowing particles of the short queue formed there.

'Coach station to pick up some luggage, then the Flackman – Earls Court,' Bellman said when his turn for a taxi came.

The cabby gave him an uncertain look before dropping the flag and moving off.

The man wearing a sports jacket and twill trousers waited until the cab was out of sight before entering the phone booth.

'He's booked in to the Flackman in Earls Court, sir. Bishop's taking over now,' he said when the call was answered.

'How is he?' Praeger said.

'Drunk, sir.'

'Hmm. Still, we expected that. We'll see.'

37

Chapter Five

Bellman woke at eight and immediately felt the urge to leave the hotel. The previous night was not altogether forgotten, neither was it very clear. He must begin clean – aware of his actions – and the hotel was a remnant of ill-considered choice. The intention to use only carefully judged decisions was there, but he worried about his resolution.

The first cigarette did not help his train of thought. Fuck Kitholm!

He got up and shaved and washed, then packed his few belongings into the shabby case, leaving the hotel without fuss.

The food he ate in a small, side-street café was swallowed with indifference; fuel.

Outside, he automatically turned to the tube station and rode to Kensington, then changed to a Circle line train. There had been other occasions when he had used the repetitive journey of the line to sit and think, staring through the window at the miles of non-distracting electrical conduits.

He recalled many things. Last of all – Sandy. He remembered her and the warm, reassuring kiss she gave him when she knew he was feeling low. 'This is a down moment, kid. If you hadn't died, this wouldn't be happening.' His stomach gave an immediate lurch. The fact was true but it was as though he was blaming her.

With Sandy there had been few bad times and those that had appeared were quickly smothered. Like the time he had been worried about work – worried for her sake because violence was imminent and he had not known how to warn her that he might be hurt. Without knowing the extent of his problem she had stood, hands on hips. 'What's the matter, Bellman, they getting to you?'

He had laughed delightedly and made love to her there and then.

Well, they *had* got to him. And paid the piper in advance.

The train made one of its numerous stops and he got off without bothering to check where he was. It turned out to be Notting Hill Gate. When he checked his watch he was surprised to see that it had gone ten and he knew he must have made two circuits of the system.

The woman in the flat-finding agency was practised in pessimism. When she heard Bellman describe the type of flat he was looking for, she shook her head. 'It's almost impossible to find anything at all these days,' she said, eyeing him, assessing his fee-paying potential.

Bellman sat with his case beside him. 'It must also have a telephone,' he said as though he hadn't heard.

'Do you know what you're asking, Mr ...?'

'Bellman.'

'... Mr Bellman. I think the price of an apartment such as you describe would be ... prohibitive.' She turned to a small card-file. 'I may be able to find you a room where there is a telephone arrangement with ...'

'How much?' Bellman said brusquely.

'Well it ...'

'No. I mean for a decent flat – with a telephone.'

'Really, there's nothing that ...' She stopped as he dived into his pocket and produced the roll of money.

'I don't know how you assess your fee,' he said, flicking through the notes.

Her eyes were fixed on the cash. 'It's a percentage but ...'

'I'm not interested,' Bellman said, peeling off a section of notes and waving them in the air. 'There's a hundred there. I want a flat – rent up to, say, thirty-five, forty a week.

If you get one for me, the money's yours, irrespective of anything else. If it's not enough, say so – I'm not raising the ante. I'll go somewhere else.'

The woman fluttered. 'Well, I didn't think you would want something in that range. Even so . . .'

Bellman began to replace the money.

'There may be . . .' she began hastily, stopping with relief when the money reappeared.

'What?' Bellman prompted.

'There is a lady nearby – Fortis Crescent. She lets the top floor of her house. There are two rooms – one with an integral kitchenette – and a bathroom. It is separate from her own, ground floor accommodation and has its own side-entrance. The rent is forty pounds a week. No other part of the house is let. She lives alone.'

'Separate telephone?'

'Yes but . . . ah . . . she does like to have someone who is recommended.'

'So recommend me,' Bellman said, waving the money.

It hurt but she said, 'But I don't know anything about you, Mr Bellman.'

He sighed and raised his eyes to the ceiling. 'I'm self-employed – contacts in the travel world. I arrange private tours for visitors and so on. I used to work in London but recently I have been engaged up north. Now I want back.' He threw the money down on the desk. 'I promise not to puke on her petunias or piss in the sink. Now, if you feel you can recommend me, let's get going.'

She attempted to register disgust but the effect was spoiled by her eyes which were clamped to the scattered banknotes. She lifted the telephone receiver and began to dial.

'Mrs Anstey? Ah. It's Mrs Keel . . . yes . . . the agency. I think I've found someone to replace your nice Mr Hammond,' she gave Bellman a defiant glare on the word 'nice'. 'I've done all the necessary checking, I'll forward the . . . oh, well, that's very kind of you. I'm sure you will find him

suitable. It's a Mr Bellman . . . yes . . . I'll send him round.'
She listened for a few moments then said, 'Thank you, Mrs Anstey . . . yes, almost immediately.'

When she replaced the receiver her cheeks were touched with pink. 'She's waiting for you.'

'Don't let it worry you,' Bellman said. 'We all have to tell a few lies now and again.'

She picked up the money. 'I hope you will be considerate. Mrs Anstey is a nice woman.'

'As considerate as you were,' he said. 'The address?'

She wrote on a piece of paper and handed it to him.

He took it and said, 'Thanks, and don't worry. I'm not another Jack-the-Ripper.'

108, Fortis Crescent was in the select part of Notting Hill, standing on the rising ground of Campden Hill, overlooking Holland Park Avenue. Bellman inspected it from the gardens at the rear, the hallowed territory of sprawling greenery kept solely for the occupants of the adjoining dwellings. Each of the houses on the crescent had its own short run of garden separated from the private sector by low, iron palings or trimmed hedges.

The house itself was red brick and old, the upper floor dominated by a large, wide-view window, slightly out of keeping with the rest of the building. Bellman liked the look of it. He circled the narrow walkways to the front entrance.

Mrs Anstey *was* nice. A fading person whose looks could be termed 'genteel', she fluttered her hands as she showed Bellman to the door at the side of the house.

'I think it's convenient to have your own entrance, don't you?' she said.

Bellman agreed and followed her up the stairs. The door at the top led directly into the living-room which had the large window. The furnishings were new but comfortable and he was pleased with the overall view he had from the window. The 'integral' kitchenette was a screened area in one corner of the room, fitted with a cooker and what appeared to be an excess of tools and gadgets. He gave it only a cursory examination.

The bedroom was smaller, overlooking the crescent at the front of the house. He inspected the bathroom which led off from the bedroom, nodding politely at Mrs Anstey's various explanations.

Back in the main room he lifted the receiver from the telephone which stood on a low table and checked that it was connected.

'It's a lovely apartment, Mrs Anstey, I would like to take it.'

Her hands did a subdued tic-tac. 'Oh, I'm glad ... ah ... did Mrs Keel explain about the rent it's ...'

'Forty pounds a week. Yes.'

She watched him anxiously. 'Will that be ...'

'That's fine. A month in advance?'

Her relief was obvious. 'Well, if you don't ...' She avoided the 'unpleasantness' of the business side of the transaction by failing to complete the sentences which pained her.

Bellman reached into his pocket. 'I would like to move in immediately if you have no objections. Cash?' He began to count out notes. 'Unless you wish to check my credentials first?'

'Oh I'm sure if Mrs Keel recommends you ...' She handled the notes gingerly. 'I'll make out a rent book for you. If you want anything, you know where I am.' At the door she turned. 'I'll see about transferring the telephone to your name. I think that's ... oh, of course, here are the keys.'

When she had gone he did a short tour of the rooms again. The hint of permanence that came with a month's rent paid in advance settled strangely on him and he indulged in the odd little acts of acclimatisation which came automatically, if unconsciously; running the tap in the tiny sink beside the cooker, testing the bed with curled knuckles, and unnecessarily flushing the toilet.

When he could no longer avoid it he returned to stand by the telephone, looking at the instrument with an expression of hatred, knowing that when he rang the number which Praeger had given him he would be giving his own seal of approval.

He took the cheque book from his pocket and slowly dialled the number that was written there.

A woman's voice said, 'Selgo. Can I help you?'

'My name's Bellman. I have a message for Mr Praeger.'

'Oh yes, Mr Bellman.'

He gave her the address and telephone number. 'I think that's all he wants – for now.'

There was a pause while she wrote down the details. 'Thank you, I will pass the message on.'

He picked up the directory which was beside the instrument and searched for 'Selgo'. It was listed as Selgo Business Consultancy, Lexington Street, W1, Soho.

Closing the directory he went to the bathroom and filled the tub with hot water. He had not bothered overmuch with bathing recently; the long soak he indulged in left him with a strangely soft skin.

'He reported in,' Kitholm said.

Praeger took the paper with the information, raising his eyebrows as he read. 'Chosen an expensive area, hasn't he?'

'Perhaps it's a good sign,' Kitholm said.

'I would have thought he'd have gone for a low-class area,' Praeger mused. 'How did he land up there?'

'Through a normal agency. He nearly sent our man dizzy, riding the Circle line, before he settled.'

Praeger looked up sharply. 'Did he realise he was being followed?'

'No. He never looked behind once. I think he was just deciding where to go. You know he went boozing after he was dropped off? Spent the night in a sleazy hotel in Earls Court.'

'Yes. I saw the report.'

Kitholm watched Praeger walk away, amused at the thought that the report had not contained the news of facial injury to one of Praeger's pet operatives. That was something Kitholm had learned privately.

Bellman lay on the couch, his feet trailing over the edge. Smoke trickled upwards from the cigarette in his hand. He watched its progress with thoughtful eyes.

The events which had overtaken him and the proposed maiming of Ronald Toper seemed to be in a different world. His invidious position gnawed at him but the act of violence he was committed to left him unconcerned. At one time he would have been seriously worried by his lack of feeling.

The need for a drink roused him and he left the house and found a pub. Only half an hour remained before lunchtime closing. He ordered a pint of bitter to chase down the three whiskies he sank in quick succession. When the barman shouted, 'last orders' he called for a double. He was nearly back to normal – recent normal. The long soak in the bath had left him with little to remind him of the pain he had suffered the day before. He lifted the glass and finished the drink.

Outside he turned and met the incline of the hill as he walked towards 'the Gate'.

He was still some way short of the tube station when he was sure about the Hillman. It had pulled away from the pub as he left, now it was travelling slowly towards him on the opposite side of the road. The driver was hunched over with his head turned away from Bellman, apparently searching for an address on that side. The passenger was staring unnaturally ahead and Bellman knew the man's eyes would be swivelled towards him. When the car had passed, he crossed the road, watching the vehicle from the corner of his eye. The driver executed a 'U' turn and parked beside the pavement. The passenger door opened and a short, bubble of a man emerged to stroll along the opposite pavement in the same direction as Bellman.

He was pleased that he had identified them so easily and was content to let them follow – for the time being.

He caught a train, allowing ample time for his follower to gain the adjoining carriage, and travelled to Mile End. The small, half remembered car-hire company was still there and he had no difficulty in renting a Toyota. At least he still had a clean driving licence.

On the way back he admired the persistence of the bubble-man who followed in a hastily-summoned cab. The Hillman appeared behind him when he reached Holborn, confirming that they were equipped with radios. Apart from the proficiency in communications, Bellman was unimpressed by their technique.

He stopped at a supermarket and bought a range of food and two bottles of whisky. He displayed the bottles prominently at the top of the carrier-bag.

The drink was obligatory, not because it was his practice to drink at home – most of his soaking was done in pubs – but because he knew it would be expected of him.

He parked the car directly outside the house in Fortis Crescent and carried his purchases upstairs. Once inside he moved to the bedroom and watched the crescent. The car that had followed him failed to appear, but a man who looked like the driver arrived after a few minutes, hurrying along as though late for an appointment. He gave the Toyota a quick once-over as he passed.

Bellman left the window and opened one of the bottles. The drink went down smoothly and he carried the refill to the kitchenette where he set a steak over a low flame before puzzling over the instructions on a packet of frozen vegetables.

Since Sandy there had only been a series of rooms, mostly without cooking facilities and the act of producing a meal came strangely. He ate what he cooked, quickly, then made coffee and sat back to think.

'I see he's still boozing,' Praeger said, his eyes on the report.

Kitholm raised his eyebrows. 'That was to be expected. He's hired a car – that could be preparation for his task.'

'Or something to go jaunting in. Keep a close eye on him.'

The following morning Bellman took the car and did more shopping, this time fitting himself out with new clothes. He took no particular pleasure in the expedition; it was a means of showing a respectable front. The two ready-made suits were the only items to delay him longer than he would have liked.

He made several trips to the car with various purchases. The bubble-man was on duty again and Bellman took care to give him no cause for alarm. It was essential to lull him if he was to get a few minutes alone.

When most of his buying was done he visited a small shop in Oxford Street and bought a denim suit then wandered into a large store. The bubble-man followed and Bellman cut across the shop floor, forcing the little man to move to the rear of the premises. Still apparently strolling, Bellman left the store. A backward glance showed the bubble-man pushing shoppers aside in an effort to keep up.

The pavement was crowded. On the other side of the road Bellman saw the driver of the Hillman appear at the kerbside, indicating his direction to the bubble-man who was obscured by a mass of bodies. Bellman saw the hand-play without looking directly at the signalling man. When he saw a door cramped singly between two shops, he lowered his head and ducked inside, observing the solicitor's plaque as he raced up the stairs which faced him.

On the first landing there was a window overlooking the street. Bellman squeezed into the recess and looked down on the moving throng below.

The driver was still across the road, gesturing with out-spread palms. The bubble-man was out of sight but obviously nearby, demanding to know where Bellman had gone. Bellman waited until the driver walked on and passed his position, then hurried down the stairs.

Out in the street he turned and retraced his steps, watching for signs of undue interest in his presence. When he was sure he was unobserved he trotted to the side street, relieved to see the shop as he remembered it.

'I want a wig,' Bellman said.

The man who had approached him clasped his hands tightly at the insult. 'Yes, sir. We have some very nice *pieces*. Now, if I can explain how we set about . . .'

'Do you sell them as they are?'

'Pardon.'

'Off-the-peg?'

'Well!' The lisp came with outraged emphasis.

'I want a bloody wig and I want it now.'

The salesman did a little jig. 'We have got . . .'

'Show me,' Bellman said.

The man led the way to the rear of the shop, deliberately exaggerating his mincing step to show that he was not intimidated. A limp hand indicated a shelf with a row of bronzed heads, each with a covering of false hair.

Bellman snatched a dark one and put it on, looking at the result in a corner mirror. It was directly opposed to what he wanted, the black hair drawing attention to his face. He took it off and said, 'I want something nearer my own colour but longer, much longer.'

The salesman, caught up in Bellman's urgent mood, darted to a drawer and rummaged before pulling free a straggle of fair hair. 'It's longer than yours but . . .'

Bellman crammed it on, brushing away the fluttering fingers that tried to help him. The effect was what he was looking for – hairy, unkempt.

'It's a bit of a mess but it will soon . . .' the salesman's fingers were still attempting to touch and arrange.

Bellman removed the wig and reached into his pocket, 'How much?'

'Oh, it's twenty-five pounds. Shall I . . .'

Bellman counted out the money, refusing the offer to wrap the tangle of tresses which hung over his forearm like a stricken cat. He thrust the ludicrous mass into the bag with the denim suit and left a bewildered fairy clutching a handful of notes.

He emerged cautiously into Oxford Street but there was no sign of the bubble-man or his companion. When he was back with his car he saw the watchers, fifty yards away. Properly, once they had lost him, they had covered his transport.

Bellman drove back to Fortis Crescent and made a production of transferring his purchases from the car to the flat.

Mrs Anstey met him in the small hallway of the side-entrance and gave him his rent book.

'I was wondering,' he said. 'Would it be possible for me to use the garden? It looks so nice and...'

'Of course,' she said enthusiastically. 'Use it whenever you wish.' She took him by the arm and led him outside, pointing beside the house. 'Go down there. The small gate leads to the residents' private park. At the other end there is an exit on to the main road. It gets a little messy in the winter but it's convenient if you only need to go somewhere local.'

Bellman thanked her and went upstairs. Once inside he checked the address of Toper's warehouse in his recently-purchased street guide. The building was situated in Dalston, an area he was familiar with. He recalled the road, lined on one side by a railway running loftily above the surrounding houses, the arches beneath following the line of the track.

He traced a route and committed it to memory, then, realising what he was planning to do, reached for the whisky.

The shopping trip, which was part preparation for the task had failed to worry him, but at the thought of how he had been decoyed and trapped, his mind rebelled.

The whiskies followed in quick succession. After an hour he felt worse. 'Fuck you, Kitholm – Praeger.'

When he finally got up and reached for the car keys it was with the fumbling, dreamy actions of the drunk. Half-way down the stairs he remembered the wig and returned to cram it into a paper bag.

As soon as he pulled the Toyota away from the kerb, a grey van, which even to his watery eyes looked out of place in the quiet backwater, started up and followed. Bellman watched the van in the mirror. He was unable to see inside but knew it was part of the covering team.

He said, 'Up yours,' to the wavering image and gave a brief touch on the accelerator, noting the corresponding lift at the van's front end with satisfaction.

At the multiple lights at Notting Hill Gate he slowed. The van obediently followed suit. The traffic was unusually thin and he knew the driver of the van was in difficulty. There was nothing to hide behind and if he travelled too fast he would place himself immediately behind Bellman's vehicle.

To the uninitiated, trailing someone or something, he knew, looked simple. In fact, to do it without the quarry's knowledge was extremely difficult. A vehicle tail in London could be a nightmare. To lose sight of the objective, even for seconds, inevitably meant that the link was broken. The thought gave Bellman an idea.

When the lights ahead of him changed to amber Bellman switched lanes and swooped in front of a slowing taxi on the inside. He took the corner with one eye on the mirror, wondering what the reaction of those in the van would be to his abrupt move. There was none.

He was lucky with the bug, finding it two minutes after stopping the car and searching beneath it. Praeger's men had done the job well; placing the tracing monitor above the rear axle where its weight would assist the magnetic grip.

He slid it off and fixed it beneath the wide clearance mudguard of a parked motor cycle which also sported cowhorn handlebars, a variety of flowing tassles, and the statutory insignia of numerous swastikas.

He regained the driving seat and sat studying the street guide with unseeing eyes. The van found him five minutes later, nosing carefully into view then easing to the kerb fifty yards behind.

Two minutes later the leathered figure of the motor cyclist emerged from a shop doorway. He mounted the machine, kicked it into life and roared away in a series of practised movements.

Bellman was hard-pressed to keep within reasonable range of the wrenching spurts of the motor bike. After half a mile he gunned into a sharp left turn as the following van was unsighted by the red hulk of a bus.

The tyres on the Toyota protested audibly as he screwed it between a parked lorry and the drooping mass of a derelict car.

As he lowered the window and awkwardly craned his neck he was just in time to see the van cross the intersection and follow the route of the flying motor bike.

He murmured, 'Good luck,' and twisted the Toyota through a series of streets to link with the route he had devised to take him north.

He parked the car some distance from the arches where Toper's warehouse lay and donned the wig, immediately feeling slightly ridiculous. He felt better moments later when, with the aid of the mirror, he saw that the mass of hair completely altered his appearance. Now he was certain that any villain he might know, who frequented Toper's premises, would not recognise him.

By the time he had walked to the line of arches the whisky had less effect but his eyes still burned and his head, beneath the extra thatch, was hot and sticky.

The warehouse was easy to identify. There was a fair-sized space before the large, church-like doors which were tailored to fit the arch. A gaudy sign in red and white proclaimed: 'Pay and Take'.

Individual bastard. What was wrong with 'Cash and Carry'?

Bellman drifted towards the group of men who inevitably collected at premises like that. Those who had bought, those who were thinking about buying, and others who waited to pick at the crumbs of business which sometimes fell to the patient.

'The guvnor about?' Bellman asked.

A small man in shirt sleeves and shapeless trousers supported by a broad, leather belt, jabbed a finger at a group of three who stood separate from the others, then returned to his own conversation.

Bellman sidled around the indicated party and stood in the entrance of the warehouse, watching the helpers fill the orders shouted to them by a dun-coated man seated in the open doorway of a plywood office.

'This what you want, Mr Toper?' said a youngster carrying a large carton. The question was aimed at the group beside Bellman.

Toper was big. As he took the box from the boy, Bellman could see the fat bulging at his waist. He was without a jacket and the girth of his massive trousers was supported by a pair of crimson braces.

'That's not the one, prick.' Toper's voice was strident, alien to his size. 'Harry wants the "specials".' He threw the box at the boy who staggered as he caught it.

Toper removed his glasses and kneaded his eyes with thumb and forefinger, then passed his hand over a balding head. 'Marvellous innit? I'm surrounded by pricks – wonder I ever get anything done.' The other two nodded and smirked, anxious to keep their accepted position.

Bellman moved slowly away, standing for a few moments at the pavement's edge as though waiting for someone to join him from the warehouse. When he was sure his departure would be unremarked he turned and headed for the Toyota.

It occurred to him that the Topers of the world were all

alike. Sharking in business was one thing but this one had been fingered for something bigger. He only had Kitholm's word but he knew the type. There was no doubt that Toper was all Kitholm claimed. He wondered if it was excuse enough for the coming deed. Perhaps. But he did not like Toper anyway.

This time they were angry. Bellman knew by the hard look given him by the bubble-man from the driving seat of the Hillman which was parked outside the flat. The positioning of the car showed they knew their cover was gone and they did not like it.

Bellman ignored the car and went inside. Whistling.

'Did he deliberately lose them?' Praeger asked.

Kitholm nodded unhappily. 'Yes. He located the trace and switched it to a motor cycle. Our chaps had something of an altercation when they recovered it . . . ah . . . the machine belonged to a . . . Hell's Angel.'

Praeger narrowed his eyes. 'I hope he's not playing games. The time element is important.'

'We did know the risk,' Kitholm said, attempting to make the 'we' sound like a 'you'.

'Well, he knows the deadline,' Praeger said.

Chapter Six

In the evening Bellman considered using the garden to escape from the house unnoticed. But they were there too. The same man appeared regularly on the pathway at the bottom of the short house garden. A call to the local police station complaining of a man on private property would produce results, but he decided against it. Praeger had an investment to protect and there was no point in causing avoidable trouble – yet. But Praeger had to learn too.

He dressed himself in the denim outfit, with a warm pullover beneath it. The wig went into the slant pocket of the denim top only after a struggle. It was bulky but once he had patted it into place it was not too obtrusive. He crammed a complete change of clothing, including shoes, into a small holdall then stood with eyes closed, mentally checking his preparations. When he was satisfied he went down to the car.

This time he roared the Toyota away after a quick dash from the doorway of the house. He caught a glimpse of frantic activity in a red car at the end of the crescent but he was away and clear. Until the Hillman moved in behind him as he headed for Kensington. Bellman sighed and dropped his speed. No doubt the Hillman had been standing-off, waiting for such a break and the occupants had been alerted by radio by those in the crescent. He thought it unlikely that the Toyota had been fitted with another bug but decided to check nevertheless.

The red car, which he thought was a Rover, took over as he approached the underpass at Hyde Park Corner. Bellman changed lanes and circled the massive memorial, filtered left and cruised down Constitution Hill. He made a small effort at the traffic lights on Westminster Bridge but his heart was not in it and they were ready for him. At Lambeth North he parked the Toyota, ignoring the circling followers as he locked the car and crossed the road to the station.

He knew they would follow him on to the train but did not trouble to single them out.

When he emerged at Piccadilly Circus he headed for Soho and did a round of the pubs, ordering beer, only once weakening and calling for a whisky.

At ten o'clock he walked to Shaftesbury Avenue and hailed a taxi, ensuring that the man he had seen waiting outside the pub had sufficient time to call up the car that was hovering in the background.

He said, 'Kensington,' to the cabby but only waited until they had travelled the short distance to Piccadilly Circus before jumping out, tossing a pound note to the driver through the open window.

He dived down the steps of the Underground into the booking hall, then ran to the next exit and up the stairs, emerging into the crowd which stood on the corner of Regent Street.

When he looked across the road he saw the bubble-man standing by the entrance where he had left the taxi. The rounded figure was twisting and turning in agitation until joined by another man. There was a heated discussion but Bellman got the impression that his action was not entirely unexpected. The bubble-man even shrugged.

Eventually they walked away and Bellman left the cover of the crowd and stopped another taxi. He ordered it to Lambeth, asking the driver to make a circuit of the area near the Toyota before paying him off. The covering team were not to be seen so he drove northwards, stopping once to check the car for a bug. When he found nothing he drove to Victoria and parked the car in a square behind the station.

He reasoned that his followers probably believed the Toyota to be a decoy and had decided to quarter the area of his disappearance to try and regain contact. Whatever, he was much happier now that he was free of them.

The shop was exactly the same. Years before he had said to Sharman, 'A gun shop in this area. It's asking for trouble.'

'Looks well-protected, Sarge ... belled-up,' Sharman had said.

The alarm still appeared to be efficient, prominently displayed on the outside of the building. Bellman examined the small door at the side. The padlock was large and he knew there was also a mortise lock but the door itself looked anything but sturdy.

He had been inside just the once, taking a gun there for the owner to identify. He hoped the lay-out remained the same.

He circled the block once again before returning to the big Ford which had been more difficult to steal than he had anticipated. Even starting it by means of the fuses had troubled him. Out of touch perhaps. Or because now it was for real.

He took out the gloves which he'd used to jack the car and put them on again. Satisfied that the car was still clean he returned to the shop and scrutinised the area again. The street lights were dim and most of the houses further down the street showed only the flickering blue of television screens through drawn curtains.

Bellman trotted to the side door and lifted his foot. Crudity it had to be. After several kicks the wood at the edge of the door began to splinter, but the hasp of the padlock hung determinedly to the frame. A last, savage smash sprung the mortise and sent the door crashing inwards. The padlock, still unbeaten, uselessly held the hasp and its shreds of fractured wood.

The alarm bell raucously advertised the assault as Bellman charged inside and fumbled for the light switch.

The rear room still held the glass-fronted cabinet with its sentry-rows of beautiful shot-guns. Shoreditch had no claim to upper-class pretensions but the clients who visited the old man's shop cared nothing for that. They were mostly countrymen who came for shooting tools, sold by a man who knew about guns.

Bellman used the piece of iron he had found outside to prise up the metal bar securing the front of the cabinet. It resisted valiantly and he swore aloud, feeling the perspiration of fear dampening his body. The bar was not to be beaten but the fixing screws finally surrendered with a screech, allowing him to pull free the twelve-bore he had selected whilst desperately working.

Several boxes of cartridges were stacked alongside the weapons, a bad arrangement as he remembered pointing out. Now he checked the calibre of one, picked it up and ran for the door.

Although it had seemed an eternity to him when inside the shop he knew it could not have been long. Lights were only just appearing in the nearby dwellings in response to the clamour of the alarm.

Someone in a house opposite the shop was at a first-floor window and Bellman heard a half-hearted, 'Hey, you!' as he ran towards the Ford.

He was driving slowly along, several hundred yards from the shop when the first police car screamed by.

He parked the car a mile away from Toper's warehouse, taking time to select the spot. The section of road he finally decided on was only sparsely dotted with other vehicles. And no derelict hulks. Dumping spots were anathema to those who wanted a car on ice for a time, being natural hunting-grounds for systematic policemen.

Before leaving the car he ensured that the gun and box of shells were out of sight beneath the seat. Then he crossed the road and walked over the waste-land that separated two, tottering buildings. He chose a pile of rubble, larger than the rest, which overlooked the car and scratched among the bricks and rotting plaster until he had cleared a depression sizeable enough to take his outstretched body.

From the eyrie of structural waste he settled down to watch over the Ford.

Twice, during the night, police cars prowled by without stopping.

At eight o'clock Bellman donned the wig and left his uncomfortable vantage-point.

He was forced to walk some distance before finding the workman's café he sought. It was too far from the Ford to be comfortable but he needed to eat. Catching sight of his reflection in the glass door of the café he knew he did not look out of place. His denims were streaked with dust and the long hair of the wig gave the impression of an early riser who had no time for a comb.

The mug of tea which was dumped unceremoniously before him was like nectar after the long night wait. He ordered a fried breakfast and ate hurriedly, not wishing to linger where he might be remembered, even looking as he did.

He checked the car once, then walked a direct line along the main road until ten o'clock, then returned.

The confines of the Ford coupled with the unfeeling pressure of the gloves on his hands made the loading of the gun difficult, but he finally managed it. With the weapon resting in the foot-well of the passenger seat he started up and drove away.

On the first pass of the warehouse there was no sign of Toper. The only movement came from a van which was being unskilfully reversed towards the double doors. Bellman took the car in a wide circuit of the arches, watching the mirror for possible trouble.

When he drew up before the premises again Toper was standing by the doors, gesticulating to someone inside. A massive hulk of a man stood near the van which had finally been positioned at an angle to the main entrance.

Bellman lowered the window on the passenger side of the car, leaned over and shouted, 'Ron!'

Toper turned and looked towards the Ford. Bellman shouted again. Toper moved towards the car with a crab-like movement, bending to try and see inside.

When he was ten yards away Bellman lifted the twelve-bore and thrust it through the window space.

Toper's jaw sagged in disbelief, but he recovered quickly and turned to run.

'Don't fuck with Vic!' Bellman screamed and blasted the gun at Toper's frantic legs.

The concussion in the confined space was terrible, threatening to burst Bellman's ear-drums.

Toper's leg took most of the shot. At the moment of impact it was the supporting limb and the shattered bone collapsed him like a rubbery bowling pin, blood visibly pumping through the tattered remnants of his trouser-leg.

Bellman loosed the remaining barrel at the stationary van, seeing the circular, shot pattern appear in the soft metal of the side.

Toper was screaming as Bellman hammered the Ford away.

The journey to Liverpool Street station took ten minutes and Bellman knew he was pressing his luck. The description of the car would now be on the police radio bands. He stopped the car and got out, stuffing the wig into his pocket. Once he had closed the doors, the gloves followed.

Bellman went to earth in the Underground like a fox returning from a night hunt.

In the train he studied his own emotionless reflection in the tunnel-blacked window. Apparently Kitholm's assessment of his capability had been right.

The thought hurt. Was the ultimate low point reached when a desperate act like the one he had just committed left no impression? Even the mental question was dead, pointless.

Tiredness was creeping over him as he collected the holdall from the Toyota and returned to Victoria station.

In the 'Superloo' he hired towels and soap to scrub himself clean in the shower. When he had finished he changed into the fresh clothes, filling the holdall with the ones he had been wearing.

He hired a left-luggage locker and crammed the holdall inside, then, safe from forensic treachery, he headed for the Toyota.

During the drive to Fortis Crescent he fiddled behind the dashboard facia until his fingers found a projection where he hung the key of the locker.

The red car was outside the house. Bellman held his breath as he locked the Toyota and turned to go inside. If it was to happen this would be the time they would pick him up – fresh from the kill.

He felt the sullen eyes of the bubble-man boring into him but there was no sudden movement of men running to apprehend.

Climbing the stairs he realised he had found a contradiction in himself; he *did* still have feeling – the fear of being caught. The thought failed to please him.

Inside the flat he picked up the telephone and rang Praeger's number. The woman answered.

'This is Bellman. Tell Praeger I've done his errand, now he can do me a favour by calling off the boy-scouts who keep trying to follow me.'

'I'll deliver your message,' the woman said.

Kitholm was smiling.

'Judgment vindicated, eh?' Praeger said.

'Well, it was pretty neat.'

'How did he do it? The lead-up, I mean. I know the result.'

Kitholm coughed. 'We're not exactly sure. I have made out a report ... here.'

Praeger took the paper from Kitholm's extended hand

and read from it. When he looked up he said, 'Witnesses to the statement involving Datchett?'

'Yes. At least one man heard the gunman say, "Don't fuck with Vic" or something like that. The name could only mean one person to Toper and company.' Kitholm made a subdued, told-you-so motion with his hand. 'I think Bellman did very well.'

Praeger gave a brief nod and turned on his heel.

Chapter Seven

Bellman appreciatively absorbed the surroundings as he was led to where Kitholm sat. The waiter held a chair for him.

'Expenses must be good.'

'Adequate,' Kitholm said. 'Something to drink?'

'Scotch.'

Kitholm said, 'And the same for me,' to the waiter.

'Careful,' Bellman said. 'There lies the way to alcoholism.'

Kitholm ignored him and waited for the drinks to arrive. When they were alone he said, 'You did a good job.'

'It isn't difficult to poke a gun at a man and pull the trigger,' Bellman said, lifting his glass.

Kitholm was watching him narrowly. 'No, but to do it without leaving a single clue requires thought. You went to some lengths to be alone.'

'I didn't ask for company.'

'They made themselves obvious?'

'Yes – to me. They might have been good enough for an average tail job.'

'Why did you consider it necessary to throw them? Frightened of a set-up?'

'Wouldn't you have been?'

'Probably. Nevertheless, you were ultra-cautious.'

'Why follow me at all?'

Kitholm drummed his fingers on the white tablecloth. 'Praeger's instructions. He likes to know how his operatives work.' A faint tic appeared at the corner of his mouth. 'On this occasion, however he was dis...' He broke off, shaking his head in self-reprimand. 'Anyway, he's satisfied for the moment. Three days and the local police are no nearer identifying the gunman. The description they've put out hardly fits you.'

'You know how unobservant witnesses can be,' Bellman said, remembering the stubborn resistance of the holdall to the flames of the council rubbish heap. The stench from the burning wig was still fresh in his nostrils.

Kitholm smiled. 'I said you were good, Bellman. Apparently you haven't lost your touch.'

Bellman did not reply and there was a long silence until Kitholm said, 'The strongest instinct.'

'What?'

Kitholm blinked guiltily. 'The strongest instinct – survival. When you were . . . convalescing, you spoke as if a successfully accomplished assignment would be of the utmost indifference to you.'

Bellman tensed. The words were a reflection of his own self-criticism.

Kitholm noticed the change in Bellman and said hurriedly, 'We'll order, shall we?'

Bellman read the menu without interest. The Tentman advertised its class by the scale of its prices. He was not hungry but he ordered a fish course and told the waiter to bring him a double whisky before the meal.

'Still hard at it?' Kitholm indicated Bellman's glass.

'As much as I need. I can afford it now. I could before but the surroundings weren't so classy. So why am I here?'

Kitholm insisted on eating before explaining. Bellman ate quickly. Kitholm savoured the food, passing judgment on various dishes in knowledgeable fashion. Bellman considered the observations were nothing but half-arsed snobbery. And said so.

When he had finished eating, Kitholm wiped his mouth with a napkin, meticulously dabbing and touching. He sent for coffee and when it arrived said, 'To the next stage then.'

Bellman lit a cigarette. 'Next stage?'

'Yes. The Toper business was only the beginning. Ill-concealed threats of retaliation against Datchett have already been bandied about. He's protested his innocence of course, but no-one believes him. To spark-off the situation we are going to supply an unarguable catalyst.'

'Fancy words. I suspect they mean me.'

'Of course.'

Bellman rocked his chair back. 'These are very small fry to be the target of a special set-up.'

'They are, but as I said before, they are only the means to an end. The pains will be felt in a much higher sphere.'

'Tell me.'

'You know the complete picture cannot be revealed.'

Bellman let himself fall forward again. 'Come *on*, Kitholm, do you expect me to work in the dark *all* the time?'

'Yes,' Kitholm said simply. 'Why the display of interest, anyway? When we last spoke you gave the impression that you couldn't care less.'

'It might make it easier for me – knowing what I'm up against.'

'That's too bad.' Kitholm sipped at his coffee. 'I can go this far – Toper was being used by a man we wish to get to. Datchett's firm is also being used, but by a different concern. Set those two factions against each other and much of the work will be done for us.'

'So what has to be done?'

'Namely – Datchett.'

'To what extent?'

Kitholm made a wavy movement with one hand. 'It doesn't matter too much. Hurt. Killed if necessary.'

'That's not very precise.'

'It doesn't need to be. The attempt will be enough to set the two camps against each other.' He gazed into the distance for a time. 'Actually, Datchett's death would come as something of a bonus.'

Bellman studied Kitholm with such intensity that he shifted in his seat. 'What's the matter?'

Bellman gave a bewildered shake of his head. 'I still have difficulty believing what I hear – coming from you, I mean. You would have been the last man I would think of to be involved in this.'

Kitholm writhed in his chair. 'I truly believe in Decimate L. It's the only . . .'

'Forget it,' Bellman said, too indifferent to capitalise on Kitholm's discomfort. 'Tell me about this so-called next stage.'

'What do you remember about Datchett?'

'Thug. Usual petty-theft beginnings. Graduated to the bigger stuff – jump-ups, blaggings. Eventually controlled a few similar types down east somewhere. He hasn't been convicted for a few years but enjoys the fact that most people *know* he's involved in some heavy jobs – presumably under the guidance of the man you want to crack. That's my recollection. Things have probably changed.'

'Not so you'd notice,' Kitholm said. 'In fact that's a pretty fair précis of Mr Datchett's activities. He's had a good run. Now he has to fall. The only instruction I have is where it has to be.' He took out his note-book, flicked through the pages, then returned it to his pocket. 'One thing about villains, they're always predictable. You know about his mother?'

Bellman wrinkled his forehead. 'Lives somewhere in Hackney?'

'Yes. Hundred and forty-three Dowson Street. Datchett visits her every Friday evening before the week-end merry-go-round. He usually arrives around seven and stays with her for about an hour.'

Bellman began to laugh. Not loudly, but in a steadily growing swell of genuine amusement.

'What's so funny about that?' Kitholm asked huffily.

'The location,' Bellman spluttered. 'The psychology of it. Whoever thought of attacking him there must have criminal tendencies. Apart from the actual pain, the humilia-

64

tion of being done right on "Mum's" doorstep will be more than he can bear – assuming he lives.'

Kitholm sat with downcast eyes and Bellman stabbed a finger at him. 'It was *you*, Kitholm. Good Christ, man, you're positively obscene.' He began to laugh again.

'I was asked for my view,' Kitholm said coldly. 'I did my best to think as a villain.'

'They'll be sending you on a shooting next.'

'I don't think so. That will be left to the expert – you.'

'Any particular method for dealing with Datchett?'

Kitholm raised his shoulders. 'Not really. He has others with him when he visits his mother. They wait in the car. I presume you will have to shoot him.'

'Friday,' Bellman said speculatively. 'That's the day after tomorrow. It will have to be done then; next week would be too long between incidents.' Kitholm nodded.

'Okay,' Bellman said. 'Friday it will be. Can I take it that I won't be followed everywhere?'

'You can take it that the scene – Dowson Street – will be left clear. The rest of the time there will still be a certain amount of surveillance. Praeger insists.'

'Providing they're no more tenacious, I don't mind.' Bellman said.

Bellman was having problems with his eyes.

The sort of spectacles used by actors were useless when it came to deceiving the ultra-cautious, the plain glass of the false lenses betraying the lie.

The glasses that perched on Bellman's nose had been bought, second-hand, from a stall in Shepherds Bush market; an optician's nightmare of piled frames.

The heavy tortoise-shell surrounds added a new dimension to his face but the lenses, although only weak, caused sufficient distortion to make his head ache. He had bought them years before and used them successfully on two occasions. But not to shoot anyone.

The dim lights of the Soho club were no help.

'I don't know you,' the little man sitting opposite Bellman said.

'If you did, the last thing I would do is ask you to sell me a shooter,' Bellman said, pushing a finger at the peak of his canvas cap.

'You know what I mean,' the man said appealingly.

'Listen,' Bellman said. 'I've got "readies" here. I need a gun. If you can get me one – now – say so, otherwise piss-off and let me find somebody who *will* do business.'

The other licked his lips nervously then, suddenly decided, stood up. 'Wait here, I'll be back in ten minutes. Forty quid, right?'

'Providing it's what you say it is – and has the ammo'.'

'It has, it has.' The little figure disappeared hurriedly, a swinging door the only indication of his passage.

Bellman sipped at the watered whisky and grinned. Watered scotch to a bloody expert.

'Not just now, love,' he said to the girl who had moved to his table and made to sit down. His words halted her, the silk-shining backside hovering over the seat like a gaudy dragonfly. She did not look at him but walked away with an affronted sway.

Bellman caught the arm of a passing waiter, a muscled type who would have looked more at home in a boxing-ring than slinging drinks as he was. 'Another whisky,' Bellman said. 'This time I'll have one from the bottle that hasn't been tampered with.' He placed two pound notes on the tray which hovered above his head.

The waiter opened his mouth to protest, then realised that one note would have covered the cost of the drink – even at the club's inflated prices. 'Yes, sir.' The 'sir' emerged with the rough embarrassment of unfamiliarity. When the drink arrived it was a double and Bellman's taste-buds confirmed it was undiluted.

'I've got it, I've got it.' The little man slid into the seat, unobtrusively patting the pocket of his raincoat.

'I'd never have believed it,' Bellman said sardonically,

but the derision was lost on the other who smiled proudly across the table.

'Give it to me, then.'

The small body twitched. 'Here, guv? Can't we go in the bog or somewhere?'

Bellman wagged a finger. 'I know your type, you'll get me in there and insist on kissing me.' His tone hardened. 'Give me the bloody thing.'

The gun, wrapped in brown paper, was pushed on to his lap. He trampled the wrapping to the floor and finger-checked the automatic, ensuring that the magazine slide and breech were empty.

'Ammunition?'

The magazine emerged from the man's pocket and travelled under the table, accompanied by the same amount of neck-twisting furtiveness.

Bellman slid the rounds from the magazine. There were five. He put the bullets and magazine into his pocket, then cocked the gun. The click as he squeezed the trigger could have been the real thing.

'For Christ's *sake*, guv.'

Bellman took out forty pounds and handed them across the table. 'It seems to be all right but if there's something wrong which I can't see in this light...'

'There's nothing wrong with it. Honest. Well, if you're satisfied...' He got to his feet.

'Siddown,' Bellman growled.

The chair gave a squeal as the little man dropped down again. 'What...?'

'We leave together,' Bellman said. 'If I get lumbered on the way out I want you in reach.'

'Leave off, guv. I'm not like that.'

Bellman stood up and wiped his mouth. 'No? Then you've nothing to worry about.'

They walked out together.

Bellman wedged the gun under the seat in the Toyota and drove back to the flat.

The tail-cars had been changed but one of them was parked only thirty yards from the house. He had lost them on the way to the club. The evasion had not seemed to raise much consternation.

He went over his plans while making coffee. It was only twelve hours since the lunch time meeting with Kitholm and he already had the gun. Now he needed a vehicle.

Before getting into bed he went to the window and looked down at the waiting car. He was tempted to tap on the glass and give a wave but he remembered the times he had drawn the monotonous duty of observation and stopped himself.

It took Bellman three hours to find the van he wanted. The dark green Bedford stood in a quiet back street near the hospital. He left his car near Stamford Brook station and returned to the van.

He had a prickly sensation at the back of his neck as he drove the Bedford away. The theft had been ham-fisted and his lack of finesse worried him.

The silence which followed the killing of the engine when he reached the parking lot at Wormwood Scrubs was a relief.

The small jar of black enamel was awkward to hold in gloved fingers and the paint brush almost impossible. But he persisted. He used a straight piece of wood to guide the brush as he drew the six-inch horizontal line in two places on each side of the van. When that was done he painted the glass of the rear windows on the inside, leaving an eye-sized hole in the centre of each. The result, when he retreated to survey his work, was disappointing. It looked exactly what it was – a van, painted with pointless black marks.

He left, hoping the effect would look different at night.

The walk to the station at White City raised a thirst in him and as he back-tracked to his car, he debated the wisdom of picking up the tails who had been dumped yet again. He decided against it and found a pub by the Thames and a bottle of whisky.

The mud-oil mixture of the water flowing beside the pub, reflected his mood. Since shooting Toper he had constantly tried to analyse his feelings. And found he had none; only total indifference, if that could be described as a feeling. So what was he? Mentally ill? He shook himself. Balls! A piss-artist. Pure and simple.

He visited the van when the light was poor. The work with the black paint looked exactly as he hoped it would. The thin lines resembled the slits let into the sides of police observation vehicles; the so-called 'unmarked' transports. But to any criminal with ambition, the subterfuge was wasted; the fittings proclaimed the vehicle's calling as well as any neon sign. It was rare for a new, disguised transport to be on the streets for more than a week without its details being known to the criminal fraternity.

Bellman left the Toyota and drove the van east, leaving it among a welter of vehicles in a narrow side street. With the rotor-arm in his pocket he rode the Underground back west.

He had decided against an overnight watch on the van. If it was discovered by the police before he came to use it, he was confident of recognising a stake-out.

Praeger was the worry. Kitholm's superior knew exactly where the strike against Datchett would take place and that gave Bellman an uneasy feeling. If Praeger intended double crossing him the ideal time and location would be when he attacked Datchett. On the other hand he had been allowed to deal with Toper without interference.

It was easy to believe that his usefulness was only in the early stages, but would he be able to anticipate the parting of the ways?

He left the train and found a telephone.

He was not sure if it was the same one, but a female voice answered.

'I want to speak to Mr Praeger,' Bellman said.

'I'm sorry he's not here at the moment.'

'Kitholm then.'

She said, 'Hold the line, please.'

Kitholm sounded ill-tempered. 'Who is it?'

'Me – Bellman. Listen, Kitholm, I've been thinking. Tomorrow I'll be right on offer. You know precisely where I will be. I don't like it.'

'Of course we will. So what's the problem?'

'I want to be certain that none of your mob will be near the premises.'

'I've already told you ...'

'I mean *anywhere* near.'

'You have my assurance ...'

'I don't give a shit for your assurance. If I see anyone who I believe to be connected with you – the job's off. Understand?'

'Whatever's made you so jumpy?'

'I'm not jumpy. I just think you may have decided to keep an eye on things. Don't – and that includes "distance" observation.'

Bellman left the call-box and walked to the nearest pub. The car could stay where it was until the following day.

'I'm sorry to disturb you, sir, but Bellman has just telephoned.' It was the first time Kitholm had called Praeger at home.

'That's all right. What did he want?'

When Kitholm told him, Praeger said, 'What do you make of it?'

'I've had a few minutes to think about it – I believe it must be to do with the flats.'

'The flats?'

'High-rise blocks. They overlook Dowson Street. He's worried that we might post men up there.'

'Why should he be worried about that?'

Kitholm was pleased to get the drop on Praeger but tried not to show it. 'That's where *he'll* be.'

The static sounded faintly in Kitholm's ear while Praeger digested what he had said.

Finally Praeger asked, 'A rifle? Is he good enough? He must be out of practice.'

'I think we must...'

'Will the overwatch men be using those buildings?' Praeger said tetchily.

'More than likely. You directed them to use anywhere advantageous.'

'Cancel the overwatch,' Praeger said and the line clicked dead.

Chapter Eight

Bellman woke with a terrible pain in his shoulder. The previous night's drinking had been monumental even by his standards. The resulting anaesthesia had allowed him to sleep in a contorted heap.

It took ten minutes to massage life back into the limb.

While the coffee was heating he visited the bathroom. 'That's more like the Bellman I know,' he said to his red-eyed, stubbled reflection.

He lay in the bath, coffee and cigarettes on a nearby chair and processed his thoughts. When he had covered every point that came to mind he returned to the immediate. The first action must be to test the automatic.

After breakfasting on toast – all his stomach could stand – he left the flat.

The Hillman was waiting in the crescent; two faces watched from behind the windscreen.

To make it easy for them he walked to the main road and stopped a taxi. It was not far to the Toyota and fifteen minutes later he was driving round Shepherds Bush Green. The Hillman faithfully followed each move he made. It took three attempts and a slice of luck with an articulated lorry before the shimmering image disappeared from the driving-mirror.

He headed north with a sigh of relief which quickly changed to bellowed curses as he became certain of the identity of the battered-looking Vauxhall which followed his route.

For five hectic minutes he indulged in an uncaring series of grinding turns and tyre-screeching drifts through the streets of a shocked Harlesden. The Vauxhall, despite its aged appearance, hung on determinedly.

He had just decided on what to say to Praeger if the police should intervene, as was inevitable if the mad, careering ride was to continue, when the same thought seemed to occur to the occupants of the Vauxhall. It slowed and dropped away.

Not until half an hour afterwards was he fully satisfied that he was tail-free. A spark of sympathy for the un-defeated driver of the Vauxhall flicked through his mind.

Two hours later he was on a stretch of the A1 which he thought would suit his purpose. He filtered off to the left and followed the road which looped over the main carriage-way and into the countryside. With nothing in sight but a distant moving tractor he stopped the car and took out the automatic.

A collection of rubbish lay scattered in a mud-ridged gateway. Bellman selected an empty oil-drum and stood it upright in the field before retreating and raising the gun.

When he squeezed the trigger there was an unsatisfactory 'crack', unlike the blasting detonation of his favourite Webley .38, but the oil-drum moved and a small hole appeared off-centre. He fired once more, noting that the second hole was near enough to the first to claim reasonable accuracy for the weapon.

After heaving the canister into the ditch he turned the Toyota and drove back to London.

The Hillman and Vauxhall sat in the crescent like dis-gruntled, mechanical animals. Bellman entered the house without giving them a second glance.

He spent half an hour cleaning the gun and oiling the working parts. When he had finished he wrapped it in a cloth and put it beside the clothes he had laid out ready for the evening.

The brush that stood in the corner of the kitchenette was too long for what he wanted. It took twenty cursing minutes to shorten it by nine inches with a kitchen knife and wrap it in layers of newspaper, with a final covering of corrugated cardboard. The result, he thought, looked as near to a covered rifle as could be achieved.

He changed into the clothes he had got ready, wondering if his struggle with the decoy gun was necessary. He had been deliberately vague about the address in Dowson Street when Kitholm asked him – he knew the area well – but had Kitholm assumed he would use the vantage of the over-looking dwellings as he hoped he would?

Why was he fighting, anyway? If Kitholm's new ruthless image was to be believed, Bellman knew he would produce enough evidence to smother him whenever it was necessary. The fact that little of it would be authentic would only give the whole affair an extra taste of bitterness. And that only applied if a terminal method was not used.

Bellman left the flat with the automatic bundled together with the canvas hat and spectacles. The wrapped broom-handle he carried at the trail, ostensibly guarding it from the view of the watchers in the car. He prayed briefly for a block in their mental processes when they tried to figure out how he had transported a rifle to the flat.

The cars only followed as far as Marble Arch before dropping away.

Bellman doubled-back twice to ensure that there were no replacement vehicles at his back, then drove to the East End.

At six-fifteen he was in the van and moving towards Dowson Street. A circuit of the area revealed nothing out-wardly suspicious so he began a regular patrol – large sweeps with Dowson Street as the hub.

He had donned the hat but left the spectacles in his pocket.

He did not see the silver Mercedes arrive but it was parked outside number forty-three when he returned from a circuit of the neighbouring streets.

Although it was dusk, Bellman waited for ten minutes before turning the Bedford towards the Mercedes and driving past. He parked on the forecourt of the nearby apartment block, leaving the vehicle at an angle so the plain sides directly faced the silver car.

There was no interior door to divide the driving compartment of the Bedford from the main body, but it was dark inside, giving the illusion of a dimmed and separate section. Bellman backed into the rear of the van and waited.

Dowson Street was made up like many others in the area – old houses on the way down; new flats on the way up. There were a few in-between pieces of open ground which awaited the builders. Number forty-three was the centre house in a remaining terrace of five. The crumbling brick hutches cowered beneath the looming modern concrete in structural terror.

Bellman only had a short wait before seeing movement in the Mercedes. When he had driven by, he had seen that it contained two men; one in the driving position, the other sprawled untidily in the rear.

It was the man in the back seat who moved, leaving the car and swaggering to the door of forty-three. A figure appeared in the doorway in response to his knock and he indicated the van where Bellman crouched. The one who came from inside the house stepped out to follow the other's pointing finger.

It was four years since Bellman had seen Datchett – a brief glimpse of an arrogant, protesting man in a police, charge-room. He had changed very little. Even under the inadequate street-light, Bellman could see that, if anything, he was heavier. The shoulders looked as powerful as ever, but the body had the bellied, overfed puffiness of indulgence.

Datchett moved forward a few steps, turning his face up to the light. His trousers were dark and Bellman could see that the shirt reflected the light as only expensive silk can do.

For a moment Bellman thought he had miscalculated and Datchett was going to approach the Bedford, but he did not, raising a hand to his eyes instead, pretending to shield himself from the glare of the overhead light as he looked towards the van. The man from the car followed suit. The ever-eager servant.

'You all right in there, Bill?' Datchett directed the question through cupped hands, the echo of the discordant bellow rebounding from the walls of the concrete giant above. The question was followed by a shout of laughter in which the the side-kick dutifully joined. Finally Datchett made a masturbatory jerk in the direction of the van and swaggered back to the house. His companion climbed back into the Mercedes.

Before Datchett disappeared he made an exaggerated sweep of the arm to look at his watch. ' 'Bout half an hour, Bill. After that we're going to the Trident. Expect to see you tagging along.' There was more laughter as he closed the door.

Bellman was satisfied. There was nothing more likely to please the animal courage of the villain than to openly flout his contempt of 'Old Bill' – the police – when he was on safe ground. Nevertheless he was sure that Datchett would be out before the promised half-hour, the irritating presence of the enemy working on the system.

He was right.

The door of the house opened precisely twenty minutes after Datchett had gone inside. Bellman could see that the bullish figure's head was turned, reassuring some unseen inmate.

Bellman set the spectacles across his nose and climbed into the driving seat, swearing quietly when his thin gloves snagged on a projecting screw. He started the engine, engaged the gears, and moved towards the Mercedes as Datchett crossed the pavement.

Datchett now wore a coat and as the Bedford approached he threw back the lapels then hooked his thumbs over his belt in a time-honoured show of unconcern.

As the van drew level with the posing figure, Bellman

braked to a halt and lifted the gun from the floor. Ignoring the distorting lenses, he sighted on Datchett's heart and fired.

The expression on Datchett's face hardly changed. The police just did not aim guns at people – unless they were similarly threatened – so the sudden materialisation of the gun was totally incomprehensible to him.

The bullet was not. But it killed him.

Bellman never knew if it was good shooting – considering the spectacles – or pure luck which sent the bullet exactly where he aimed it, smashing through the rib bones, the distorted lead moving the heart away from its connecting veins and arteries. For all practical purposes, Datchett was dead before his last, concertina action dropped his head to the ground.

The driver of the Mercedes had been lounging behind the wheel, emulating his boss by curling his lips and showing a mouthful of contemptuous teeth as the Bedford halted. Blind courage moved him from the position and half-out of the car a second after Bellman fired. Instinctive prudence caused him to duck and leap aside as Bellman turned the gun on him.

The man in the rear seat sat frozen.

Bellman accelerated away, dabbed the brakes at the end of the street, and began the turn. With the van at a crawl he looked back. The driver was crouched over Datchett with his companion about to join him. Both faces turned towards the retreating Bedford. The driver straightened from his inspection of the body and headed towards the Mercedes.

Bellman used the two remaining rounds to deter him, the quick 'crack-crack' starring the Mercedes's rear window opaque. Both men disappeared behind the vehicle in a flurry of flailing limbs.

Bellman knew where he wanted to dump the van but was forced to wait until two teenagers, sidling down the line of cars, saw the slowly moving Bedford and swung away. He turned the van sharply beside a towering lorry, stopped the engine, and threw the gun into the rear compartment. After removing the hat and spectacles he walked away from the vehicle, reaching the Toyota three minutes later. Twenty minutes afterwards he was again opening the door of a locker on Victoria station to bundle the gloves, spectacles and headgear inside.

There were no waiting cars outside the house in Fortis Crescent. Inside Bellman bathed, scrubbing furiously at his wrists and forearms knowing the precaution was pointless, but pleased to be occupied. When he was finished he returned to the living-room and sat chain-smoking until he considered the time was right to telephone Praeger. Strangely, the thought of pouring a drink did not occur to him.

The telephone rang at ten-thirty, ten minutes before Bellman's own decided time. It was Praeger.

'Very good, Bellman,' he said.

Bellman remained silent.

'Did you hear me?' Praeger said, the irritation apparent in his voice.

'Yes.'

'I see. The strong, silent killer.'

'Bollocks, Praeger. You want to say something – say it.'

'Oh dear! What a bad start. I only wanted to congratulate you . . . extraordinary lengths.'

'What?'

Praeger's voice rose. 'I said extraordinary lengths – both of evasion and execution. Evasion referring to the disguised approach, of course.'

'When dealing with men like you it's an obvious precaution. It was no part of the agreement for me to be followed everywhere in any case.'

Praeger's thin laugh echoed over the line. 'As I remember it there was no agreement otherwise . . . however, you've made your point. There will be no surveillance from now on.'

'Big deal.'

'Don't get out of hand, Bellman.'

Bellman said, 'Bollocks', again, but felt a stomach-twinge at the latent threat in Praeger's words.

'Our friends, the police, are not very happy,' Praeger continued. 'The East End is rife with rumours of assassin policemen. It's a little near the truth. Was it wise?'

'They'll find the van.'

'They've already done that. Indeed, it's almost on exhibition at the local station. At the moment it's being worked over by the fingerprint boys, but it is parked near enough to the station gate for the rubber-neckers to confirm that it was a theatrical piece – keeps the natives happy.'

Bellman waited. He knew his attitude was annoying Praeger but couldn't bring himself to ease the situation with a few polite words.

'We'll be in touch,' Praeger said finally.

'I suppose you will,' Bellman replied.

'It would appear that we have a surprise on our hands,' Praeger said.

'I did say he was good,' Kitholm ventured.

Praeger inclined his head. 'True, but even you under-estimated.... Sniper!' The word was uttered with total derision.

Kitholm moved uncomfortably. 'It was the obvious answer.'

'Precisely,' Praeger said, staring fixedly forward. 'Suddenly Mr Bellman has become very important ... however, we must ensure that we don't grasp a tiger by the tail.'

When he had left the room, Kitholm did a mental recitation. 'Or a nigger in the wood-pile ... or a cat among the pigeons ... or a spanner in the works.' He searched for other tags. Praeger's was best.

Chapter Nine

'*Gang Warfare on London's Streets.*' '*Three Shootings as Street Battles Rage.*' '*Commissioner: "Intolerable. These Monsters Will be Stopped".*' Bellman read the stories below the headlines. There was little variation. The rumblings in the East End of London had grown steadily until, on Saturday night, open warfare erupted between the Datchett and Toper factions. It was obvious that other scores were being settled in the general furore – real and imagined.

Many of the happenings had been too late to catch the Sunday editions, but the Monday nationals gave extensive coverage to the battles that had carried over from the Saturday night, dimmed, then flared again on the Sunday evening.

The score was one man dead and twenty-three wounded by gun-shot or knife. In one incident in Mare Street, Hackney, two car-loads of men had carried out a running battle in a style reminiscent of Chicago in the 1920s.

The newspaper reports affected Bellman.

He had remained inside the flat on Saturday and Sunday drinking, but not desperate, depressed but in no need of further diversion to take his mind off the killing of Datchett. After reading the reports on Monday morning he headed for the pubs and oblivion.

The persistent ringing finally woke Bellman. It was ten am. He lifted the receiver, said, 'Later', in a slurred, furry voice, and crashed the instrument down again.

For ten minutes he sat and stared into space, the empty

bottle at his feet. His suit was splattered with mud and patterned with tram-line creases.

When he came out of his reverie he looked longingly at the coffee-making equipment, denying himself with a shake of his head and heading for the bathroom.

The hot water washed away the sweat and drew the cramped aches from his body.

He was sitting on the couch with a large mug of coffee before him when Kitholm rang again.

'Spartan but clean is the expression, I suppose,' Kitholm said, eyeing the barn-like dimensions of the one-roomed Thomas Binn.

'It's different,' Bellman admitted non-committally.

'Definitely.' Kitholm's tone was only a degree below caustic.

'If I'd known you were likely to produce an orgasm, I'd have suggested a pie-and-eel shop,' Bellman grunted.

Kitholm said nothing. His recent dealings with Bellman had given him a certain immunity. But he considered it more necessary than ever to play the superior. 'Why did you suggest this place? It took me hours to find it.'

Bellman used the bottom of his beer-glass to join together the several rings of spilled ale on the scrubbed-wood table. 'I like it here. I also wanted to avoid somewhere of your choosing – starched waiters and endless discussion on what wine we should have.'

'We won't be subject to any of that talk here,' Kitholm agreed, surveying the place again.

Bellman stood up. 'Shall we eat?'

He enjoyed Kitholm's awkwardness as a man in a striped apron handed them knives, forks and plates before pointing to the sides of beef and mutton, spitted at the end of the counter.

Bellman carved thick slices of beef with the chained carving-knife, then handed it to Kitholm. As he piled his plate with roast potatoes and Yorkshire pudding from the recessed, metal containers, Kitholm struggled hopelessly with the meat.

Bellman returned to the table with his plate, then ordered more drinks at the bar.

When Kitholm returned to the table he was looking ruefully at the massacred meat on his plate. 'I never was much good at this kind of thing,' he said.

'It'll taste the same,' Bellman said with a touch of conscience.

They ate slowly, Bellman in particular enjoying the meat with its streaks of running red. When they had finished, Bellman visited the counter and returned with coffee.

They moved to the side of the room and sat in large chairs, separated from the other eaters by vast areas of space. Kitholm seemed to be more comfortable when clear of the rudimentary dining section. 'That was one hell of a rumpus you caused,' he said.

'I thought that was the idea.'

'It was, but the repercussions have been more violent than we expected.'

'What should I do? Go back and say I'm sorry?'

Kitholm gave a small cluck of amusement. 'Hardly. The action has been successful, that's the important thing. The camps are well and truly at each other's throats. The events that have followed Datchett's death have overshadowed the actual killing. There've never been so many arrests for GBH and so on.'

Bellman said, 'Good,' and lit a cigarette. 'What now? Is this meeting the prelude to more mayhem?' He said 'mayhem' with a deliberately theatrical air.

Kitholm dabbed at his mouth with a handkerchief. 'Yes. We're moving out of the lower strata. From now on the objectives will be bigger – the biggest, in fact.' He crossed a leg and tapped his knee with a short forefinger. 'You will remember the original discussion. The real targets are the top men – men who, up to now, have been untouchable.'

'I remember,' Bellman said, 'but I wasn't given any details.'

'You wouldn't have been told anything, other than your own part, if it could have been avoided.'

Bellman said, 'Up yours', and waited.

Kitholm's cheeks twitched momentarily, then he carried on. 'When you disposed of Toper and Datchett and subsequently ruined those who employed them, it was necessary path-clearing. The way is now open for us to attack the next objectives – Pool and Cliveson.'

'Sounds like a firm of solicitors.'

'No. Nothing like. They are the biggest of the new criminals. Each has his own outfit. Warwick Dunn Pool is a very rich man, inherited money mostly, but he's added to it in a variety of ways – stockbroking deals, property developments, gaming enterprises ... an endless list. Oh yes, and crime of course. He's one of those strange phenomena society throws up every now and then – a wealthy man who cannot resist illegal pickings. He enjoys life in the family tradition – county set, South of France, and so on. He is married and his three children, two boys and a girl, receive the best education that money can buy. His wife is a doyenne of numerous charities and Pool himself belongs to all the best clubs. No weak links as far as illicit sex is concerned – or any others for that matter. His mode of life keeps him clear of criminal playgrounds, and consequently free of attention from police intelligence departments. He is going to be a very difficult man to beat.'

Kitholm sipped at his coffee before continuing. 'Anthony Cliveson is something of a different proposition. He's a self-made man who began life in the north. There, with a small capital and a large will to succeed he entered the second-hand car business and, by the use of strong-arm methods, soon had the motor trade in several major towns well and truly tied up. He moved to London ten years ago. Cliveson's far from well educated, but he has a natural feel for business and as soon as he arrived on the local scene he sensed that methods which won the day up north would create more problems than they solved down here. So he went respectable, or ostensibly so, at least. He invested wisely in well-run clubs and made a killing in the property market during a very profitable period. Only gradually did he inch a finger into the criminal pie, but now he is well established. His name is not strange to the intelligence files, but at best he only features in the "suspected of" sections. His legal advice is the best available.'

Kitholm threw his arms wide, then slowly brought his hands together. 'That is one of the things that Pool and Cliveson have in common – the best advice. Both men have a host of front men in the shady-dealings department, and they are similarly possessed of an eye for an opportunity and a consummate greed. There,' the hands flew apart, 'the likeness ends.'

Bellman shifted in his seat. 'Neither of them sounds like a pillar of society, though Pool might appear to be on the surface, but nothing you've said stamps them as extraordinary.'

'Perhaps not,' Kitholm acknowledged, 'but you can take it from me, if they can be dealt with, the whole edifice of organised crime will crumble.'

'I'm right in assuming that you've told me something of their backgrounds because dealing with them is not going to be as straightforward as the action against Toper and Datchett?'

'You have it in one. The lesser lights of each organisation can be considered expendable, but as far as the principals are concerned certain rules have to be observed.'

'I understood that the rules went out the window when your department was formed.'

'To a great degree, they did, but by rules I really mean the avoidance of self-defeat. If Pool or Cliveson, or both, were merely disposed of, the action could back-fire. With Pool in particular the outcry would be enormous. Nevertheless, if their deaths were all that was needed to contain the menace – they would be sanctioned. As things stand, their passing would only serve to bury their dealings deeper, leaving the field open to others within their organisations. No. The answer is to destroy from the inside. That way the destruction will be complete, with no Phoenix ready to rise from the ashes and continue business.'

'One thing's for sure, Kitholm. If flowery phrases fought crime you'd be a one-man army.'

Kitholm glowered at Bellman, but he did not allow his annoyance to further intrude. 'If we can wreck either or both of their empires it will spell out a general warning that no-one will dare ignore.'

'Yeah, yeah. The "whole edifice" bit. Get to the ways and means.'

'Patience, Bellman. Although both organisations have concentrated on the same areas of crime on previous occasions, their meetings have brought no clashes; a few gentle bumps perhaps, but nothing serious. Pool and Cliveson are not aware of each other's aspirations, though they are coincidentally alike, but at the moment they are both interested in one aspect of crime, and there lies our opportunity.'

'The two camps will come up against each other and the sparks will fly?'

'With a little help from us. We believe that they are already aware of competition without knowing its exact source, and without someone telling them they may never know. The intermediaries may get to know their counterparts, but there is little danger that the identities of the top men will be revealed because both organisational structures are designed to prevent just that.'

Kitholm stopped and looked around the room as though he had just arrived. When he turned his attention back to Bellman he was disappointed to see him staring into space, apparently oblivious of the strategic break in the explanation.

'Which, in your opinion, is the most lucrative angle of crime at present unexploited by the big boys?' he snapped. Before Bellman could reply he went on, 'I'll tell you: women – brass – the high-class stuff in particular. In recent years organised prostitution, like many other things, has been without a figurehead. A few élite groups cater for the top custom; they make a great deal of money, but they would make even more if they troubled to concentrate their efforts. The rougher trade is handled by the continually warring networks in the West End. A few individual ponces run one or two girls, and that's about it. Disjointed.' He shook his head as though regretting that things were not better organised.

'Let us stay with the so-called "classy" side of the scene. A large percentage of the money earned from prostitution comes from the new-rich, the arabs. They have an insatiable appetite for our girls and they are willing to pay incredibly high fees for their services. Recently some of the providers of those services have been crossing swords over who should get the lion's share of the middle-eastern trade. The strong-arm side of Cliveson's organisation has actually been approached for help. That roused Cliveson's interest and he soon recognised the potential. He's naturally attracted to the type of business and he plans on becoming the new Messina.'

'There was more than one Messina,' Bellman said inconsequentially.

'Cliveson probably considers himself the equal of several,' Kitholm said. 'Pool, on the other hand, was alerted to the current position in quite a different way. His world is one of high-finance and many of his clients feel the need for female company once business matters have been attended to. Pool arranged for any such requests to be passed on to the call-girl operators, but after a time he realised that he was virtually giving money away. His present intention is to regroup the various stables under a section of his organisation.'

'Where does all this information come from?' Bellman asked.

Kitholm shook his head sadly. 'You can't help digging, can you, Bellman. You don't need to know where it comes from. The important thing is that the facts are true.' He paused briefly and considered what he had said. 'I can tell you this much,' he said, relenting slightly. 'We have contacts in both camps. Most of them are in the lower echelons, but they can tell us quite a lot. Also we have a constant flow of ... other information. Piece it all together and a pretty clear picture emerges. Be certain of one thing – Pool and Cliveson are on a collision course.'

'So why not let them cut each other's throats?'

Kitholm nodded. 'That would appear to be the obvious solution, I agree. But it wouldn't work. Pool and Cliveson are both shrewd men, they would recognise that open conflict would do nothing but damage both their causes, and they would work out a compromise. We believe we must play on their greed – create an atmosphere of distrust between them so that their reasoning deserts them and they declare war on each other. If this happened it would be bound to escalate, resulting in the destruction of both their empires.'

'One of them might decide that the prize is not worth fighting for and throw his hand in. That would mean happy birthday for whoever remained.'

'It's a possibility, but once they've involved themselves to some degree they will be most reluctant to retire gracefully, especially as it would mean kissing goodbye to the money they've already laid out.'

Bellman was suddenly anxious to end the talk. 'So what do I do?'

'I will give you an idea on how to begin, after that you have pretty much a free hand. Results are all that we're interested in.'

'I'm very honoured.'

'So you should be. I don't think you realise how difficult

it was for me to persuade Praeger that you were the best man for the job.'

'Why did you bother? Could it be that if your insistence was eventually justified your personal reputation would be enhanced?'

'Your opinion of me is unimportant,' Kitholm said. 'Let me give you the rest of the information then, at least, we will be able to part company. Pool's enquiries have been conducted through a man named Brantner who is usually employed in the property side of the business. Brantner is young, late twenties, and though he's inexperienced, criminally speaking, there is no doubt that Pool considers him very capable, otherwise he would not entrust him with an important new venture. Brantner has edged into the scene very cleverly, keeping to the periphery while learning the ropes. He's managed to recruit a couple of the rare girls who had kept themselves free of "protection" by hovering around moneyed men and acting as Mr Fixit when one of them saw a woman they fancied. He gets about quite a bit. Favours the Dayton. Know it?'

'Yeah – the casino.'

'Right. There have been other Pool-inspired probes, but the main action is with Brantner. Cliveson is fronted for by Terry Elson. You won't know the name because he's a recent import from Manchester. About three years ago he collected a con up there for GBH. A man with a conviction may sound a poor bet to act as a front man, but Elson's shrewd, a cut above the average assault merchant, and a reputation for violence isn't a bad thing if you're going to muscle in on heavy stuff. Elson's been more straightforward than Brantner, going directly to the girls under protection and suggesting that a more comprehensive scheme would be to their advantage. Existing ponces have faded rapidly. Elson also moves around, but his main hangout is the Loom. He can nearly always be found there at some time during an evening.'

Bellman lifted his eyebrows. 'I know the Loom. Haven't

been there for some time but they used to be pretty choosy who they admitted.'

'Still are to some extent. Elson has no problems.' Kitholm examined his fingertips. 'That's more or less all I can tell you. It may seem very little, but I can assure you, organised prostitution on a grand scale is a very definite possibility. We think you should join the club scene; become as knowledgeable about the workings of the girls and their minders as you used to be. Use any brass you think may be able to help; expenses are provided. If you can contact Brantner, Elson, or both, then do so. After that it's for you to decide how to cause the maximum amount of dissension. If violence comes into it, and I suppose it will, Elson must be the first to go.'

'Why Elson first?'

'Because we think that Cliveson's reaction will be more positive than Pool's. Especially if he's made to believe that Pool is responsible for whatever befalls Elson.'

Bellman chewed his lip for a time, then said, 'It's one thing to avoid being recognised in the few seconds it takes to shoot someone, but something else to move about clubland with impunity.'

'I'm sure you'll think of something,' Kitholm said.

'Why can't I hit Elson and Brantner outside – not get involved with them personally?'

'Because it wouldn't work as it did with Toper and Datchett. These are clever people we are dealing with from now on. And we need to know more about their plans; the details of possible replacements, anything you can find out. I warned you that this would be more difficult. There will be no gang warfare as a result of a single incident – at least, it's highly unlikely. It would have been simpler to do as you suggest, and safer for us – you wouldn't have been told the details for a start – but it would not work.'

Bellman stared unseeingly across the room. When he finally blinked and focused on Kitholm, he said, 'I can do it. It will take time.'

'How long?'

'A week. Maybe longer. And that's before I'm on the scene.'

'Explain that.'

'This needs a new approach. A new identity for me. I would leave here for a short time – come back as a new face on the London scene. The background is important.'

'You have a free hand. It should be all right – providing you don't take longer.'

'What about those little men who have been following me about?'

'That's all finished, you know that. Surveillance of you has ended. We are taking a chance on your good faith.'

'More likely you realise it's a pointless exercise.'

Kitholm reached into his pocket and came out with an envelope. 'Another five hundred.'

Bellman took the money. 'At least the expenses are good.'

'They're likely to be heavy where you're going. There's more if you need it – within reason.' He watched Bellman pocket the money. 'You wouldn't get very far with that amount if you decided to ...'

'Does it hurt, Kitholm? Dealing readies out and not asking for a receipt? Surely it must offend your rule-book mind ... Kitholm, the man with sub-paras instead of grey matter.' The reason for the attack was not clear even to Bellman. He thought it was probably because he was not in control of his own destiny, and Kitholm happened to be near.

'We expect to hear from you within a week, then,' Kitholm said, standing.

'No. I said I would be back here in a week. It will take as long again to filter into the scene. It's unlikely that you will hear from me earlier than the end of the second week.'

'Now look here . . .' Kitholm stopped as Bellman began to withdraw the envelope from his pocket.

Bellman watched Kitholm's jerky exit with great delight.

'How does he intend to approach the problem?' Praeger asked.

Kitholm said, 'I didn't ask.'

'Don't you think we're entitled to a certain amount of prior knowledge?'

'I believe that Bellman is the type of man best left to devise his own scheme. His two recent assignments prove my point, I think.'

Praeger's eyes narrowed, but his face was averted and Kitholm could not see the displeasure. 'Bellman's successes do not necessarily mean he's trustworthy.'

'I'm sure his interest has caught,' Kitholm said. 'He would do the job for its own sake.'

Praeger turned quickly. 'I sincerely hope you are wrong. That would be bordering on professionalism. We employed Bellman because he's a derelict and therefore expendable.'

Kitholm said, 'Yes, sir.'

Chapter Ten

Bellman shopped for food and drink, took it to the flat, and stayed there for two days while he worked out exactly what he planned to do. During that time he drank part of the stock of whisky he had bought, but he was never intoxicated. He began to grow a moustache.

At seven pm on the second day, he knew he had found the answer to the problem. An hour later he embarked on the first step – visiting various clubs and casinos, where he made application for membership under an assumed name. The Loom and the Dayton both received visits; at neither place did he encounter any objections. When he decided that he had covered as much ground as was necessary, he told himself that he had earned a decent drinking bout.

The following day, a Thursday, Bellman woke with a hangover which he only mastered with a fierce onslaught of coffee. When he felt reasonably human again, he went below and saw Mrs Anstey who fluttered and clucked at his insistence on paying a further two months' rent in advance.

'There's really no need, Mr Bellman. I'm quite happy with the present arrangement.'

Bellman wondered how she had failed to see his several drunken ascents of the stairs, mentally comparing her with other landladies – particularly the odious Mrs Clarke. 'I insist, Mrs Anstey. I may be away quite a lot during the next few weeks and I'd hate to lose the flat.'

'Oh, I'm sure that won't happen until you are ready to leave yourself.' She handled the sheaf of five-pound notes as though they were wet. 'It is a moustache you're growing, Mr Bellman? I'm sure it will suit you.'

Bellman was thankful when he was back upstairs. He packed a case and took it down to the car.

A few minutes after twelve noon he crimped the Toyota in a tight turn of the roundabout at Apex Corner and swung on to the A1 proper – and the beginning of his search.

When he entered the first transport café an hour later he knew his dress of slacks, slip-on shoes and thin jacket was not in keeping with the dungarees and boots of the seated truck drivers but he did not let it worry him.

The café had plastic-topped tables and a long, serving counter behind which a man in a clean, white apron shouted orders through the hatch at the rear. A disembodied voice answered each shout with a bored, 'Okay.'

Bellman ordered his fry and collected it when called.

Truck drivers were scattered in groups throughout the café, seemingly congregated according to their geographical origins, if dialect was an indication.

A corner table was occupied by a drive-weary family, the husband drooping with fatigue while his harassed wife tried to cope with two grizzling children.

There was only one other female present, a young girl sitting at a table with two men. She had long, dark hair which hung in straggled skeins on each side of a thin face. Her clothes were creased and a hole in the knee of her tights drew the eye's attention like a pallid magnet. The men ignored her whilst they ate. She was far from pretty.

Bellman finished his food and collected another tea before spreading a newspaper on the table before him, reading with detached interest, oblivious of the surroundings. Two teas and ninety minutes later the faces had changed but the dress and conversation were nearly the same.

Bellman had perked up twice, both times when a girl entered. The first was accompanied by a car driver who was obviously her husband and the second by a trucker who patently was not.

The girl with the trucker was a horrific mess of frizzed, red hair and panda eye make-up.

Bellman had afforded neither women more than a single glance.

He sighed and folded the paper. When he slid the Toyota away from the café and headed north again, the long stretch of road ahead of him reflected his mood. He had not expected it to be easy. Neither had he thought the prospect would look so bleak.

In the hours that followed he entered three more road-side cafés. Seven girls came under his scrutiny. All failed. Some were too old. One was definitely too young. None of them had anything but the tired, gritty look of the mobile prostitute. This was to be expected, but Bellman was searching for a difficult to define, exploitable quality which he knew could sometimes be found among the transient colony of road-girls.

He abandoned his search at ten that night and booked in at a guest house, fighting the temptation to call at the nearby pub, and losing.

The following day he ranged as far as Doncaster and returned to Grantham before resting for the night. He was discouraged, not only by the fact that he had failed to see the type of girl he was looking for, but also because none had come even near to his specifications.

His only consolation was the moustache, which was growing. Though far from fully formed it covered his upper lip and drooped obediently below his mouth at the corners.

It was the next day, Saturday, that he found her.

The café was off the main road, partly hidden by trees. This time he saw the sign on the grass verge which he had missed on several other occasions. He was pleased to find somewhere new, becoming increasingly aware of the odd looks he was being given in revisited cafés from those used to the rebounding trips of commercial truckers, but suspicious of yo-yo Toyota drivers.

He needed the coffee he ordered, having driven for an unbroken two hours.

The place was smaller than most and lacked the cloying stickiness of the larger establishments. There were only six tables. A box of a counter stood at the rear wall. To all appearances only two customers were inside, men, sitting at separate tables but conversing loudly across the intervening space.

Bellman was collecting his drink from the fleshy pink-faced man who dwarfed the small counter when he heard a female voice say, 'Piss-off and let me alone.'

When he turned he saw that one of the men was making obscene gestures at a girl who stood stiffly upright in the corner behind the door as though anxious to disassociate herself from the surroundings.

She had long, brown hair which needed combing but looked clean. The face below the hair was also long but without the usual attendant thinness. A broad forehead balanced the firm chin and slightly prominent cheek-bones accented the merest touch of Asiatic slant at the corners of the eyes.

She was tall. Bellman estimated that, close up, she would only stand a couple of inches shorter than himself. Her bust was small, raising only slight mounds under the pink-grubbiness of her sweater. Perhaps her most striking features were the long, slim legs which were beautiful and, beneath anything but the dusty, black skirt, could be magnificent. She wore once-white sandals and her feet were dirty.

Through the tawdriness shone the quality Bellman had been searching for: an aliveness which unconsciously defeated her present mood; the promise of humour in the flecked eyes; youth; character.

Bellman took his cup to a table and sat so that he could see the girl without directly facing her.

The teasing man said, 'What's your name?'

'None of your bloody business,' the girl snarled.

'What's *your* business?' the second man cackled.

The girl ignored him and walked to the counter. 'Give me a tea, Fred,' She spun a coin on the plastic covering and leaned over to catch something the fat man said in a quiet undertone. 'Who them?' she said loudly, turning to look at her tormentors. 'Nah! They don't bother me. I doubt you could make one man from the pair of them.'

The man sprawled nearest the door produced a five-pound note and crackled it suggestively between thumb and forefinger.

The girl said, 'Put it away, your missus'd kick your arse if you even spent half a quid of that.'

The man behind the counter gave a bellow of laughter which somehow managed to convey that the game was over.

The men at the tables got to their feet and left.

'How'd you end up here, Jo?' the one named Fred asked. 'Not often I see you.'

The girl wafted a disgusted hand and sat down heavily. 'Christ! I don't know. I got this punter way up ... oh *somewhere*. Not a trucker – guy in a small van, traveller or something. Anyway, on the way down he's telling me that we'll put up for the night, so I'm secure, right ...? Yeah?' She tossed her head. 'The bastard stopped for petrol and when I got back from the Ladies, he's gone.'

'It's a hard life, right enough,' the heavy man said. 'Now why don't you ...'

'Fred. FREEED!' She was on her feet, pirouetting, an accusing hand making a finger revolver which pointed at his huge stomach. 'No conversions, Fred.'

The big man smiled sheepishly, including Bellman in the apology, and walked through a door behind the counter.

Bellman lit a cigarette and stared straight ahead, his eyes avoiding the girl.

'You hear that?' she said belligerently.

He turned and looked at her. 'Yes.'

'And what did you think?' Her eyes were running over him. Assessing.

Bellman gave a disinterested shrug. 'What do you want me to say? You know your way around ... Okay ... So what?'

She moved over to him and stood spread-legged. 'Got a cigarette?'

Bellman flicked the packet on the table but didn't offer to open it for her.

She took one and stood waiting.

'Christ!' Bellman said. 'You do like the treatment, don't you?' He held his lighter out to her.

Without taking her eyes from him she clicked the lighter into flame, the action proving her worldliness: identification by feel; a life of travelling cigarette lighters.

'Sorry,' she said, sitting on the chair opposite him. 'It's been a pig of a day. I shouldn't have tried to take it out on you.'

Bellman only shrugged.

'Hey!' she said. 'You're not very friendly, are you?' Her elbows were resting, flanked by her hair which brushed the table as she thrust her head forward to peer at him.

He shrugged again.

She studied him suspiciously, sensing he was more interested than he appeared to be, but he met her eyes and she gave up the scrutiny. After smoking silently for a time she said, 'You interested?'

'What?' Bellman was surprised at the suddenness of the question.

'In me. Fancy me?'

'I'm interested,' Bellman said carefully.

'Depends on the price, I suppose,' she said knowledgeably. 'A fiver?' The price came in a quieter voice. Open to negotiation.

'I said I'm interested. Come for a drive and I'll explain.'

She said, 'Oy, oy!'

'What's wrong?'

'I just got dumped by one like you.'

'Leave off. I'm not a kink.'

'They all say that.'

Bellman reached inside his coat and peeled off two notes without revealing the bundle. He handed them to her. 'Ten pounds. Does that help?'

She took the money but looked at him doubtfully. 'It's good pay ... what goes with it?'

'For the money? – merely a talk, I promise. I'm not a crank. You can get out of the car at any time you want.'

She decided quickly, scooping up her large, floppy handbag. 'Okay. Let's go.' She walked to the door without a backward glance.

Bellman drove steadily, keeping to the slower lane.

The girl sat at an angle, her back resting between the seat and the door. One leg was folded beneath her. She said, 'So?'

Bellman glanced over at her and smiled. 'Fancy moving up a few leagues?'

She studied him for a time, then her shoulders began to shake as she laughed silently.

'Why are you laughing?' he said.

She pushed away the hair which had fallen over her face. 'Sorry. It's just that I had you figured for something different.'

'Like what?'

'Oh, I don't know ... "How did you start in this game? Wouldn't you like a regular life – roof over your head" perhaps.'

'Get many offers like that?'

She made a little squeak of amusement. 'Often. They never come to anything.'

'What happens?' He was not really interested but was anxious to keep her talking. Conversation regularised any new relationship; made it more comfortable; usually.

She acted with an exaggerated concern. '"Come home with me," they say. "I'll introduce you as my girl. You can

98

have a new start."' The chuckle was harsh – bitter. 'I've taken them up a couple of times – just to see what would happen. You should see how they begin to fall to pieces about fifty miles from home. Christ! They make me sick.'

'I'm not offering that.'

'I know.' She looked at him carefully then said, 'You're a ponce.'

Bellman kept his eyes on the road. 'Yes.'

'Funny. You don't strike me as one.'

'That's why I'm successful.'

The girl pointed a finger at him, sighting her eye along it. 'If you're so successful how come you're recruiting road-girls?'

'Not girls ... girl. You.'

'Don't give me that.'

'I don't tell lies,' he said quietly.

His tone silenced her and she lowered the accusing finger. Then, 'London?'

'Yes.'

'What happened to your last girl? Or do you run more than one?'

'Just one. She left me to work in a club on a regular basis.'

'And you let her? I thought you usually "disciplined" girls who did that.'

'I don't work that way. I would but it causes unnecessary trouble. If you come with me you'll live in a reasonable pad and get enough money for new clothes – good ones. You would be working in top-class surroundings.'

She watched the road for a long time, occasionally glancing at him, swift, searching peeps. Finally she said, 'Why me?'

'Why not?'

'I wasn't the first girl you came across.'

'No. I've been searching for three days. Some girls have it – others don't. You have.'

The uncertainty showed in her voice. 'I seem to have

heard that before. Why not take up a local girl? One from London, I mean?'

Bellman drummed his fingers on the steering wheel. 'I could do that, but it's better to start with a new face. The mystery element's essential when you're working the top trade. Down there they've seen it all before. A new face and ... youth. That works.'

She began to laugh again, not stopping until he gave her a long, questioning stare. 'Sorry,' she said. 'It's your manner – so direct. It may be wrapped up in different words but your offer means get on your back and earn.'

'Of course.'

'I do that already.'

Bellman gave a cluck of disgust. 'For how much? Christ! Don't you see what I'm offering?'

'I keep all my earnings,' she said stubbornly. 'Ponces take most of what a girl works for.'

'You keep half of what you make with me, and that would be twenty times what you make on the road.'

'That's generous – from a ponce.' She accentuated the word deliberately, watching for a reaction.

'It is. I'm not greedy. The earnings are big.'

She shook her head. 'You're too good to be true.'

Bellman shrugged. 'Try me.'

'It's not a unique situation. I've heard that this has happened to other girls.' Her voice portrayed a certain amusement.

With the easing in their relationship and the absence of obscenities her speech was not unattractive. Bellman guessed that she was from the Midlands, but there was something else, some indefinable element.

'I still don't see why it's me that's getting this never-to-be-repeated offer,' she said.

'I've told you. You have something – and you're young. How old?'

'Twenty.'

'Balls. Eighteen – maximum.'

She nodded vigorously, smiling. 'Just.'

'There you are. But don't think that only you would fit the bill. If you refuse, I'll look for someone else.'

'For another three days?'

'Longer, if I have to.'

Suddenly she said, 'No thanks,' and shook her head, the long hair flailing.

Bellman said nothing but slowed the car as he approached a lay-by.

When he had stopped the car she opened the door and got out. 'Sorry,' she said, leaning down, watching his face.

Bellman lifted both hands from the steering wheel in a gesture of acceptance. 'It's okay.'

The door slammed and he edged the car forward, nosing the bonnet into the road.

The metallic din made Bellman duck involuntarily as she banged her fists on the roof of the Toyota. When she had opened the door and dumped herself back in the passenger seat she said, 'Christ! I was only testing ... you nearly drove off.'

Bellman laughed at her indignation.

The girl said, 'Joanna – Jo.'

Bellman said, 'Michael – Mike.'

Chapter Eleven

'I'm afraid I have an ulterior motive, Mrs Anstey,' Bellman watched her face through the veil of fern which framed the flowers. 'My girl is staying in London for a time. She was here last night and I want her to remain with me for the duration of her visit. It may seem old-fashioned but I thought I should see how you felt about it.' He smiled openly. 'The flowers are a bribe.'

She stood with the bouquet at arm's length, one hand draped across her breast. 'Oh, they're beautiful, Mr Bellman. You had no need to do it. What you do is your own affair. I would only object to week-long parties or arson.'

Climbing the stairs, Bellman wondered if he had over-done the subservient bit. On balance, he thought not. Had it suited him he would have moved Jo in and to hell. But landladies were sometimes a breed to be pampered. He knew.

Jo emerged from the bathroom as he entered the flat. She was using the ends of a large towel, which was draped across her shoulders, to scrub furiously at her soaking hair. Apart from the towel she was naked. Her breasts jiggled with the movement of her arms. She had a narrow waist and the legs confirmed earlier promise; slim calves and surprisingly full thighs curving upwards to the thick bush of hair at her belly.

Bellman observed her in a single, sweeping glance and turned away to fiddle abstractedly with a pile of newspapers and magazines. 'Another bath?'

'I told you last night – I'm a nice clean girl. Seriously –
I am. Some road-girls are really scrutty.'

There was a protracted silence until she said, 'You're
something else, you know.'

He turned reluctantly. 'What do you mean?'

The towel now followed the line of her body. She had
crossed her hands, covering herself as far as her knees. When
she slowly raised her arms, the towel fell away again and
she surveyed herself critically. 'Well, I'm not that bad, am
I? I thought ponces always sampled the goods. What's with
this "you take the bed – I'll sleep on the couch"?'

'I told you. It's no reflection on you. I don't dabble
much, that's all.' He spoke gruffly. The possibility of having
to explain himself to a prostitute had not occurred to him
when planning his move.

'Hey!' she said delightedly. 'You're not a first, are you?'

'A first?'

'Yeah – a queer ponce.'

He was forced to smile. 'No. Anyway, I'm not so sure it
would be a first.'

She was serious again. 'I'm too small there, aren't I?'
Her eyes were on her breasts which she studied with an
angry expression.

'They'll do,' he said shortly.

'Maybe arabs like them like that.' Her mood swung
again. 'I'm not sure I like this arab business. My trade
may have been low-class but at least I could choose.'

'Yeah,' Bellman said. 'Between a nice sweaty trucker
who'd been on his arse for hours or a weedy little traveller
who didn't want to touch you but tried to get you to blow
him as he drove.'

She held up a thumb. 'That's my boy – immediate
perspective.'

'That's right,' he said. 'In any case, I only mentioned
arabs as a possibility. Big money is what matters. Now get
some bloody clothes on, otherwise I'll buy your new rig-
out myself and my tastes are dated.'

'Don't you dare.' She fled, long legs flying, feet skidding on the mat by the door.

Their first stop was at a denim-palace – at Bellman's insistence. 'You can't turn up in a real joint dressed like that,' he pointed at the black skirt and worn sweater. 'Looking scruffy in denim is all right. In your present gear they'd send for the Salvation Army.'

In a pre-washed denim suit from the palace and shirt, shoes and underwear from a chain-store, Bellman's preconceived picture of her began to emerge.

'What did you do with your old clothes?' he asked.

'Dumped them in a bin in the toilet after I'd changed,' she said disinterestedly, holding out a leg to look at the flare of the trousers.

'Some old cleaner will think she's made a find.'

She sniffed. 'She wouldn't if she knew the action they'd seen.'

In the Regent Street shop they were attended by a friendly but *svelte*-awesome saleswoman. Bellman whispered, 'What's your dress-sense like?'

'Better than yours,' Jo returned, looking around with an interest devoid of deference.

'Don't forget, the accent's on evening clothes. You won't be able to get exclusives but with three hundred to spend you should manage two or three acceptable outfits. We can get others later.'

Jo nodded, then surprised him with her straight-forward handling of the assistant. Only once was he forced to grab her hand as she made a threatening gesture at the woman's retreating back as she swished away with a rejected item.

Bellman was uncomfortable in the woman's world of gowns and near-silent movements. The superior tolerance afforded him by both females annoyed him. He was pleased when they had finished, carrying the purchased garments down to the Toyota with a profound sense of relief.

When Jo moved towards the passenger seat he stopped

her. 'Here's fifty. Float around and buy the bits and pieces you women always seem to need. You know the address of the flat – get a taxi when you're ready.'

She looked at the notes then regarded him sorrowfully. 'Some girls would consider this a fair hit and have it away.'

'Then they'd be stupid. There's plenty more where that came from. You be all right on your own?'

'Sure. I've been in the big city before, you know. Don't worry.' She stuffed the money, masculine fashion, into the pocket of her jeans. 'See you.'

'Don't buy jewellery,' he called after her. 'I'll see to that myself.'

She waved an acknowledgement without looking back.

He telephoned from the flat and said to Kitholm, 'I need more money – another five hundred.'

'We didn't expect to hear from you yet. You said a fortnight.'

'I said a fortnight before I'm on the scene. Do I get the money?'

'What's the angle?'

'Do I get the money?' Bellman repeated.

There was only a brief pause before Kitholm said, 'Yes.'

'Good. Put it in the bank, I want to use it today.'

'It will be there within an hour.'

At five pm he began to worry, but Jo appeared ten minutes later, erupting into the flat in a welter of packages and plastic carrier-bags. 'Wait till you see, Mike. Wait till you see.'

He was amused at her enthusiasm, letting it gradually dwindle before producing the two small boxes.

She caught her breath when he strapped the wafer-thin gold watch to her wrist but when the necklace of simply-designed, heavy gold links was around her neck she said, 'Jes-SUS,' and ran to a mirror to stare in disbelief.

'And they're *yours*,' Bellman said. 'Not just for window-dressing.'

She turned slowly, a finger touching her chin, eyebrows raised in a parody of haughtiness. 'Remote and hard to get, you said. Yes?'

Bellman clutched his head. 'I didn't say impossible.'

She laughed and flounced to the couch, holding out a hand to him. 'Mike.'

He took her hand but remained standing until she pulled him down, guiding his hand behind her waist. She pushed against him and looked into his face, then shook her head. It was a question.

Bellman shook his head too. 'Now look, I've told you . . .'

'Okay, okay.' She gave him an impulsive kiss on the cheek and immediately reset the mood by drawing her head back in mock-horror. 'Fuck me. That was right passionate wasn't it?'

Bellman grinned and stood up. 'And you can cut out the bad language. From now on you're Jo – it's a good name for the business – and you're the daughter of an old-established English family. A girl with breeding who has left the rails slightly; available – at a price – but your sexual experience is limited. You're prepared to do it for money but are pleased to learn at the same time. They should love that.'

'Let's hope I don't forget myself and tell them their time's up.'

'For Christ's . . .' Bellman swung round.

She was laughing, a hand at her mouth in trepidation. 'It's all *right*. I was only kidding.'

He subsided, pointing at the kitchenette. 'See what you can do in there.'

She displayed a childish delight in cooking, producing the finished goods like a magician. The food was not bad, but Bellman kept the compliments to a minimum, feeling a need to reassert himself after her teasing.

Over coffee she said, 'You must have a drawback, Mike. When do I find out about it?'

'I drink.'

'I hadn't noticed.'

'I've been under control recently. You'll see. When I drink – I drink.'

'Get violent?' she asked the question without fear.

'No. Just keep away from me.'

'When do I see you boozed?'

Bellman stood up. 'In a few hours. Stay here and study the make-up books or whatever. Remember – simplicity's the aim.'

He left her and walked down the stairs with a curious feeling of reluctance. The urge to drink was pressing him hard but it was the first time a witness would be present to see his homecoming.

He drank deliberately, realising he was performing the act to keep his word to her, as well as fulfilling an urge. The alcoholic toning-down he had disciplined himself to during the days of the search gave the drink more kick. At ten o'clock he had difficulty in standing. An hour later he opened the door of the flat and fell to the floor.

Jo emerged from the bedroom and looked down at him. 'You weren't kidding, were you?' she said.

After a struggle she managed to remove his shoes and trousers. Half-consciously he flapped clear of his jacket. She cajoled and levered him to the couch then covered him with a blanket.

When she recovered the clothes from the floor she saw the bulge of money in the inner pocket of the coat. She glanced at the comatose Bellman and removed the notes, counting them with fast, efficient flicks, ending with a whistle of surprise. 'Who's looking after who?'

Bellman gave a liquid belch.

They began with the tourist trips: Westminster Abbey, the Tower of London, St Paul's, Buckingham Palace.

'Why?' she asked.

'You have to know about these things. Your cover indicates that you received a good education. Suppose a punter asked you about Buckingham Palace? You'd look pretty stupid if you had to admit you'd never seen the place.'

'Listen, if a punter wants to know about Buckingham Palace when I'm at work on him – I'll go straight back to the Great North Road for a refresher course.'

The next day he took her to the traditionally moneyed institutions: the Dorchester – 'Nice. Look at all those old Johns.' The Savoy – 'See what you mean about foreign influence;' the Hilton – 'Yank Johns.'

She broke in the evening: a small restaurant in Chelsea with a fussy wine-waiter insisting that she would enjoy the wine he recommended – at nine seventy-five. 'Listen, prick-face. At that price I'd want the bloody vineyard. Bring me a beer.'

Bellman did not speak while driving back to the flat.

She said, 'I'm sorry.'

'Too late, kid. You blew it. Those prices aren't extortionate in those kind of places.' He rolled the car to a stop at traffic lights and turned to her. 'Once more, Jo, and you're out – on your way back to that big main road and the two-quid punters. You'll have your bit of jewellery. It won't last long.'

'You don't mean it.'

'Don't I? One more slip and you're on your way.'

In the flat she hovered anxiously until he told her to go to bed.

She was awake before him, placing coffee on the table by the couch. Bellman thought the message had got through – she was a notorious late-sleeper.

By the fifth day she was accepting anywhere he took her without surprise. Even the top restaurants held no fears for her. After a brief survey she would settle to the task of eating.

Bellman knew it was time to move on. He did not want her to acquire the sultry, bored look of the indulged.

Chapter Twelve

She looked superb.

Bellman had insisted on being present when she applied her make-up. Cosmetics were a mystery to him but he knew the result he wanted to see. Now that she was beginning to make her own contribution, she was serious and eager to please.

Her long hair, expertly cut now, hung down her back, ending in a straight line below the shoulders. A touch of blue at the eyes and a warm lipstick with a soft sheen gave her a simple but expensively-finished appearance. Jo herself had added the slight hint of colour which accentuated the bone structure of her cheeks.

Her teeth were very white. When she smiled the result was completely sexual. She was not a beautiful woman but it was impossible to deny her magnetism.

He had tried to guide her towards an impression of youth lacking complete innocence; knowledge lacking over-experience.

And he had succeeded, he thought. Which was something, considering the well of her life.

A brief moment of doubt disappeared when he looked at her again. She was smoothing her dress, turning to see the effect of the moving material. He had asked her to wear the dark-blue gown which was simply cut and clinging, hinting at her legs beneath.

'You look great,' he said, the words coming to him strangely. 'Now – accessories. Just the watch and evening bag, I think.'

She clutched at her neck. 'What about my . . .'

'No leave the necklace. You're just right.'

She did not argue.

Bellman gave his own, hastily bought suit, the once-over. It was stylish and surprisingly comfortable for a first-time wearing. The Italian shoes he wore were not what he would normally have chosen but fitted the part.

His hand went up to his moustache before travelling over his head to the lengthening hair at his neck. Ideally he would have liked more time to grow himself into a new appearance, but he was convinced he could carry off a change of identity successfully – unless he were directly confronted by someone who knew him well.

Jo noticed his own self-criticism. She patted his chest. 'Don't worry, you look great too.' Then. 'Can I ask why?'

'Why what?'

'The moustache – it's very new. And your hair. I think you used to have it shorter.'

'Let's just say, a fresh start. I'll be breaking new ground insofar as surroundings go. I don't want any old hangers-on near me.'

She said, 'I see,' but sounded unsure.

When he telephoned for a taxi she expressed her surprise. 'What's wrong with the car?'

'Nothing. But this way we're free agents. A Toyota doesn't exactly give a Ritzy impression, either. Later I may buy a decent set of wheels.'

In the cab he said, 'Once more ... name?'

'Jo. No other details.'

'Approaches – propositions?'

'They have to see you.'

'Where do you live?'

'I never tell – even if pressed.'

'Good. Anything you don't understand, you ask me. Right?'

'Okay.'

Bellman said, 'That's about it, then,' and used a finger to tilt her chin so that she was forced to look at him. 'There is one more thing, Jo – don't cross me. You'll get the opportunity. Don't take it.'

She looked into his eyes without flinching but the words made her shiver inwardly.

Bellman was pleased to change the subject. 'The fancy places we've been visiting recently were just for training. Where we're going now is for real.' He looked out of the window as the taxi braked to a stop. 'And here we are – the Loom. It's purely a night-club with cabaret – the lot.'

In the reception area Bellman used a confident manner to ease their way through the formalities.

Their entry to the bar, separated from the main floor by a lattice of wrought-iron, gave him the first public confirmation of his faith and judgment in Jo's appearance. Though not exactly crowded, the atmosphere in the bar changed noticeably as every head turned towards her.

Bellman ordered drinks and they sat at the bar, knees touching the upholstered front.

A man approached and introduced himself as the manager, asking Bellman his requirements. After a brief talk he left and spoke to a waiter.

Bellman nudged Jo. 'Newcomers are always vetted by the top man.'

'Why vet anyone? I would have thought that providing you have the money to pay, you're welcome.'

Bellman made a negative movement. 'Not so. Particularly us. They have to be careful.'

'How do they know what I am?'

'They're probably not sure but assume to be on the safe side.'

'So what problems could I cause?'

Bellman lit a cigarette and studied the tables through a gap in the ironwork. 'Well, they know what goes on but they have to ensure that a certain amount of discretion is used. The sort of facilities you offer can be good for business. They can also be troublesome if they attract the wrong types.'

She followed his gaze. 'The prospect's not exactly fantastic as far as I can see.'

Bellman said, 'It's early yet.'

They had been shown to a table and were half-way through a meal when Jo put her fork down. 'Mike. When's it all going to happen?'

He looked at her in surprise. 'Be patient. It will take time. To get the best custom we have to be selective. I don't mind a longish reconnaissance, why should you?'

She pouted before taking up her fork again. 'You've been pretty good to me. I want to ... well ... repay you.'

Bellman laughed. 'That's probably the first time someone in your position has complained because she's *not* working.'

She said nothing, looking at him from below lowered brows, her expression a mixture of sadness and anger.

Bellman failed to see her look, busying himself with wiping his mouth, anxious that he should not make an elementary mistake this early. The comparative quiet of the club worried him now and he did not want unwittingly to transmit his doubts to her.

The entertainment began with a small, darting man who flitted about the tiny stage extolling the virtues of those who would shortly appear. His place was taken by a blonde singer, accompanied by a band huddled together at one side.

To cover his disquiet Bellman ordered champagne, chivvying Jo into a lighter mood. The entertainment was good but not extraordinary and their moods reversed. Bellman sat with a cynical, glum forbearance while Jo watched with a lively interest, over-applauding each act.

No single happening transformed the atmosphere but eventually it was noticeable that a lighter, general mood prevailed. Mixed groups appeared and filled the tables. Couples searched for and joined friends already seated while several all-male parties surveyed the scene with a touch of arrogance before allowing themselves to be ushered to their places.

With the influx of new life the band played rejuvenated music and the waiters moved into a higher gear.

Jo looked at him suddenly. 'Things seem to be livening up.'

Bellman nodded agreement.

'What exactly is the position here?' she asked. 'With girls, I mean. Does the club employ any?'

He said, 'No. Many places do but this isn't one of them. You could bring the wife – so to speak. Clubs which have pushy hostesses find themselves with an all-male clientele. That is why people like us are tolerated here – welcomed, in fact. At least, as I explained earlier, the discreet ones are. We provide for those not already fixed-up.' He got up. 'Stay here, I'm going to wander around. Don't worry, just remember what I've told you.'

To the manner born she gave him a limp wave and turned her attention to the comedian who was desperately attempting to gain the diners' attention.

Bellman ordered a drink and sat with it at the bar. Watching Jo he was reminded of clear-water angling. The bait was on view but, at first, apparently invisible to the fish. She sat with studied unconcern until a waiter bent over her, murmuring in her ear. She looked at him and smiled, giving a gentle shake of her head. Five minutes later a young man in evening dress was at her side, one hand resting on Bellman's vacant chair. This time there was no smile but a dismissive wave of the hand.

Bellman watched the man return to his table and the eager, expectant faces of three older men who sat there. The expressions changed as the propositioner spread his palms, explaining the rebuff.

'Perfect,' Bellman said as he sat down beside her again.

'Two offers to "join the gentlemen" refused. That's perfect?' she said indignantly.

He said, 'Wait,' and waved for more champagne.

The waiter had barely left when the youngster was beside the table, edging into an empty seat. 'Could I have a word with you?'

Bellman turned slowly, eyebrows lifted.

'I ... ah ... I just asked the young lady if she would care to join our party.'

'And what did she say?' Bellman said unhelpfully.

'Oh ... well ... she ...' he stopped in an agony of indecision.

Bellman lit a cigarette and surveyed the uncomfortable figure. 'Don't worry, you're on the right tack, but ...' he turned to glance at the three men, 'what have you got there? Out-of-towners?'

The relief flooded out. 'Yes. Yes ... I'm glad you understand. I'm ... arranging their evening.'

'I know. Jo here is a bit out of their class, though.'

'Oh?' The eagerness was open. 'I can assure you they have plenty of ...'

'Money?' Bellman gave the other a hard stare. 'Look, you're pretty new at the game. She's out of their class. Understand?'

'Oh ... fine. Well, I'll be going.' He left with a dignity he obviously didn't feel.

She said, 'Why?'

Bellman grinned at her. 'You seem to be saying "why" every two minutes.' He leaned back and let his gaze wander over the floor. 'He's young ... just landed a better-class pimping job. His clients have money but they're only here for one night.'

'So?'

'So they're not what we want.'

'Money's money – surely.'

'It's not the right money.'

She looked at him with puzzlement but kept quiet.

'Did the waiter say who else it was who wanted an introduction?' Bellman said.

'I didn't ask ... just said no.'

'Good,' he said infuriatingly.

It happened on his second cast. Bellman had left Jo again, seating himself at the bar. Before he could order a drink a hand touched his arm. When he turned he saw a square face close to his own. He was a big man, dressed informally but expensively. A blue shirt emphasised the powerful chest beneath the dark suit.

'You're new,' the man said.

'So are you,' Bellman said and turned away.

The other showed no reaction but studied Bellman through part-closed eyes. 'New in here, I mean.'

Bellman turned back. 'Always a first time and all that.'

'I'm not sure about you.' The words were quietly spoken but there was an undertone of menace.

'What the hell are you talking about?' Bellman allowed his voice to rise.

'You're working the girl. Don't deny it. I know the method.'

'Who's asking?' Bellman stood up. 'No. Don't answer that. I don't want to know.' He leaned close to the other's ear. 'Piss off and let me graft.'

The big man shrugged. 'If it was up to me I probably would, but one of my people wants to meet the girl.'

'And who are your people?'

'You need references?'

'No, but I like to know who I'm dealing with – that's to say, I like to know how they're fixed.'

'They're fixed.' The flat statement was accompanied by a hard stare. 'You seem very particular.'

Bellman lowered himself to the seat again. 'She's expensive – very expensive.'

'That's no problem. How much?'

'Two hundred. And she's a straight lay. No variations. She's only a kid at the game.'

The laugh came grittily. 'Aren't they all.'

'I mean it.' It was Bellman's turn to give a hard stare,

balancing concern for his charge with latent threat – the ponce who knew his job.

'They're over there,' a large hand indicated the far side of the floor where there was a small, raised section, further separated by vertical louvres of heavy plastic.

In the spaces between the hanging slats there was a glimpse of heads bent in conversation. They appeared oblivious of the singer's efforts.

'I'm Clay.' There was no proffered hand.

'Mike,' Bellman said, still watching the group.

'Clay's my second name.'

'Mike's my first.'

Clay sighed. 'Shall we cut the smart chat. Okay, so you're new here and you feel you should be careful. That's all right with me. You operate sensibly – just don't tear the arse out of it. I'm employed to vet people, so that's what I do.' There was no hint of apology in the words, only an explanation.

Bellman responded at once. 'Fair enough. Just understand one thing. I'm new *here* – not at the game. I have a nice young girl there – and she *is* young. If your people are interested and they have the money, well, we'll meet them. That means without a promise that we'll actually play.'

Clay's smile was a surprise after the grating laugh. 'A particular ponce?'

'Yeah!' Bellman said. 'A particular ponce. Nowadays you have to be particular. We've already turned down two offers.'

'I saw,' Clay said, motioning to Bellman. 'Collect the girl and follow me.'

There were four men and two girls at the table. They stopped talking as Clay began the introductions: 'Peter.' Weighty with hooded eyes; encumbered with an excess of rings, cuff-links and an unfashionable tie-pin. 'Henry.' Small, grey-haired. 'John.' Fat and sweating. 'Marcia.' Black-haired, crows-foot traces at the eyes. 'Terry.' Heavy, confident, well-turned out, with a hint of ostentation. 'Jane.' Tiny with auburn hair accentuating a pale complexion.

'This is Jo,' Clay moved her forward with a touch of his hand. 'Oh, yes – Mike.' The pause and off-handedness were a separate explanation.

The men had nodded and smiled at Jo. The women were more cautious, giving only slight, downward flicks of the eyes at a possible competitor.

They all ignored Bellman.

He did not mind, expecting it. While the reshuffling caused by their arrival was carried out, he stood back, moving only slightly to edge near the one who had been introduced as Terry.

It was easy to see that Jo was intended for the vulture-like, Peter, who moved an adjoining chair and fussed her into position beside him.

Bellman had no difficulty in placing himself where he wanted.

There was a call for more glasses and the attendant palaver of filling them. Peter held the floor with the minimum of noise, a hand indicating an empty glass, a lift of the large head silently demanding attention before speaking.

The conversation had no theme and no direction, being a hotch-potch of business anecdotes, exaggerated accounts of experiences mixed with a spattering of jokes.

By some nebulous intimation, Clay and the one named Terry were excluded from the conversation. As was Bellman. The females were allowed to participate because they were what they were.

'First time in here?' The question was pitched low so as not to disturb the talk at the end of the table.

'Yes,' Bellman said. 'Mike – Mike Cater.'

'Terry Elson.' The surname was spoken with deliberation, probing for recognition.

'We're from the Midlands. We don't know many people down here yet,' Bellman said.

The explanation seemed to appease Elson. 'You'll find it different down here – more difficult.'

Bellman mentally debated how he should answer. Meeting Elson on his first night had been a stroke of luck. He recognised that the mention of potential 'difficulty' showed a lack of subtlety on Elson's part – or a brash confidence in his own ability. It was probably a mixture of both. Whatever it was, Bellman had no wish to get their relationship off to a bad start. Neither did he want Elson to think he was easy meat. He took a long pull at his drink.

'Jo's new at the game. I'm not. I don't think the big city will intimidate me.'

Elson looked speculatively at him. 'Know your way around, do you?'

'London? Sure. Excuse me a moment.' He motioned to Clay, unobtrusively but firmly.

Clay did not react immediately, waiting the statutory period of time which would show Bellman just where he stood in the descending line of importance of those present. When he did finally move it was to approach slowly, bending casually between Bellman and Elson. 'What?' The tone of question was purposely designed to emphasise the reluctant movement.

'I want to get something straight,' Bellman murmured. 'If the big fellow – Peter, is it? If he wants Jo, he has to weigh in before the action. With me.'

Clay drew back slightly. 'I handle anything like that. I'm Mr Hull's assistant. You'll find the arrangements satisfactory.'

'I won't unless I'm paid first.'

Clay gave a weary sigh. 'You're in a new scene ...?'

'Cater.'

'... Cater. You're in a new scene. Tread carefully and you'll earn.' He turned away.

Bellman's hand streaked out and grasped Clay's elbow. The smile never left Bellman's face but the strength of his grip could be seen by the indentations in Clay's suit. With steady pressure he drew Clay nearer. 'You've been giving a lot of instructions, Clay. Now listen to some. Unless I've got two and a half in my pocket before Jo leaves – there's no deal. She stays with me.'

'You said two,' Clay said, glancing along the table to see if the exchange was being observed.

'That's right, I did. But the rate's gone up since you began throwing your weight around.'

Clay's colour deepened, the only visible indication of the inward struggle. Discretion won. 'All right.' He pulled to break Bellman's grip.

Bellman released the captive arm slowly.

'Can you back your words?' Elson said as Clay returned to his seat.

'I'm no hard man,' Bellman said. 'I just like things to be done properly.'

'So I see,' Elson said, tilting his chair back.

The group had now split unequally. Bellman and Elson were left alone at one end of the table as the others gathered around the presiding Hull at the other: an unequal see-saw of adult playtimers.

'Where's your girl, then?' Bellman asked.

Elson's head jerked sharply upwards. 'Me? I haven't got one. I'm not one of them. What I mean is – I'm just a spectator. More like ...'

'Me?'

'Christ! No. I'm just showing an interest. ... Look, we'll have a talk soon. It's a bit awkward at the moment.'

'All right,' Bellman said equably. 'Tell me – who runs the other girls? Clay?'

Elson grinned. 'Clay would love it if he heard you say that. No. Like he said, he works for Peter Hull. Hull's big business – electronics and Christ knows what else. The other two are not exactly poor but they rely heavily on Hull for a slice of the cake. Anyway, when they're on the town it's Clay's job to arrange the entertainment. The girls are from a telephone. Understand?'

'Call-ups?'

'Yeah – exclusive.'

Bellman eyed the girls critically. 'They don't look top class to me.'

'Depends how you view it. You're lucky, your girl's young. Those other two come well-recommended. They'll provide the right kind of action when asked.' Elson gave a guarded laugh. 'I think Hull was feeling a bit jaded. He decided he didn't want a bird – until he saw yours.'

'He's got good judgment,' Bellman said. He was watching Jo as he spoke, anxious that she would create the right impression. He need not have worried. She was drinking but still had the actions of the sober. Her eyes met his and, though her expression did not change, she managed to transmit a message of assurance.

Hull was on his feet and waving a champagne bottle. 'A drink for all, then we're leaving. It's been nice, gentlemen.' The dismissal was aimed at Bellman and Elson. Clay included himself in by nodding understandingly.

As the general departure began, Clay arrived at Bellman's side. 'Here. Two hundred and fifty.' The notes were in a flat wedge, held so that Bellman could take them unobtrusively. 'That's the last time you'll ever pull the "upping" stakes with me.'

'I shouldn't think it would be necessary a second time,' Bellman said. 'Where's she going now?'

Clay retrieved ground. 'You've got your money. The girl will be returned tomorrow. That's all you need to know.'

'Good business,' Elson said, watching Bellman dispose of the money.

'Yes. It will get better too.' Bellman held out his hand. 'Nice to meet you, Terry.'

Elson shook hands. 'Sure, Mike. See you around soon, I hope.'

'We'll be here or somewhere not too far away.'

Bellman managed to wink at Jo without being observed

as she glanced over her shoulder at the exit. He watched from the door as Hull's Bentley sighed to a halt. Jo gave a lightning, comic roll of the eyes as she was handed into the car. Bellman returned to the bar as the other girls were escorted to the vehicles which followed the Bentley, a pecking order of Jaguar and Rover.

After several large whiskies, Bellman left and returned to the flat.

It was strange, using the bed again.

Chapter Thirteen

'It's one big bloody joke!'

She was sitting on the edge of the bed, shoulders shaking with laughter, head forward, hair swinging.

Bellman opened his eyes slowly. Hurting.

Then she was on her feet, twirling in the early-morning light.

'What's the matter?' Bellman croaked.

She stopped and held her hands out wide. '*Him* – that Peter. *What* a sexual athlete. Early to bed and what happens?' She circled a thumb and forefinger. 'Nix. He's like a bit of string. I try to help and guess what? He *stops* me. How about that?' A hand went to her forehead. 'Do you know how we spent the night? *Cuddling* for Christ's sake.' She giggled and assumed a mock-serious attitude. 'He did roll on me a couple of times, on the second occasion he sort of half-managed it. I got the idea it was for *my* benefit. After a time I got the message – told him he was a raging bull. He was like a little boy with his first bike.' She flopped down on the bed again. 'Did he actually *pay* for that, Mike?'

'Two hundred and fifty.'

'*What*?' She let herself fall across his legs. 'I don't believe it. I could do ten of them without stopping for breath.'

'Don't be coarse,' Bellman said and eased himself painfully from the bed. 'You might have made the tea before waking me.'

She said, 'Sorry, I didn't think of it,' then, 'Hey!' When he turned she was pointing at him. 'You're in the nude, Mike.'

Bellman swore and fumbled his way into pants and trousers.

When they were facing each other across the table, steaming tea-mugs between them, Bellman said, 'Here,' and counted bank-notes into her hand. 'A hundred and twenty-five. Use a tenner to open a post-office account, then give the book to me. Do what you like with the rest.'

She stared at the money in her hand. 'I still can't believe it.'

Bellman said, 'Try. Now get some sleep in.'

'I was hardly disturbed last night,' she protested.

'Do as you're told, otherwise you'll begin to get the haggard look. Bad for business.'

She riffled fingers through her hair. 'Wow! Organisation. Mike, I'm excited, I want to buy ...'

'Shop when you like, sleep when you like – as long as you *do* sleep. Be here for five o'clock, that's all I ask.'

She spoiled the elaborate salute by executing it with out-thrust tongue.

When they entered the Loom again, less than twenty-four hours had elapsed since their last visit.

Elson was at the bar. He lifted a hand in recognition and motioned them to join him.

'Terry,' Bellman uttered the terse greeting as he slipped on to a stool beside Elson, beckoning Jo to the adjacent seat.

Elson stopped her before she was seated. 'Move along a few places, sweetheart. Mike and I have business to discuss. I'll send you a drink.'

Jo lifted her eyebrows at Bellman. He hesitated, then nodded. She moved out of earshot and edged on to a seat further down the bar.

Bellman lit a cigarette. 'The next time you want her out of the way – ask me first.'

'What I have to say is for you only,' Elson said grimly. 'I have a proposition.'

'Go on.'

'It's very simple. I'm offering protection. Wait!' he said as Bellman's head reared. 'This isn't a shake-down. You probably don't know what's happened recently. Things are moving on the brass scene – changing. When I say protection I mean a part of a bigger scheme. A ...'

Bellman slid off the stool. 'I don't need it.'

Elson grasped Bellman by the arm. 'Don't be hasty. For a start, the girl would be steered towards some decent work and soon ...'

'And soon I'd be out on my ear,' Bellman said, shaking himself free. He motioned to Jo. When she was by his side he said, 'Thanks for the drink we didn't get,' and pushed Jo gently before him.

Elson watched them walk away then turned to his drink.

Bellman made a point of ordering a table in view of Elson but stayed only long enough to display his independence.

At the exit, Jo said, 'What's wrong? Why are we leaving?'

'Pastures new,' Bellman said.

'Did Terry Elson say something to upset you?'

'Yes – but it fits.'

'Huh?'

Bellman shook his head and waited for her to climb into the taxi. She entered with a show of furiously-wiggling fingers indicating non-comprehension. It occurred to him that she would never be speechless while her fingers and eyes remained intact.

Bellman was writing his false name in the membership book of the Dayton when a discreet cough from the receptionist made him open his wallet and select the pristine membership card from among the others.

'I'm sorry, sir, I see that you're a new member,' the receptionist said. 'We know most of our customers and don't need to trouble them.'

Bellman said, 'That's quite all right,' and ushered Jo towards the deep-carpeted stairs.

'Are you a member *everywhere*?' she asked.

'Just the places that matter,' he said, remembering the

early-morning trips to collect the custom-printed envelopes containing the cards from various clubs before Mrs Anstey could see the strange name on them.

Bellman made only one circuit of the gaming-floor before seeing a group of men who interested him. There were six in the party; four were dark-skinned and dressed in expensive-looking suits which rested on their slight frames as though they were the traditional dress of the desert instead of the flowing robes and sandals normally associated with the Middle East. The other two were unmistakably English. The first, a tall grey-haired individual, had the sharp nose and supercilious expression of struggling aristocracy while his companion was smaller and younger, confident but eminently approachable.

Bellman turned to Jo. 'Move about, kid. Play the girl alone bit. If you get any propositions don't blank them out completely. Just make sure they know you have a minder.'

She moved away with a small lift of creamy shoulders.

Bellman changed twenty pounds into gaming-chips and made a desultory tour of the American-roulette tables, casually watching Jo's progress through the screen of oblivious punters. After twenty minutes' aimless wandering he could see she was bored, moving to sit at the edge of the area and ordering coffee from the waitress who served her with the perfunctory attitude reserved for lone females who were seldom good for a decent tip.

She was not alone for long. Her rueful smile at an eager blood was a lesson in non-hurtful rejection. The second approach was from a middle-aged man who spoke to her earnestly, head lowered in studied politeness.

Bellman admired her friendly smile and the apologetic movements of her hands as she explained that her unattached state was only temporary. The man left with an understanding nod.

The third bite was from one who actually looked like a fish. He was obese, flopping into the chair beside Jo like a landed carp, arms dangling. Bellman could see that the words issuing from the slobbery mouth were brief and to the point. He moved away from the protective screen of players and crossed the floor to where Jo sat.

'All right, sweetheart?' he looked down at her, ignoring the sprawling figure in the nearby chair.

'I was just saying . . .' the fat man began.

Bellman turned to him. 'Piss-off, fat-gut.'

'Wha . . . ?'

'You heard.'

It was an effort for the man to haul himself clear of the chair but when he had finally managed it he scuttled away, throwing anxious backward glances in Bellman's direction.

'Wow!' Jo said. 'Can't say I would fancy that all over me, but couldn't he complain to the management or something?'

'If he was a big spender – yes. But he's not. His type is easy to recognise – likes to be where the action is without getting too involved. Unless he can pick up something free. He'll be only too pleased that *we* don't complain.'

'I'm sure you're right. Just the same, if he'd wanted to play I would have. . . .'

'Let me be the judge of who you go with.'

'Yes *sir*,' she said as he moved away.

He looked back at her. 'And that's another thing. Stop saying "wow" and things like that. You sound as though you should be wearing a gym-slip.'

She allowed her tongue to protrude very slightly. 'And *that's* bad for business?'

Bellman gave a resigned sigh and retreated into the crowd.

After two hours Bellman was bored and frustrated with the lack of action. The group of six which interested him showed enthusiasm only for the play. They stood at a roulette table watching each other's efforts with a mixture of amusement and condolence. Bellman had followed their play and seen that the stakes were high, a single spin of the wheel often carrying two, or three hundred pounds belonging to one or more of the swarthy members of the group. The tall man and his younger colleague did not play, occupying themselves in watching the efforts of the others.

A good win would be greeted with congratulations accompanied by an undercurrent of derision at the inevitability of eventual loss. The actual money seemed to be of no importance.

Half an hour later there was movement. First one and then another would spend longer with his head averted from the play, eyes searching for a new interest. After a final exclamation of disgust at the behaviour of the ivory ball the group drifted away from the table to meander without apparent purpose among the other tables.

It was the tall Englishman who eventually subsided into a chair near Jo, seemingly tired of the endless excursion. He looked up at the assembled group with one finger tracing his jaw line. The languid eyes flicked from one speaker to the next. There appeared to be some dispute as to what the next move should be. One gestured towards the restaurant, the remainder demurred.

The man who Bellman believed to be Brantner stood patiently waiting for a decision.

The minority of one prevailed, the group moving towards the restaurant in a straggling file. As they moved off, two glanced towards Jo. She was sitting with legs crossed, apparently relaxed and happy.

When they had disappeared, Bellman joined her. 'Feel like eating?' he said.

'Cor! Fank you, guv,' she said in a dreadful imitation cockney. 'Me stomach fought me froat had bin cut.'

'Don't tempt me,' Bellman growled. He guided her round the gaming floor before approaching the restaurant. 'Don't want to appear too eager,' he said.

'Who to?' she asked.

'I'm interested in a party who have just gone in.'

'You know, Mike. I'm really puzzled now. Why . . .' His warning glance stopped her.

She contained herself until the first part of their order arrived. In the middle of extracting prawns from the cloying sauce she raised the tiny fork and stabbed it in his direction. 'I don't think you're being straight with me.'

'How do you mean?'

'Well,' she sucked a tooth indelicately. 'I admit I have no experience of ponces,' she used the word hesitantly, 'but I would say I have struck lucky with you. All the same, I'm here to earn, surely – for both of us. I find it strange that you don't take all the work available. You've laid out quite a bit for trimmings,' she indicated the dress and watch, 'and so far the investment hasn't been recovered. What sort of business mind have you got?'

Bellman avoided her eyes. 'Are you grumbling?'

She looked hurt. 'No ... but, well, it just seems ...'

He covered her hand with his own. 'Jo. Trust me. I know what I'm doing. You won't lose out moneywise.'

She looked down at his hand in surprise. 'It's not that. I've seen and done more in the last few days than I would ever have done on my own. If it ended tomorrow I wouldn't complain.' She looked at the surroundings. 'I love all this. Who wouldn't – if they came from the sort of life I was leading? But, as I said, I'm not in the picture. You're keeping something from me. I feel it.'

Bellman released her hand and sat back to stare into the distance. Her questions troubled him. Her *intuition* troubled him, and he did not know how to answer. He could undoubtedly bully her out of her inquisitive role but was reluctant to do that. To upset her would mean that he would not be able to rely on any future order being obeyed. Apart from that, he had a natural aversion to anything which might interfere with the strange relationship which seemed to be developing between them. And how many girls would have accepted the good life and not cared about earning their keep? Most.

'I won't deny there's something in what you say,' he said quietly. 'Neither can I explain. I only ask that you trust me. If at any time I feel you should know more – I will tell you.'

She sat perfectly still for a long time, watching his face earnestly. With a sudden movement that made him start, the now-familiar finger-waggle burst into action. 'Okay. That's fair.'

The complete acceptance pleased him.

Bellman had seen that their presence was noted by the six men who were eating together. At one time Jo was obviously under discussion, all eyes centring on her. He insisted on hurrying to finish the meal.

'What now?' she said as they left the restaurant. 'The bar?'

Bellman shook his head. 'No just stay near to me. We'll watch the play.'

'Excuse me,' the interruption came before they were half way across the floor. It was the younger Englishman who had waited so patiently with the arab clique.

Bellman turned and waited with upraised eyebrows. Despite his earlier easy manner the other's confidence was tested as he searched for the proper introduction. 'I ... ah ... I hope you don't think this too impertinent of me but I ... we, that is, haven't seen you here before.'

'We haven't been here before, that's why,' Bellman said.

'I see. Well ...'

'I think I can put your mind at rest,' Bellman smiled and held out his hand. 'Mike Cater.' He indicated Jo. 'This is my girl – Jo – and yes, she's a professional.'

'Don – Don Brantner,' the relief was audible. 'It's very difficult sometimes. You know, you could have been a normal couple, that is ...'

'I know what you mean. You're with the arabs?' Bellman said bluntly.

Brantner winced slightly. 'Yes. I prefer to call them gentlemen.'

Bellman ignored the reprimand. 'And they're interested in Jo? Good. I hoped they would be.'

'You mean you deliberately ...'

'No, but they looked like the wealthiest people in here.'

Brantner seemed to appreciate the honesty. 'I see,' he said with a small laugh. 'Well now, if you would like to be introduced?'

'I'm afraid tonight's out,' Bellman said sorrowfully. 'She already has an appointment but contacts are always useful. Perhaps another time?'

'You have just the one girl?' Brantner was back in his former, confident groove.

'Yes. She has style enough for a dozen.'

'Mmmm.' Brantner's eyes confirmed the sound.

Bellman placed his hand lightly on Brantner's elbow. 'If it would help you, Jo could go with you for ten minutes, you know – meet your clients.'

'They're not exactly clients,' Brantner said, his voice sharpening a fraction. 'I'm just showing them round. I'm not a ...'

'Christ!' Bellman's voice was low with disgust. 'We haven't been on the London scene for long but it seems to be full of men claiming not to be anything. It's funny, anything to do with brass brings on a sharp attack of embarrassment but there's never any objection to the financial benefits.'

Brantner watched Bellman lighting his cigarette with unusual interest. 'What makes you say that?'

Bellman slowly expelled smoke. 'I'm used to straight talking. The other evening we came across someone like you – an arranger. He was also reluctant to admit he was pimping. Which is what it amounts to – even though it is in reverse.'

'Who?' The question was pointed, ignoring the taunt.

'Come *on* now,' Bellman remonstrated. 'You should know better than to ask. Would you like to introduce her or not?' he concluded, changing the subject.

'Yes, of course,' Brantner said, taking Jo's arm. 'Perhaps we can talk again, sometime, Mike.'

Bellman waved off-handedly. 'Sure. We'll be around.' He looked at Jo. 'I'll be in the bar.'

When she returned Bellman was twisting the stem of his glass, peering into the pinkish depths of a Campari.

'Good God!' she said. 'I've seen it all. A lady's drink. What's the matter with you?'

'I try to keep to the less potent stuff when I'm working. Hadn't you noticed?'

'Can I have the same?'

Bellman ordered her drink and said, 'How did it go?'

She watched the green-coated barman pour the Campari, insisting on serving her own ice. 'With them? – Okay. They were all eyes and there was a definite air of disappointment when that Don fellow said I already had an "engagement".' She ended the sentence with a lift of the eyebrows.

Bellman ignored the silent question. 'Happy with them?'

'As customers?' She made a show of open palms.

'Let's move.'

'Where now?'

'Home.'

'*Home*?' She was wide-eyed with incredulity.

Bellman pushed his glass away. 'Drink yours up too. Work's finished for tonight.'

'I hadn't noticed it had started,' she muttered as she followed him out.

Chapter Fourteen

Bellman did not wake until ten the following morning. He found it impossible to believe he could have slept so long without complete intoxication.

There was a note propped against the ash tray on the coffee table: GONE SHOPPING – BACK MIDDAY.

He straightened the couch and made himself tea. He was flicking idly through a magazine when Jo returned.

He gave her ten pounds. 'Do an about-turn and shop for some stuff we can eat picnic-style. Get a bottle of wine too.'

She paused in surprise, then threw her collection of parcels on the couch. 'Great. Where're we going?'

Bellman was embarrassed by her enthusiasm. 'Don't get all worked up, we're not going anywhere special. It's a nice day, though. I thought we'd have a change.'

She skipped to the door, then ran back and rummaged among the parcels. When she found what she wanted she threw it, hitting him on the chest. 'Here, for you. It's nothing much.' She was gone, the door slamming behind her.

Bellman waited until the downstairs door banged shut before opening the parcel. Inside was a mohair sweater. He tried it on and found that it fitted. The dark green colour was to his taste, inasmuch as he had any preferences nowadays.

Jo returned with bread, a cooked chicken, coleslaw and a variety of sandwich fillings. A separate box contained frozen éclairs.

She produced the wine with a shouted 'Olé' then paused to peer at the label. 'Don't know what it is but it looks classy.' She put the bottle down. 'Hey! Did you like your present?'

He said, 'Yeah. Nice. Now let's get the sandwiches made.'

She made a cross-eyed face at his back and carried the food into the kitchenette.

Twice during the journey she asked where they were going but Bellman only smiled and returned to the mechanics of driving.

He stopped the car on the hill. Below, the long expanse of grass dropped steeply then rose sharply half a mile away. The grandstands were empty but looked invitingly friendly under the warmth of the sun. White running-rails emphasised the contours of the downs and the sharp turn of Tattenham Corner.

Jo got out of the car and stood gazing across the shallow valley. '*Now* tell me where we are.'

'Epsom.'

'It's great. Is this where the Derby's run?'

Bellman joined her. 'Yes, the start's over there,' his finger pointed back then traced the course. 'They race along there, down the hill and up the straight to the winning line ... there.'

A few other cars were scattered haphazardly on the grass but none near enough to disturb them. They spread the food a few yards from the Toyota and ate without speaking. The wine was too sweet for Bellman's taste but he professed to enjoy it. When they had finished they lay back, faces to the sun.

She said, 'Christ!' quietly.

'What?' Bellman turned his head to look at her.

She was staring skywards, eyes flickering against the light. 'I was just thinking. Tell me a month ago that I would be as happy as this and I'd have said you were mad.'

Bellman said nothing. When he looked at her again he saw she was crying, silent tears tracking down her cheeks. 'Here. Turn it in.'

She gave her face an angry scrub with the heel of her hand. 'Sorry. Don't worry – I'm not coming the poor-girl stuff. I don't usually blubber for no apparent reason.'

Bellman looked away as she smeared her face some more. 'You disappoint me. We're together for business. This is just for a change. Don't let it get to you.' The words came out harshly and neither the tone nor the content had been exactly what he wanted, but he let them stand.

Her face was composed again. 'Okay. I said I was sorry. It won't happen again.'

Bellman blundered on, knowing he was saying the wrong things but unable to stop. 'You know, to hear you now I would never have guessed you were on the game. Good education?'

It was her turn for the knife. 'What are you saying? What's a nice girl like you ...'

'I didn't mean ...'

She flapped a hand to silence him. 'You're entitled to know, I suppose ... Good home – Lincoln. Local education until my parents were divorced – then a boarding school. I was quite bright – no genius, but adequate. When I finished school, well, I don't know what happened. I tried work – office stuff but it was no good, not for me, anyway. I was keen on both my parents – couldn't believe it when they broke up. Mum remarried. My father went to London. He wrote to me. I even saw him a few times.' Her fingers twisted into the grass and wrenched some free. She threw it skywards. Some of the greener, heavier blades landed on her face. She blew them away with exaggerated raspings from distended cheeks. 'You know the rest – broken home, the international excuse. I screwed around – didn't enjoy it much but there was always plenty who wanted to try me, so I thought I might as well earn a living from it.' She smiled grimly, a fleeting mask. 'You know how it goes ... after the first few times, it's easy. So ... that's it. Joanna Tine. This is your life.'

Bellman squinted along the line of his legs, aligning the

winning post with the end of his toe. 'It's not a unique story.' The words were commonplace but his tone gave them power; coldness.

She turned on to her stomach and raised herself with straining arms. 'You know something? I feel better now.'

He swivelled his eyes towards her, suspiciously, but still fell. 'The burden shared angle?'

'No. Because I know I'm dealing with a bastard.' She sprang to her feet and walked away.

Bellman watched her. She was strolling through the parched grass, kicking at tufts like a child. When she raised her head it was to view the surroundings as though they were completely new and not the subject of an hour's inspection.

They were approaching the flat when he said, 'I'm sorry.'

'You've no need to be.'

'There was no reason for me to be that hard.'

'Why not? You were right – we're in business.'

When he stopped the car in the crescent she got out quickly. 'Come on, boyo. Let's get grafting.'

Bellman muttered 'Fuck it' to himself as he followed her into the house.

Chapter Fifteen

They arrived at the Loom at eight. By eight-thirty they were involved with a north-country businessman who had approached them when they entered. Once certain of Jo's availability he made a great show of inviting them to his table and standing the meal.

The man blanched when Bellman told him it would cost two hundred pounds for Jo's company but he agreed, immediately calling for the bill.

'Wants his money's worth,' Bellman said as they were led away from the table.

'He'll get it,' she promised grimly.

When they had gone Bellman headed for the bar and drank steadily. Elson arrived as Bellman called for his fourth whisky. He was alone and before he turned towards the bar he stood on the edge of the floor and surveyed the scene. Turning, he saw Bellman and sat down beside him, pointing at the part-filled glass. 'Drink, Mike?'

'Thanks. Whisky.'

'Where's Jo?'

Bellman finished the drink and pushed the glass towards the waiting barman. 'Working – customer from here.'

'Thought any more about what I said?'

Bellman lifted the refilled glass. 'No. Funny thing – it must be open season on ponces. I had a similar offer last night.'

'Oh?' Elson's eyes were bright, unmoving. 'Who was that from?'

Bellman gave a dismissive shrug. 'Don't know. It was some fellow in the Dayton. Don somebody.'

'Brantner?'

'What?'

'Don Brantner.'

Bellman pointed his finger. 'That's him. Know him?'

'Everybody does,' Elson said. 'He's nothing.'

'You could have fooled me. The people he was with were money. And I mean money.'

'Foreigners?'

'Yeah – so?'

Elson shrugged. 'Did you do business?'

'No. Jo was already booked but the options were left open.'

'Does that mean you'll be working together in the future?'

Bellman downed the whisky and clapped a hand on Elson's shoulder. 'Money's money. I liked his set-up. Thanks for the drink, Terry. I have to be going.'

He made for the door with the knowledge that he had planted the seed. All that remained was to see if it grew. He gave it perhaps a day. In his experience such maturing could be exceptionally fast.

Outside, he paused to take stock, wondering where to go to ease the craving for more whisky which had overtaken him in the last hour or so. He swore when he looked at his watch and saw it was eleven. The pubs were closing so it would mean the effort of entering another club or the lone whisky bottle in the flat.

He chose the bottle and his own company, taking the whisky straight from the bottle as he sat on the bed. Intake without enjoyment. The bite was there but the echo was sour instead of jolting and welcome.

It took longer than usual before the lights dimmed and the room tilted. He barely managed to undress himself before sliding between the sheets.

He noticed a trace of perfume which he failed to identify; or understand.

She was on form again; completely reverted to her flippant, pre-Epsom manner.

'Here's me, working me fingers to the bone and what do I find when I get 'ome?' she pointed an accusing finger at Bellman. 'Me ol' man – pissed as a newt.'

Bellman stirred, watching her fold his scattered clothes through pain-filled eyes. Even in his stupefied state he could recognise that the recital was as much for her own benefit as his. The words were calculated to disperse the antagonism of the previous day.

'I'll be surprised if you only worked your fingers,' he said, trying to contribute to the truce.

She swung round and grinned. 'He was more active than the other bloke but I wouldn't reckon his wife's overdone if last night was a big event.'

Bellman groaned and held his head. 'Spare me the details.'

'Tea coming up,' she said. 'See – I never make the same mistake twice, do I?'

'Thank God for that,' he said feelingly.

She brought him the tea and sat on the edge of the bed. 'We went to a pretty crummy hotel. I think he'd saved up for his big night out.'

'He was loaded,' Bellman said. 'Just showing his northern caution, that's all.' He asked her for his coat and took out the money, handing her half the fee.

She fingered the notes. 'Thanks, Mike. Can I have my post office book? I think I should save some. It's not in my nature but you've given me a conscience.'

He lit a cigarette and blew smoke upwards as he shook his head. 'No. The book stays with me. Make your own arrangements – a bank – no, you'd have problems with references ... put some in a building society.'

She swatted at him with the notes. 'Good idea ... towards me old age, you know. Now. Can I have the bed?'

She asked no questions when he told her he was going out alone. 'Okay. I fancy a night by the television.'

When he was at the door he said, 'See you, then.'

A hand appeared over the chair and gave a wave. He did not leave until a leg followed, giving a spot-light kick as the fingers of the hand changed into an obscene gesture.

It was difficult for him to observe the Loom. The entrance was recessed between other premises and the road, a continuous line, offered no bend to form a concealed vantage point.

Bellman parked fifty yards from the club, lowering the window of the Toyota so that, periodically, he could peer out and get a partially-obscured view of the doorway.

Elson arrived after Bellman had been watching for an hour, handing the keys of his car to the doorman who drove it past Bellman before turning into the narrow mews which led to the garage at the rear of the club.

Bellman waited for twenty minutes before leaving the car and ringing the Loom from a call-box, asking for Elson.

Elson must have been in the bar for he answered almost immediately.

'Terry? – it's Mike.'

'Who?'

'Mike – Mike Cater.'

'Oh yeah?' Elson sounded less than enthusiastic.

'About your offer, Terry, you know, the thing we were talking about. Can we meet?'

'Why?'

'Something's come up. I'm interested.'

'Perhaps I'm not – now.'

'Don't mess me about, Terry,' Bellman pleaded. 'If you're with someone I'll understand but ...'

'All right. Where will I meet you? Here?'

Bellman made a low, frightened sound. 'Christ! No. Can you make it to the Red Lion. Know it?'

'The one off Curzon Street?'

'Yes.'

'All right, I'll be there in ten minutes but I don't see what ...'

'It *is* urgent, Terry. I wouldn't have called you otherwise . . .'

'Okay. I'll be there.'

Bellman returned to the Toyota and made the short trip to the pub. He was in a corner seat when Elson arrived.

'What's the matter, then?' Elson said when Bellman had bought him a drink.

'I've been warned off.'

Elson's glass halted abruptly on its upward journey. 'Who by?'

'That's just it – I don't know. Earlier I took Jo to a pub we usually visit before clubbing – one near Marble Arch. We hadn't been there two minutes when *three* of them pull me. A big bloke and two others.' Bellman gave his shoulders the ritual twitch. 'I'm not easily scared but *shit* – they meant business.'

'What did they say?' Elson was impatient for the story, not Bellman's phony heroics.

'The big one did the talking, said there was no room for individual operators, I was either to team up or leave the game altogether.'

'What did you say.'

'Say?' Bellman snorted. 'Fuck-all. I grabbed Jo and we left. Smartly.'

'You've no idea who they were?'

Bellman made a point of studying Elson's face. 'No. I thought you might be able to tell me.'

'Me?'

'Look, Terry. All I ask for is a quiet life. If they were your mob, say so and . . .'

Elson glanced disgustedly at Bellman and lit a cigarette. 'They were nothing to do with me.'

Bellman beat a fist into an open palm. 'Who then?'

Elson shook his head, his eyes unfocused as he thought. 'You're sure you've never seen them before?'

'No, at least, I don't think so.'

'What does that mean?'

'Well,' Bellman rubbed worried fingers through his hair. 'I think I might have seen one of them before – in the Dayton.' He let his hand fall away. 'I don't know. The Dayton's class – these were real heavies.'

Elson looked up quickly. 'You saw Brantner in the Dayton.'

'Yes.'

'Was the chap you recognised with him?'

Bellman frowned. 'I didn't say I recognised him. His face seemed familiar, that's all. Anyway, if it was the same one, he wasn't with Brantner, that's certain. This chap was just stooging around, you know, like some blokes do in a spieler.'

'But could he have been with Brantner. Even though you didn't see him actually speak with him.'

Bellman lifted his shoulders. 'How would I know?... Come to think of it, though, he was never far away from Brantner's group.' He passed a worried hand across his face. 'I didn't realise Brantner was in with anything heavy. He doesn't look the part.'

'*He's* not,' Elson said emphatically.

Bellman ignored the point. 'What should I do?'

'That's up to you. You say you're not scared.'

'I'm not but, well, team-handed – that's something else.'

Elson snapped his fingers. 'Do nothing for now. I might know more about it when I see you again. Will you be around tomorrow?'

Bellman shrugged dispiritedly. 'I thought I'd keep my head down for a while.'

'Okay. Where can I get in touch with you?'

'Is it all right if I contact you,' Bellman asked timidly.

Elson gave him another contemptuous look. 'All right. Ring me at the Loom sometime. Leave a message if I'm not there, I usually call in most nights.'

Bellman got to his feet. 'Thanks, Terry. See what you can find out. I won't forget.'

'Too right you won't. You had the opportunity of coming in with ...'

'I know,' Bellman said. 'I should have ... Christ! What's the use ... I didn't think anything ...' He made for the door, leaving the sentence unfinished.

Elson watched his drooping exit contemptuously.

Kitholm's voice openly showed relief. 'Thank God. Where have you been, Bellman?'

It was two days since Bellman's meeting with Elson. Two days of short journeys to nearby restaurants; a visit to the cinema and long hours by the television. The period was made more difficult for Bellman by Jo's unquestioning acquiescence to whatever he suggested.

He began to think he preferred her when she was inquisitive and awkward.

'I've been working,' Bellman said.

'Oh yes?' Kitholm allowed his sarcasm to show. 'Might I ask what you've been doing?'

'Has there been any friction between Pool and Cliveson ... in the brass department, I mean?'

'No. You're the man on the spot, I understand. You would have heard.'

'I haven't been around for a day or two.'

'Why not?'

'It sounds as though you already know but in case you don't, I have contacted Brantner and Elson. A couple of days ago I did something which I hoped would light the fuse. I've been standing back to await the results.'

'You sound as though you're reading the instructions on a firework,' Kitholm said acidly. 'What exactly did you do?'

'If you haven't heard, then it hasn't been successful. And don't ask what it was. You left it to me. Remember?'

'I am aware of that, Bellman, but we want results. You appear to have chosen a very nice companion for your jaunts. Perhaps you've forgotten the objective.'

'My so-called "nice companion" is a brass. I'm working

her. You now have a high-class ponce on your books, Kit-holm.' He glanced towards the door of the bedroom to ensure Jo could not overhear. The sound of a dropped clothes-hanger followed by a hearty oath reassured him.

'. . . results. Remember that, Bellman.' Kitholm was saying.

'Calm down, Kitholm. I only wanted to know if you'd heard anything. I'll be in touch.'

Bellman replaced the receiver and closed his eyes to think. The telephone rang again almost immediately.

'This is Praeger, Bellman.'

He said, 'Oh yes?' very politely.

'I'm not happy. You were told to take Elson out.'

'No. That was suggested as a possible necessity but the method of disruption was left to me.'

'I'm telling you now. Deal with Elson.' Although it was devoid of Kitholm's rising inflection, Praeger's voice had a definite edge. Urgency almost.

'All right,' Bellman said and let the telephone fall heavily.

Praeger jerked the telephone away from his ear and turned to Kitholm. 'Do I detect a flaw in Bellman's methods?'

'I don't think so,' Kitholm said hurriedly. 'Whatever he did may have had an effect we are unaware of.'

Praeger looked at Kitholm with disparagement. 'That's not very likely. I want some real action.'

'At least his cover is original.' Kitholm's statement was almost a plea.

'Bellman is never short on originality,' Praeger conceded coldly. 'Let us hope he puts it to good use again.'

Jo made no comment other than nodding when Bellman told her they were recommencing business.

Elson found them in the bar at the Loom, minutes after their arrival. 'I'm pleased to see you, Mike,' he said, lifting a hand to Jo at the same time. 'Peter Hull's in there. He's been asking for Jo.'

'I thought Clay did his arranging,' Bellman said, before burying his nose in his glass.

Elson's jaw tightened. 'Clay's employed by him but I now look after his entertainment arrangements.'

Bellman raised his eyebrows. 'This something new?'

'I'll explain later. How about letting Jo go through to him?'

'All right,' Bellman said and touched Elson's sleeve as he rose to escort Jo away. 'Don't forget it's payment in advance, will you?'

Elson gave him a long, hard stare before he moved off. 'I'll be right back.'

Bellman sipped at a beer as he waited for Elson to return.

There was no preamble once Elson was seated at the bar again. 'Where have you been? You said you were going to phone me.'

'I told you I was going to keep my head down for a while. That's what I've been doing.'

'I made a few enquiries about those three – zilch.'

'That's why I decided to emerge, I mean, they could have been a small mob trying to horn in, couldn't they?'

'Unlikely, I would say.'

'The situation's hard to understand,' Bellman said regretfully. 'Time was when everything was organised.'

Elson turned on him in surprise. 'I thought you wanted to be left alone?'

'I do, but if it's a choice between a little money or none, well, the answer's obvious.'

Elson gave him a satisfied pat. 'That's sensible. We can do business.'

'What about those others?'

'Forget them.'

'Brantner?'

'Forget him as well. He's not organised.'

'And you are?'

'We're ... getting that way.'

'Who's we?'

Elson's mood changed suddenly. 'You ask a lot of questions for a man who only runs one girl.' He finished his drink and set the glass down on the bar. 'It strikes me that you're a prick, Cater.' He put his hand in his pocket and drew out a sheaf of notes. 'Here. Two hundred. You're only getting the full whack this time. We have to talk about the future another time.'

'When?' Bellman said, pocketing the money.

Elson paused then took out his pen, writing on a piece of paper torn from a small note-book. 'I'm not guaranteeing to be in here as often as usual. I'll be moving around quite a bit now. Ring me at that number tomorrow – at six.'

Bellman took the paper and put it away.

Elson stood up. 'I have to get back to the others, some of them aren't fixed up yet. See you.'

Bellman finished his drink and left. He did a short pub-crawl before returning to the flat and the bed with its unaccustomed scented sheets.

Jo woke Bellman at ten.

'You're late,' he said when he saw the time.

'He was all bright and bouncy this morning. Insisted that I share breakfast with him. The waiter who served it was a right little sniggerer – nearly got the back of my hand.'

'Hotel?'

'Yes. Same one as last time. Near Baker Street. I don't think he believes in taking his spare birds home. Perhaps he's got a wife there, though.' She handed him a mug of tea. 'Mike?'

Her tone made him look up. 'What?'

She stood up and turned her back to him. 'Terry Elson said the situation will soon be changing. He didn't say how exactly, but I think he was trying to say he would be taking over from you.'

Bellman sipped the tea. 'So what's the problem? You'll still be in work.'

She turned, eyes blazing. 'What do you mean? Do you

think you can let me go just like that? Don't I have any say in it? I don't want to work for that ... that ... bastard, or anyone else come to that. If you intend to ...'

Bellman held his hands in front of his face in mock fear. 'Whoa! Hold on ... nothing will change.'

She calmed immediately, studying his face intently. 'Are you sure? Don't kid to me, Mike.'

'I'm not kidding.'

A quick stride brought her beside the bed to look down at him. After another searching study of his face she suddenly clapped her hands. 'Great! ... Right – it's bath-time for me, then bed so you'd better vacate. Unless ...' She fluttered her eyelashes outrageously.

'I'm getting up,' Bellman growled.

When he heard her splashing in the bath he pushed the door open and went in, making for the wash-basin.

'Oh, *sir*,' she said, crossing her hands across her breasts.

'I'm in a hurry,' he said, lathering his face. 'Anyway, you're wasting energy – you could cover them with a couple of fingers.'

She laughed. 'Bastard,' and scooped water at him.

He searched for two hours before finding the block of flats he wanted. His route was complicated, never taking him far from the central area or moving too near the suburbs.

He made a point of staying away from the flat while Jo was sleeping, occupying himself by browsing in the shops and department stores, particularly the book sections, an old pursuit which seemed strange to him now.

She was up when he got back, just before six. He gave her half the money which Elson had paid him and some extra notes, telling her to go out and re-stock the drinks cabinet.

'You want me out of the way while you use the telephone,' she said astutely, but took the money and left.

Bellman rang the number Elson had given him. A woman's voice said, 'Denning's.'

'I'd like to speak to Mr Elson.'

'A moment.'

He heard the buzz of an extension then a voice said, 'Elson.'

'Hello, Terry. It's me – Mike Cater ...'

Elson said, 'Yes, yes,' hurriedly. Bellman was pleased, the tone showing that Elson wanted to say as little as possible over the telephone. 'Can you meet me tonight, Mike, say a couple of hours time at ...'

'Sure, Terry, but before you say any more, listen for a moment ... I've come up with something on those fellows we talked about ...'

'The ones in the pub?'

'Yes. I've found out who one of them is, at least I think ...'

Elson cut him off. 'That's good, Mike, but we can't talk about it right now. Tell me later.'

'All right,' Bellman said, 'but can you pick me up. I have some photographs. The man I'm talking about is on them. I don't want to carry them about with me, though. I've been told the chap's name but it doesn't mean anything to me. You might know more.'

'Don't say any more about it for now, just tell me where to find you.'

'Do you know Parren Court – Paddington?'

'No, but I can find it.'

'I'm at hundred and ten – eighth floor.'

Bellman gave more directions and ended by saying, 'I won't be there until nine—that be all right?'

Elson said, 'Fine. See you then.'

Are we working tonight?' Jo said when she returned, lumping a loaded bag on the floor.

'I am – you're not,' Bellman said shortly, his tone preluding further questions.

She made a face at him but said nothing.

He left at seven-thirty and drove to Parren Court.

The apartment block was not yet two years old. At the foot of the building the landscaper's attempt to capture the well-established look had only partly succeeded. Grass showed in weak patches and the mixed bag of shrubs drooped wearily with the effort of fighting for establishment on the steep mound which supported the structure.

Bellman used the lift to reach the eighth floor which was at the top. The doors of the lift opened on to a corridor running both sides of the shaft. Apartment doors studded the walkway on either side, their heavy wood composition proving that the designers may have been under pressure to utilise the space available but still remained alive to the security angle.

Bellman's footsteps were absorbed by the rubberoid composition of the floor as he took the right-hand section of the corridor and walked to the end. He pushed through the reinforced-glass door and stood at the head of the stairs, a spectacular sweep of fashioned iron, descending in a spiral of tight loops until the hand-rail disappeared into the leaves of a massive rubber-plant on the distant ground floor.

He took one short, downward glance before retreating to the lift, satisfied that everything was as he had found it a few hours previously. Music, filtering through the door of one apartment, reminded him that any encounter with the nearby occupants would be sudden and unavoidable. The lift took him silently down, the action helping to soothe his sudden doubts.

He had parked the Toyota where he could see the entrance of the drive, a short ski-jump of concrete, providing a timid driver's nightmare.

Inside the car he wiped a thin film of moisture from the windscreen and waited.

Elson arrived a few minutes after nine, the Ford Granada pausing at the entrance sign before taking the rise in a sudden, confident spurt.

Bellman left the Toyota and followed the glaring tail-lights on foot, arriving as Elson alighted, stretching and looking upwards. He swung in surprise as Bellman greeted him.

'Just got back myself,' Bellman explained. 'Come on, I'll take you up.'

'Looks a nice place,' Elson said as they waited for the lift.

'It's okay,' Bellman said off-handedly, breathing a silent sigh of relief as the doors opened on an empty elevator.

'Tell me about these photographs, then,' Elson said when they were ascending.

'In a while. See what you think of them first. By the way, Terry, I don't want to get involved in any heavy stuff, you know what I mean. I wouldn't like to think you'd tell anyone I'd shown them to you.'

'Of course I wouldn't.'

'What about that woman who answered the telephone? Do you think she might have . . .'

'Don't worry about it. I always make sure I'm not over-heard. Relax, Mike, no-one even knows I'm here.'

Beautiful – prat. Now let everyone keep snug indoors.

Bellman reached into his pocket and took out a set of keys as the doors opened on the eighth floor. He felt a sudden warmth at his arm pits. The unreal detachment of the Toper and Datchett episodes was gone, replaced by a physical tightness which bound his chest.

A burst of laughter, guillotined by a closing door, reached them from the floor below as Bellman led the way along the corridor.

'I can see why you need to earn regularly,' Elson said as Bellman paused by the end apartment. 'This place can't be cheap.'

Bellman lowered the poised key. 'It's not. And with the prices they charge you'd think they would do something about this, wouldn't you?' He turned to the stairway door and pushed it open, releasing it as Elson followed him on to the landing.

Elson's arm automatically lifted to stay the heavy glass

and Bellman pivoted, driving his fist deep into Elson's unprepared belly. The punch travelled through a wide arc, the momentum causing Bellman's right foot to lift as he followed through.

For a moment he thought he had under-estimated Elson's physique and fitness when the expected jack-knife failed to occur. Only the blunt features registered the blow, a wide eyed stare of incredulity which changed to pain as the eyes glazed and the head dropped.

Bellman smashed both fists down on the offered neck and Elson completed the fall. Some inner mechanism made a gesture, a weak attempt to grasp Bellman's foot but the fingers only splayed over the shoes, lacking the strength to curl inwards. Soft living and easy victories had betrayed Elson to himself, suppressing his once natural urge to view every situation with a suspicious eye.

A quick glance through the glass showed Bellman that the corridor was still deserted. He lifted Elson with difficulty, the dead weight folding over his hands and arms as he levered the shoulders onto the iron of the hand-rail. As he dipped his hand to clutch the buckling knees, Elson made a small noise which could have been, 'No.'

Bellman heaved him over.

The centre space of the well was large enough to take a body. But not one that twisted and turned as it fell. Elson struck the ironwork at the junction of three separate floors. Once with his head and twice with his legs. His arrival at the bottom came up clearly to Bellman: the indescribable sound of human flesh in violent contact with the immovable.

Bellman gave the scene of the encounter a quick once-over and returned to the lift.

On the ground floor he turned towards the stair-well, the need to ensure that Elson was dead pulling at his guts. Voices and the sound of a closing door stopped him in mid-stride. When he edged forward he saw a couple on his left, the woman bent over her handbag with the panic of one who believes she has just locked herself out. Her white-haired companion stood nearby feverishly searching his pockets for his own key.

They did not lift their heads as Bellman left.

Inside the Toyota he twisted the interior mirror and looked at himself. The face that was reflected back was pale and strained. He told himself it could also be the effect of the street lights.

Watching the main entrance of the building he saw the couple from the ground floor emerge, fears apparently dispelled, and walk towards a car. They paused momentarily as a sports job rocketed up the incline and slithered to a halt, disgorging three shouting, waving youngsters.

Bellman gave up the idea of examining Elson and started the Toyota. His departure was controlled. Unhurried.

But only just.

When he opened the door of the flat the flickering light of the television was casting crazy, distorted shadows over the furniture and walls.

'Hi,' Jo twisted in the chair to look at him.

Bellman did not answer but switched on a small light and poured himself a drink. 'Want one?'

She shook her head, watching him curiously.

He threw the drink to the back of his throat and poured another before sitting down and staring unseeingly at the screen.

'You all right, Mike?' she asked.

'Yes. Why?' he asked without looking at her.

She muttered, 'Ask a question – get a question,' and turned away.

Bellman sat slumped, moving only to draw the bottle nearer. Soon he was drinking and refilling the glass with hardly a break in the movement.

Jo became progressively stiller as the level of the bottle dropped.

The cigarette dropped from Bellman's fingers when

there was only an inch of whisky left. She rescued it and guided it back into his fingers. His only reaction was a weak motion of his head. Shortly afterwards he was asleep.

She got to her feet and looked down at the unconscious figure. 'When you tie one on you really make a job of it.'

She moved the bottle and glass out of his reach and undressed him. It was only necessary for her to swing his feet up when she had finished but the effort made her gasp for breath.

When he was stretched out and covered to her satisfaction she switched the light off and went through to the bedroom.

Chapter Sixteen

'The phone rang twice. When I picked it up no-one answered.' She spoke in the act of closing the door.

Bellman stood in the bedroom doorway a towel draped round his neck. 'Where've you been?'

She lifted the bag. 'Shopping,' then, 'Foooood.'

He returned to the bedroom and dressed. Back in the living-room he said, 'I want to make a phone-call.'

'Does that mean I have to go out again?'

'The bedroom will do,' he said brusquely.

The door closed sharply behind her.

Praeger answered.

Bellman said, 'I suppose it was you who rang?'

'Yes. A girl answered. Where were you?'

'Pissed – out cold.'

'I'm sending Kitholm to see you.'

'Why?'

'He will tell you all you need to know . . . here he is now.'

There was a pause then Kitholm's voice said, 'Bellman?'

'Yes.'

'Meet me in the Tentman – half an hour.'

'All right.'

The line went dead and he called out to Jo. When she appeared he said, 'I have to go out. I want you to stay in until I get back.'

She said, 'Okay.'

'I'm not sure what our next move will be. I need you handy.' The explanation was also an apology of sorts.

Kitholm said, 'Effective,' and stared at Bellman's moustache.

'What? ... Oh, this ...' Bellman had grown used to his appearance.

'The hirsute look suits you. It's amazing how a simple growth can alter one's image.'

'Yeah,' Bellman said drily.

'We won't be eating but you can order a drink if you like,' Kitholm said and led the way to a small room off the restaurant.

'Coffee,' Bellman said.

Kitholm's eyes showed his surprise, then dimmed. 'Oh ... yes.' He looked accusingly at Bellman's drawn features as though he had not seen them before.

They sat at a small table and waited until the coffee was served. Kitholm was twisting his fingers in an alien, undisciplined movement.

When the waiter had gone Kitholm tested the coffee then said, 'That was violent.'

'Elson?'

'Yes.'

'Is he dead?'

'Christ!' The expletive was also foreign to Kitholm's usual behaviour.

'I wasn't certain,' Bellman insisted.

Kitholm looked at him disbelievingly. 'A pulverised head, compacted body, broken legs – arms. Good God, he couldn't be deader.'

Bellman strugged. 'I was prevented from checking. There can be some amazing survivals.'

'You did throw him from the top floor?' Kitholm said as though he couldn't believe what he was hearing.

'Yes. Is it listed as a murder?'

'The investigation is only just gathering momentum. It will be treated as murder, though, there's no doubt about that.'

'Then Praeger should be happy.'

Kitholm sighed. 'He's delighted. Now to the new business.'

'So soon?'

Kitholm sat straighter. 'The body wasn't found until ten last night. Cliveson's firm didn't know until this morning. They're going mad.'

'That was the idea.'

'Yes, but their reaction hasn't been exactly what we expected.'

'There hasn't been time for a reaction, surely.'

'Their immediate concern has been to replace Elson with someone who can take over where he left off. They may begin the retaliation when they're more certain of the facts.'

'That's understandable. So let's wait.'

'Praeger says no. A man named John Briller is to jump straight into Elson's shoes, figuratively speaking. He's more of a thug than Elson was. He's to be taken out – quickly.'

Bellman's cup clattered to the saucer. '*Whaaat?* Now listen to me Kitholm. The idea was to set the two camps against each other. It's got to be given time to work.'

'But they're replacing Elson.'

'So what? They'll get around to squaring Elson's death. I put the mix in for Brantner – Pool's man. They'll figure Pool's firm for the killing sooner or later. Then watch the action.'

'There has been talk among Cliveson's mob of lone ponces being intimidated by a strong-arm team of Pool's men, is that what you mean?'

'Yes.'

'Cliveson didn't appear to be very worried.'

'He will be now that Elson's gone.'

'Praeger says no.'

'Praeger can get stuffed.'

'He calls the tune,' Kitholm reminded.

Bellman savagely stubbed his cigarette and immediately lit another one. 'How come you know Cliveson's plans so soon?' He held an imaginary telephone to his ear. 'Intercept?'

'The information is correct,' Kitholm said obstinately.

Bellman sat with fixed eyes. Occasionally he would lift the cigarette to his lips and draw deeply but the action seemed to be purely automatic, with no pleasure gained from it.

When the cigarette had burned down, he said, 'Will I be able to pick up this Briller character in the same way as Elson?'

Kitholm tried to control his relief but it still showed. 'Yes, yes. He'll be on the scene tonight.'

'You'll hear from me,' Bellman said and stood up abruptly.

Praeger said, 'How did he take it?'

Kitholm looked at him pointedly. 'He jibbed. Said we should give the situation time to develop.'

'Since when has Bellman been giving the orders?'

'I'm bound to say he has a point.'

'We have to keep the pressure on,' Praeger said and walked away.

Kitholm watched him leave then sat down behind the desk with a sigh, drawing a pile of papers towards him. His face relaxed as he began to read. The written moderator. Order in the printed word.

Chapter Seventeen

'Terrible thing wasn't it, sir, about Mr Elson?' The barman in the Loom served Bellman's and Jo's drinks automatically, a careful eye on their faces to see what effect his words might have.

'Yes,' Bellman said, 'terrible.'

Denied the opportunity of retelling the story the barman walked away.

'What about Terry Elson?' Jo asked.

'He died last night.'

'*No!*'

'Yes. He was found at the bottom of a flight of stairs in an apartment block.'

She said, 'Christ. Suicide?'

'Either that or he was murdered,' Bellman said matter-of-factly.

'You didn't say anything earlier,' she said accusingly.

'I meant to but I forgot,' he said. 'Anyway, I'm shedding no tears.'

'It's funny – him dying, I mean, after what he said to me.' Her voice lowered dramatically. 'Do you think he tried to take over from someone and they objected – a violent one, I mean?'

Bellman laughed loudly. 'I don't know – or care. It suits us, that's for sure.'

'You're a callous devil,' she said.

They were on their second drinks when the noise of an incoming group drowned the subdued conversation and quiet music from the floor. There were three men and four girls, all talking and laughing at the same time. One of the men was Clay. They by-passed the bar, heading directly for the area of tables. As they were passing where Bellman sat, Clay noticed him and murmured something to the man at his side. They both stopped and Clay guided the one he had spoken to towards the bar.

'Cater. This is John Briller.'

It was a terse introduction, underlined by the merest nod from Briller.

Bellman gave an equally conservative inclination of his head.

'That's Jo,' Clay said, watching Briller's face.

Briller said nothing but stared at her as though examining something in a market. He was only of average height but the bullish, sloping shoulders, together with the dark hair and blue-stubbled chin, gave him a very definite presence, which, Bellman decided, had been the reason he was chosen as Elson's replacement. A man patently not to be tangled with. Lacking in intelligence, perhaps, but one who would slavishly obey orders of any nature.

Clay said, 'Heard about Terry, did you?'

'I heard he was dead, that's all,' Bellman said. 'What happened? Somebody top him?'

'Yeah,' Briller interrupted.

'I hope they get him – the one who did it.'

Briller turned his attention solely to Bellman. 'Old Bill? – no chance. Don't worry, though, the matter will be attended to.' His use of the oblique jargon of impending retribution slotted Briller firmly into the niche of violent man.

Clay moved uncomfortably under the words which were so alien to the surroundings. 'We're having a busman's holiday,' he said by way of compensation. 'John, his mate and myself – and a few girls.'

'Not looking after Peter tonight, then?' Bellman asked.

'No. John here is taking over that side. We're just ...'

'Sampling the goods,' Briller interrupted, leering.

He pulled at Clay's arm. 'Come on.' As he steered towards the main floor he looked over his shoulder. 'See you another time.' The words were addressed to Bellman but the look that accompanied them took in Jo.

When they had gone, she said, 'Christ! No thanks.'

'Don't worry, he'll never get near you,' Bellman promised grimly.

They stayed for a further half-hour with Bellman staring thoughtfully into his glass. His decision to move came suddenly, taking her by surprise.

He drove to the Dayton and pronounced it 'dead', similarly disposing of two more night-spots before deciding on a brand-new location.

The Hearts and Diamonds was a small gaming club in the centre of Mayfair where Bellman had encountered difficulty trying to join its restricted list. He had finally succeeded by paying far more than the stipulated fee.

Inside, it was busy. Bellman recognised two faces from gossip-column photographs and an MP who had not yet featured there but appeared to be trying to put the matter right. A lesser-light of the film world was recognised by Jo who drew Bellman's attention to her in subdued but excited tones. At first, the club gave a compacted, slightly claustrophobic impression. The two floors of public rooms were a series of small units joined by cramped, stubby passages, lit by fussy, miniature chandeliers. But once inside the rooms the hemmed-in feeling vanished as though part of an illusion.

'It's weird,' Jo said, staring around with puzzled eyes.

Bellman silently agreed but did not reply, leading her up a short flight of steps to the restaurant. The atmosphere inside was in complete contrast to the whirling drone of the roulette wheels and the quiet murmur of the crowd in the gaming rooms. The room was bright and long, giving its own exaggerated idea of available space. Waiters moved swiftly and silently among the tables.

Bellman's survey of the occupants was brief but allowed him to see what he wanted. He let a waiter show them to a small table then buried himself in the menu.

He did not raise his head when Jo hissed, 'Hey, there's that bloke we met in the Dayton, you know – Don – the one with the arabs. He's got someone with him.'

'I know.'

'Oh.' She sounded disappointed. 'Do you ever miss anything?'

'Stop rubber-necking,' he said as she craned to peer over his hunched figure.

She sat back and pouted.

Bellman ordered with deliberation, the promise of the menu touching a long forgotten chord. Jo followed his choice of lobster for the main course, barely suppressing a giggle when he went into a serious huddle with the wine-waiter over the appropriate accompaniment.

'Getting quite the gourmet, aren't you,' she said artlessly, when they were alone.

The food was superb. When they had finished and were sitting with coffee and lighted cigarettes she said, 'You know something? That was an education. Who would have thought that eating could be such an experience.'

Bellman smiled at her intensity. 'You're getting a taste for the good life.'

'Yes,' she said, then narrowed her eyes against the smoke. 'Don't worry – I know it can't last for ever.'

He considered it a strange remark. In his experience females usually believed everything agreeable *was* for ever, or indulged in delusions which prohibited warnings being made to the contrary.

'He's coming over – Don,' her voice had adopted the conspiratorial note which always amused him.

His eyes were already flicking round to find Brantner.

'Mike . . . Jo,' Brantner spoke before reaching their table, continuing the greeting as he joined them and eased into a vacant chair. 'I'm sorry but I didn't see you come in, otherwise I would have asked you to join us.' He waved vaguely in the direction he had come from.

Bellman said, 'Don't worry. I saw you were busy.'

Brantner nodded. 'I'm with a businessman – Swedish.' He twisted his lips into a small quirk of disapproval. 'A late arrival. I laid on entertainment for a mixed party earlier on – gentlemen from the Middle East and some Germans. Strange bed-partners.' He smiled at the image. 'The result is I'm short of a girl for my friend back there. Interested?'

'Jo?' Bellman said. 'Sure. If you like she'll join you in the bar. Better for you.'

Brantner nodded gratefully. 'That's a nice way to operate Mike.'

'Two hundred – that's my not-so-nice-side.'

Brantner unobtrusively fingered notes from his wallet and slid them to Bellman.

Bellman put the money away and said, 'That was a shame about Elson.'

Brantner's attitude was immediately alert. 'Elson? Yes ... heard any more about it?'

'No, but I've seen the man who's taking over from him ... Briller – nasty.'

'I ...' Brantner severed the sentence. 'I must get back. We'll talk soon perhaps, Mike. Your prices aren't outrageous but ... a different working arrangement perhaps?'

'We'll see,' Bellman said. 'Take your man through to the bar, then. Jo will follow.'

'Is this another club where they accept our presence?' she asked when Brantner had gone.

'Not bloody likely,' Bellman said. 'It wouldn't take much to get barred from here. You have to be double-careful. Come on,' he spread notes beside the bill and led her into a gaming room.

When he saw Brantner take the stairs to the bar, followed by a man of undoubted Scandinavian colouring, he gave her a gentle push towards the steps. 'See you later.'

She gave a casual wave and left him.

He watched Brantner oversee Jo and the client's departure from the darkness of the Toyota. They had left in a taxi and Brantner had returned to the sophisticated

atmosphere of the Hearts and Diamonds. Bellman pro-
grammed himself for a long wait but Brantner appeared
again ten minutes later, climbing into a cream sports car
parked a few yards from the club entrance.

The proximity of the car to the club was an indication
of Brantner's standing in the Hearts and Diamonds. It was
not unknown for an all-powerful doorman to blacklist a
millionaire who tipped poorly and dispatch his chauffeur
to wait away from the jealously-guarded precincts, where
the vehicle would inevitably be towed away if left un-
attended for more than a few minutes.

Bellman soon had serious misgivings about his decision
to follow Brantner. The other's flashy driving – wide, over-
taking swings, coupled with fierce blasts of acceleration –
did not lend itself to an unobtrusive tail job. But the journey
was short. Brantner parked outside a block of flats just off
the Edgware Road at its southern end and walked inside
without a backward glance.

Free of immediate problems, Bellman returned to the
flat, making a large container of coffee and setting it over
the burner. He laid two packs of cigarettes beside the stack
of paper he had placed on the low table then walked through
to the bedroom and changed into comfortable slacks and
sweater.

He took a sip of coffee, lit up a cigarette and began to
think hard.

Chapter Eighteen

It was the insistence that worried him: Praeger's insistence on the erasure of another life – Briller's.

His other worry was – why was he worried? He had killed two men and criminally injured another, so why the concern?

Because he could find no answer, his brain jolted. The careful preparations were forgotten. The coffee cooled. Only the cigarette was used, and that without recognition of what he was doing.

His thoughts followed no pattern; instead he was among a jumble of recollections: Datchett and his failure to recognise imminent death; Sandy; Toper with his overweight flight and collapsing leg; brief glimpses of previously forgotten police episodes and the drinking sessions following a successful investigation; hangovers; hours of tedious observation and the intoxicating moments of action when everything suddenly came good; Elson, bouncing off the ironwork and the noise of his body meeting the floor far below; Sandy again; Praeger.

Praeger. The name stayed with him as the nauseous tumbling inside his head slowed down.

Bellman did not know how long he sat after the nightmare ended, but the sweat was still trickling down his face when he became aware of his surroundings. He looked in surprise at his hands. There was no cigarette; the stub in the ash tray was no part of his memory.

He wiped his face and unsteadily crossed the room to pour a drink, taking it in a single swallow. He put the bottle away, then emptied the cold coffee from the mug and refilled it from the container.

He lit another cigarette and reviewed the frenzy he had just experienced. He still could not understand why it had happened. He felt no remorse, so why . . .? Then he realised he craved understanding; understanding – not justification. His head hurt. Reasoning had been at a minimum since Sandy. He lifted his head suddenly. Sandy was dead. Acceptance. It gave him no great uplift, the thought hung heavy on him, but now at least he knew he could live with it.

He reached for the paper he had laid out on the table. If he wanted to understand, he had to begin somewhere, and facts in black and white were always easier to comprehend than elusive thoughts.

How many women were currently practising prostitution in London? Class prostitutes, not the army of cheap, short-stand sellers, but the immaculately-groomed girls who waited by a telephone, or for an introduction from their minders. Like Jo.

Bellman searched his mind for figures – statistics. He slipped back into the trained, disciplined method of years before. Then he up-dated, using recent observations and snippets of information he had overheard in the clubs, items from clients, girls, barmen, waiters.

Say a hundred and fifty girls. Be conservative. Say a hundred.

A hundred at two hundred pounds a night . . . twenty thousand pounds. Christ! Be conservative again. Not all of them worked every night, and they did not all charge two hundred pounds. So . . . say fifty worked at an average of *one* hundred pounds. You could not get more conservative than that. Five thousand pounds. More reasonable. *Seven* nights a week. Thirty-five thousand pounds a week. Christ again.

Fifty-two weeks a year.

Bellman totted up the figures. One million, eight hundred and twenty thousand pounds a year. In cash. And that was conservative.

Kitholm had been so right. A fountain of money with no figurehead to control it. Prices and profits lost in the individual dealings and unrecorded arrangements of escort clubs, massage parlours and God-knows how many other outlets.

So. Control only the best. Ignore the small trade. Let it satisfy critical society's appetite for vice convictions.

More conservatism – call it a million and a half. And the top class was used by the top class – financially speaking. The highest payer secured the best merchandise. And the highest payers would be the successful: successful businessmen; successful traders; successful anything, providing money was the measure.

There was something else. The contact of pleasure-seeking but legitimate men with the outpost of crime represented by the paid girls could only be advantageous to one side – ignoring the pursuit of pleasure – and that was to those who sought information necessary to promote crime.

Bellman snorted as a paradox struck him: Lochard's theory of the principle of exchange would work to benefit the element who usually suffered from its truth; the theory that stated that when two objects met, each would leave a trace of itself upon the other.

Bellman stared at the figures on the paper. The potential of organised prostitution had long been recognised, had even been exploited, but it had never previously been considered as an integral part of an overall criminal complex. A million and a half was cause in itself, but the amalgamation of evil and unsuspecting innocence had devastating possibilities.

He lay back and indulged in a mental exercise of old habit, reviewing everything from the beginning – the recent beginning. He began with the approach at Victoria and the subsequent interviews and instruction sessions, trying to recall every word spoken by Kitholm and Praeger. Then the acts of destruction, human destruction. And the reasons. Always the reasons.

At the end he was still dissatisfied. He knew only what he had been told, and the awesome figures he had written on the paper were available to anyone with curiosity enough to work them out. But somewhere there was something missing. Underneath everything there was a reason; a reason for something – and not the one he had been given, he was sure. He gathered the papers together and stacked them neatly before dousing the lights and entering the bedroom. What was Kitholm's expression? A catalyst, that was it. He needed a catalyst. Sleep did not come easily.

He woke at eight and got straight out of bed. Jo arrived just as he finished preparing his breakfast, sliding a piece of toast from his plate and eating it quickly, licking her fingers clean of butter.

Bellman said, 'All right?'

She wiped the crumbs from her lips and said, 'Yep. It'll be nice to talk again, though. He wasn't much on English – we did nearly everything by sign language.'

'Must have been interesting,' Bellman said drily, handing her a hundred pounds.

'Are we going out tonight?' she asked as she took the money.

'I'm not sure. Why?'

She shrugged indifferently. 'No reason really.'

'I have to go out later. I may be gone for most of the day.'

'Okay.' She made for the bedroom. 'Ciao!'

He waited until ten before ringing Praeger. The voice was sharp with impatience.

'What is it, Bellman. I thought I'd made the position clear.'

'You did,' Bellman said, 'but I thought you would like to hear what I have to say.'

'Get on with it then.'

'I agreed to do as you suggested regarding Briller, and

I have met him. He didn't impress me. Elson was not very bright. Briller's actually dim.'

'Get to the point.'

'Shortly after seeing Briller I came across Brantner.'

'Oh?'

'Yes. Brantner is not what you might call a pushy type and though his approach to the take-over is not as direct as Elson's was, I would say that he's making progress – good progress. In fact, it's reasonable to assume that he will shortly be in a position to make an open bid.'

'I don't see what any of this has to do ...'

'But it has,' Bellman cut in. 'Cliveson's team has had a set-back. All right – it's not a permanent one, but it makes more sense to nibble at the foundations of Pool's intentions. I'm going to take Brantner out.'

The noise which came over the line was indecipherable. It could have been the beginning of a cough, or just the whistling intake of breath. Whatever it was it ceased abruptly. For a time there was only the electronic buzz of the line. Finally Praeger spoke again. This time very quietly.

'Bellman. I will say it only once. Concern yourself with Briller and nothing else – for now.'

'But surely ...'

'You *heard* me?'

Bellman still persisted. 'Brantner is no hard-man but if he's an example of Pool's employees you could find that Pool is far more dangerous than Cliveson.'

'I ...' Praeger stopped and Bellman could actually hear him breathing. 'For the last time, Bellman ...'

'All right, all right. I thought I was doing the right thing.'

'You weren't. Now ... is there anything else?'

'Yes. If it's to be Briller, I'll need more money. He goes around with more than one other in attendance. I may have to deal with them simultaneously, the method, therefore, could be complex – and needs financing.'

'I understand that you are receiving extra dividends – the girl's fees.'

'Listen to me, Praeger. That girl's my cover. Whatever she earns – she keeps.'

'Very touching. How much do you want from me?'

'Three thousand.'

Praeger's laugh was thin, mirthless. 'Ridiculous.'

Bellman echoed the sound deliberately. 'No, *you're* ridiculous, Praeger. The service you've had so far has been perfect – and cheap. I'm not asking for the money without reason. If you think the price is too high then ...'

'You'll get the money,' Praeger interrupted. 'Just ensure you use it to good effect.'

Bellman waited for a few moments then, in a normal voice, said. 'Good. I don't need it immediately. It will take time to organise. Kitholm can deliver it when I give the word – or you.'

'I presume there is a reason for not paying it into the bank,' Praeger said coldly. 'Mr Kitholm will do any delivering that is necessary. How long will this take? I don't want a long delay.'

'A few days.'

'Very well.'

'Bye, Praeger. If I need more than three thousand, I'll let you know.'

Praeger's voice squeaked in the earphone as Bellman put it down.

He looked thoughtfully at the instrument. There was no evidence. But he *knew* now.

When he lifted the receiver again he held it to his ear for some time without moving to dial. The check was not infallible but he thought he had retained enough expertise to recognise the muffled tuning of intercept relays. There was still nothing.

He rang the newspaper and asked for Peter Say. There was a long delay before a voice said, 'Say.'

'Hello, Peter. It's Mike Bellman. Remember?'

'Who? ... Oh. Yes. Mike. Christ. It's a long time.'

'Years.'

'Yes. What have you been up to? I heard ...' The voice trailed off in embarrassment.

'This and that, Peter,' Bellman said easily. 'It's a long story – perhaps a drink sometime? Actually I'm ringing you to ask a favour. Will you help?'

'Depends.' The caution in the tone underlined the single word.

'It's nothing dodgy. I'm doing a bit of private work. You know ...' The break deterred any question. 'I want someone's address and any additional information that's available. I could go through company records but it takes time. I thought with your library ...'

'Who is it?'

'Pool – Warwick Dunn Pool. Businessman, stockbroker, you name it he ...'

'I know of him. Give me your number and I'll call you back when I've got the details.'

'Can I ring you? I'm using someone else's telephone and I'm leaving here soon.'

'All right. Give me half an hour.'

Bellman said, 'Thanks, Peter,' and rang off.

He waited for forty minutes before calling the number again.

'Are you sure you know what you're doing, Mike?' Say asked. 'Pool's a bigger name than even I recalled – director of Danx Holdings, the firm that's notorious for property scoops and a whole shoot of other interests. It's not something like a divorce enquiry is it? If so ...'

'Nothing like that,' Bellman laughed. 'I think his domestic life is settled enough. This won't rebound on you. I promise.'

'Okay. You wanted his address? It's Tetham Lodge, Bailey Fall, Kent.'

'What's that? A village?'

'Bailey Fall? Yes – near Sevenoaks. Do you want his town address?'

'Please.'

'Fourteen, Merton Mews, Chelsea. Small place for over-night stops I would imagine. I have a list of his various interests here if you would like them.'

Bellman said, 'Might as well,' and took down the details dictated to him. When he had finished he said, 'Thanks, Peter, that's been a great help. As I said, how about a drink sometime? I may have something for you.'

'Sure,' Say replied. There was little enthusiasm.

Bellman was pleased with the lack of interest but he knew any further requests would not be favoured. The ex-police-man tag was not always an advantage, often the reverse, but Say, being what he was – a top-class crime reporter – would not miss the chance of adding to his reputation. He said, 'Thanks again,' and replaced the receiver.

The Toyota was grimy and the roof had a thin carpet of fallen leaves. Bellman swept some of them away with his hand, smearing the paintwork.

The main office of Danx Holdings was in the City; a glass-fronted building nestling uncomfortably between older neighbours. The flanking premises appeared to lean away from the new arrival in mortared horror.

Bellman viewed the monochrome exterior with misgiv-ings. He had no clear idea why he had come to the seat of one of Pool's possessions. He shrugged inwardly and pushed through the doors. It was always an advantage to have some contact with a central figure in an enquiry, albeit a detached one. And it was possible he could find something useful inside.

The foyer was large. A reception area at the rear was dwarfed by towering, marble pillars and the spacious approach area. Several low-slung leatherette couches were occupied and a small gathering of people waited by the lift shaft. The receptionist gave Bellman an interrogative stare through big-bug lenses but lost interest when he sat down as though early for an appointment.

He sorted through the literature scattered over the fronting table and found a prospectus listing the team of company directors, folding it and keeping it in his hand until he was ready to leave as quietly as he had arrived.

The drive into the West End was short but crammed with traffic frustrations. He debated his decision to visit the location of the Selgo offices in Lexington Street during the short runs and frequent hold-ups of the journey. It would only need Kitholm or Praeger, or any of the men who had tailed him, to catch one glimpse of him in the area to raise awkward questions.

Bellman grimaced. The only alternative was to make enquiries through others and the single call to Peter Say had already left him with an uncomfortable feeling of exposure.

He parked the Toyota in an overhead car-park then walked through the narrow roads of Soho until he came to the head of Lexington Street.

The plate which stated 'Selgo Business Consultancy' was the centre sign of three in the cream-coloured doorway. Bellman walked on after a quick glance around to fix the location in his mind. There was no obvious observation point he could use. A small restaurant and a pub were nearby but too close to the office. He experienced a sudden stab of apprehension at the prospect of meeting Kitholm over a pint and a sandwich in a pub only yards from the Selgo premises.

After walking for five minutes to escape from the danger area he entered a coffee bar and sat down to drink from an inadequately-handled cup, filled from a wheezing Espresso machine. The music, muted tape, cried for the crashing, in-person sounds of the transient singers of another era. Occupied with the problem of secretly observing the Selgo building he still found time for a fleeting sadness at the change.

It took thirty minutes to locate a small shop which sold the brown dust-coat and tools that he required. Out on the street again, he donned the coat and unwrapped the chisel and hammer, slipping them into the patch-pockets of the overall. The length of wood was awkward to hold as he stripped away his tie. A brief pause before the window of an Indian restaurant showed that the coat was too new and the trousers beneath were patently not working gear, but past experience told him that Jack or Jill Average usually failed to notice such details unless they were pointed out. By which time it was too late.

He tried three doorways in Lexington Street before finding something that suited him; a wide stairway leading to floors of separate business offices. Each landing had a recessed window with an accompanying ledge which could, charitably, be called a seat.

Bellman settled in the niche on the first floor. It was possible, with a moderate amount of discomfort, to view the Selgo doorway, forty yards away on the other side of the road.

He used the chisel to gouge some splinters from the length of wood, then prised at several protruding nails in the fascia of the alcove and scattered the resulting wood and metal debris generously about. The result looked vaguely workmanlike if unclear in object.

Then he sat to watch and wait.

From time to time there were footsteps on the stairway and a typist or man would pass, smiling at him in the manner people usually reserve for tradesmen exhibiting a skill beyond their comprehension.

Bellman prayed there was no enthusiastic amateur carpenter concealed in the offices or, worse still, a building janitor who would be bound to question him.

After two hours his legs were cramped and he was edgy with the third appearance of a man who used the stairs to visit an office on the first floor, though each time he had passed with eyes fixed firmly on the contents of a plastic-bound ledger and without any apparent interest in Bellman, or his wood-chiselling activities.

A total of nine people had either entered or exited from the doorway he was watching. None resembled his hazy memory of Praeger, and Kitholm certainly had not been among them. It concerned him that he had not recognised *anyone*. He calmed himself with the thought that Selgo was not the only business to be run from the address.

He gave it another half hour, then moved. To break an observation could be fatal but if he was to use the same viewpoint again it was essential to give it the occasional respite.

Casual observers were reassured by breaks and reappearances. Under the proper circumstances it was possible to become a long-standing institution within a few hours.

When he returned twenty minutes later his neck achingly adjusted to the twisted position necessary for observing the doorway.

Kitholm appeared three minutes after he had settled in again and Bellman raised his eyes in silent thanks to whatever had prevented their meeting.

Kitholm paused on the pavement, his feet sketching miniature dance-steps of impatience. Bellman was disappointed with the man who joined the jumpy figure and walked with him past the window. The man was taller than his impression of Praeger and the face was thin.

When he thought of the face he realised his mistake. He had never seen Praeger's features so his expectation was based on a subconscious construction, built on the foundation of a distant voice. The face did not fit the voice. That was all.

Bellman slipped down the stairs and searched the street for possible back-men to the strolling couple. When he was satisfied that there were none he moved after them.

The possibility of the stranger being Praeger was enhanced by Kitholm's attitude as he looked up at his companion. There was no doubt that he was the listener, nodding occasionally as the other made a point.

When they came to a narrow junction the two men stopped and talked at the pavement's edge. Bellman moved into a doorway and watched from the angled window. Less

than a minute later, Kitholm turned, waving an acknowledgement before retracing the route to the Selgo office.
The taller man moved on, his strides now long and positive.

Had it been a conference? A brief discussion away from
the office and possible eavesdropping?

Bellman allowed Kitholm to pass out of sight before following Praeger – if it was Praeger.

The figure, despite the advantage of its inches, was only
just visible among the distant crush of pedestrians.

After three right-angle turns Bellman grunted with
pleasure at the evasion. He had closed the distance to half
of what it had been, sufficiently close to see that there were
no amateur backward glances or poorly disguised checks
in reflecting windows, but the circuitous route proved his
professionalism.

He was ready for the abrupt turn when it came, turning
into a shop even as the other's stride faltered, preparatory
to swinging round. The action was practised, normal, lacking the urgency of one who was suspicious of being followed. From his position behind a rack of paperbacks, Bellman could see that the thin face showed nothing more than
ordinary caution.

He left the shop and crossed the road, pleased again when
his quarry turned sharply into a garage on the right.

The exit from the parking lot carried into a one-way street
so he positioned himself fifty yards from the concrete shute,
sheltering in the lee of a kerbside fruit stall.

Two cars left the garage with occupants who did not re-
motely resemble the man who had walked with Kitholm.
When the sleek body of a Jaguar appeared, Bellman made
a mental wager, and won.

He noted the registration number then waited until the
car was out of sight before collecting the Toyota from a
garage almost identical in appearance to the one which had
housed the Jaguar.

Jo said, 'Great timing,' when he entered the flat.

Bellman looked questioningly at her as he removed his coat.

She said, 'Ta-Raaa,' and pointed towards the kitchenette. 'I'm cooking a meal – steak.'

'What would you have done if I hadn't come back until later?' he said drily.

'Eaten it myself, probably. I'm a pretty good cook, you know. Mind you – after steak and chips I get lost for ideas.'

He admitted the food was good when she asked him, teasing her for the faint blush of pleasure his words had produced.

They shared the washing up. She said, 'Nice innit? Me an' me ol' man ...'

'Stop calling me your old man.'

This time she was not subdued, laughing and spinning a plate, only saving it from destruction at the second grab. 'We working tonight?'

The question caused his stomach to tense. His 'No,' emerged as part of a growl.

Afterwards they sat in front of the television. Bellman watched the screen with unseeing eyes while Jo studied it intently, only to leave her seat and prowl the room like an unsettled cat.

Bellman cleared his mind and turned his attention to her wanderings. She was wearing a shirt and jeans. Her feet were bare. He stood up. 'Come on. We'll go for a drink.'

Her face came alive for a moment, then dropped. 'Where?'

'Just to a pub. No need to change.'

'Great!' she was gone, returning immediately, punching an arm into a small coat.

'Anyone would think you'd been caged for a month,' he said, dressing more leisurely.

He drove to Chiswick, parking in a road beside the Thames. The daylight had nearly gone but the temperature was comfortable, bearing the slight sultriness that followed a warm day.

They sat at a wooden table outside a pub, silently watching the changing shapes of reflected lights in the moving water.

Bellman's thoughts were briefly invaded by a memory: the same elusive mixture of warmth, distant sounds, people, the easier pace of evening. But this time there was no anguish.

He stood up. 'Fancy walking?'

She looked from him to her glass, still part full, then got to her feet.

They followed the tow path, gazing at the river and peering irreverently into the windows of the houses beside the walk.

When their steps brought them to an iron railing guarding a sharp turn at the head of a flight of stairs, they stopped.

Bellman stared for some time at the lights on the opposite shore then observed Jo from the corner of his eye.

She was leaning on the rail, stomach resting on crossed forearms. Her weight was supported by one leg, the foot of the other raised, toe absently stretching and relaxing. The long hair had fallen forward, obscuring her face.

She said, 'It's lovely.' Very simply.

And Bellman was lost.

He touched her shoulder. She flinched slightly then lifted her head, eyes searching his face. He took her chin in one hand, holding it while he kissed her. She did not respond, apart from closing her eyes.

Without another word they retraced their steps.

The interior of the car seemed cold when they entered it. Jo sat stiffly upright as he drove.

In the flat Bellman took her directly to the bedroom. She paused before undoing the last button of her shirt. 'Mike ... it was nice ... beautiful ... but perhaps it was the atmosphere which affected you, you know, warm evening ...' Her voice trailed away when he did not answer. She tried again. 'You don't have to ...'

Bellman climbed into the bed and held out a hand.

She shed the rest of her clothes quickly and slid between the sheets, putting her arms around him as he reached for her. When they kissed it was with close, warm movements, gentle nuzzlings of true affection. He explored her breasts with his hand, cupping them in turn and kissing them, then ran his hand down to her stomach and into the hair between her legs. She remained passive, only opening her thighs when his fingers persisted.

Bellman's desire was not an urgent thing but a steadily rising need. A need for her. It did not strike him as strange that she was moving tentatively, confining herself to small, stroking movements on the side of his face. She was a woman who had known so many and could only advertise herself by simulated enjoyment of a client's pounding.

She made a small sound when he spread her legs and entered her, then she was quiet. With her warmth around him Bellman was forced to control himself as the long period of barrenness incensed him. He rode gently until she finally responded to the deep, cleaving strokes, tuning her own movement until they were together.

He heard her cry, high pitched, demanding, and momentarily glimpsed the long, white legs as they lifted.

Afterwards they lay quietly, exchanging the reassuring caresses of lovers.

He was on the edge of sleep when she said, 'Mike,' very quietly.

He forced his eyes open. She was on her stomach, head raised, observing his face, her eyes were compressed into narrow slits of intensity.

He said, 'What is it?'

She put a hand on his chest and scratched gently. 'I want you to know ... that ending ... it wasn't ... acted.'

He put his fingers to her mouth as she desperately searched for belief. Her face gradually softened and she put her head down beside his.

Chapter Nineteen

In the morning he talked to her. They had brought the coffee to the bed and drunk it there. Smoking. Sharing.

He told her about Sandy. About the police. The drinking. Attempting to explain what had happened. She listened without surprise.

When he came to the reason for finding her he dried up, not wanting to lie but finding it impossible to be truthful. All he could find to say was, 'Everything is not as it appears. I'm not a true ponce but I can't explain.'

'I don't care,' she said.

'The future is ...'

'Don't talk about the future. I'm lucky to have had this much. I don't mean the money ... You.'

They made love again. This time it was a wild, physical thing. Total giving.

Afterwards, when Bellman's heart had slowed and the noise in his head had cleared he reviewed the beauty of the exchange: the unique acceptance on his part, feeling as he did for a girl he had sent to other men. A prostitute. And her naïve faith in what she felt for him was unblemished by her profession.

A cynic, he knew the world could be a strange place. But not this strange.

'The next few days will be different,' he said. 'I have things to do where you won't be included.'

She said, 'Fine,' and kissed him.

They talked very little over breakfast. He encouraged her to go out alone.

When she had left he found the book where he had

recorded the number of the Jaguar and rang the registration authority, hoping the system had not changed.

It had not. And the clerk who gave him the information did not ask to ring him back at the station he had said he was ringing from. 'The vehicle belongs to a Mr Vincent Rolland, eighty-six, Rawl House Lane, Flockley, Guildford, Surrey.' The details were recited too quickly and Bellman had to ask for a repeat. When he was sure he had recorded them correctly he gave an off-hand 'Cheers,' and put the telephone down.

He stared at the paper, disappointed. Although he knew that the name Praeger was a pseudonym he still felt there should have been some indication that Rolland and Praeger were the same man. If only Praeger had been an unimportant middle name or something.

Since when had anything been simple?

The mews in Chelsea where Pool had his town retreat was small, cobbled and deserted. Bellman drove past with little interest, anxious only to locate it for possible future reference.

It took longer to find Pool's family home.

Once he had left London and turned off the major roads, Bellman found himself travelling along narrow lanes flanked with overhanging hedges whose branches caught at the roof of the Toyota.

The map showed Bailey Fall as a small village but when he had found it, there was still no sign of Tetham Lodge. Unwilling to ask directions at the single shop-cum-post office he toured the neighbouring roads but still failed to find the house. Finally he turned the car towards a tree-topped hill, seeking to view the countryside from a height which could reveal a single dwelling.

He was nearly at the top of the hill when a drive appeared on the left where a polished wood sign stated 'Tetham Lodge'. Bellman drove on, catching glimpses of the house through the screen of trees. The hill flattened on the crest, revealing an expanse of unhedged grass. He parked the car and walked away from the road, attempting to see the house from the rear. After three hundred yards he saw a break in the trees and made towards it. The wood was corralled by a wooden fence and the gap was guarded by a gate. He stood at the boundary, seeing that the missing trees were an avenue with the house just visible at the end. Two definite ruts showed in the mush of leaves and long grass but there was no evidence of recent use.

The cut-off view of the house showed a door and long windows with leaded frames. An arm of wistaria groped at the door and he guessed that the front and side would be covered with the twisting trunks.

There was no sign of life.

The trip to Guildford was necessarily devious but he found Praeger/Rolland's house easily enough. Flockley village was a product of the advent of the motor car and its ability to cut the travelling time to London. The houses had been paid for by those wealthy enough to purchase acres of open country set along a quiet road. The result was a long, sprawling village with no depth, the few intersecting lanes leading only to farmland.

Rolland's house stood fifty yards off the road. The area at the front was taken up by a sweeping drive, curving in a semi-circle, the central space filled with healthy rose bushes. The house was red brick, crowned with a green-tiled roof. It was expensive but not in the Tetham Lodge bracket.

As Bellman cruised by, a woman in yellow blouse and slacks walked from the house towards the mass of rose bushes, wicker basket and gardening gloves at the ready.

He turned the Toyota towards London, disappointed but uncertain of what he had hoped to learn.

The flat was empty. He paced the room, stiff from driving, reading from the list dictated to him by Peter Say. The catalogue of Pool interests was long but none gave him inspiration. Neither did the string of directors on the Danx prospectus.

His ruminations were interrupted by Jo who arrived looking windswept and healthy. She said, 'Hi!' and kissed him on the cheek.

'Where are the parcels?' he asked.

'What parcels?'

'You usually come in laden down.' The talk was purposely light and of no consequence. He still felt a touch of embarrassment at his new-found feelings for this crazy, trusting, finger-waving, eye-rolling, lovable creature.

She thrust her hands deep into the pockets of her coat and looked at him from beneath lowered brows. 'I've been a *good* girl – not spent a thing ... well, hardly. I had a snack. Apart from that – nothing.'

'So what have you been doing?'

'Walking. Kensington Gardens, Hyde Park, Marble Arch,' she clasped her hands like an excited child. 'Mike, it's been terrific. Without going far I've seen Peter Pan's statue, the Serpentine, the big monument at ...'

Bellman laughed at her pleasure.

She raised her fist in a threatening gesture. 'I know it must sound very ordinary to you but I found it exciting, you know ... normal.'

Her eyes searched his face to see if he understood, showing relief when he laughed again but without disparagement.

'And *now*,' she said, raising her arms dramatically, 'I want my fellow.'

Bellman cast a glance at the papers he had been reading, then put them away and caught hold of her hand.

Bellman woke early, the last hours of sleep made restless by the nagging feeling of a job unfinished, hardly begun.

He placed a tea beside the bed and said, 'Stay there.'

She said, 'Happily,' and turned over.

In the living room he used the telephone directories to

record the appropriate numbers beside the list of businesses owned or influenced by Pool.

He had decided to short-cut the company-search method and at nine-thirty he began a telephone campaign aimed at discovering the name of every director on each of the many boards. Depending on the attitude of those who answered he used a combination of charm, half-truths, and downright lies to get the information he required. He met with difficulty only twice. On both occasions he asked for a higher authority, was given it, and promptly obtained the facts he requested. He found time to smile at gullibility which apparently never changed.

At eleven he terminated the last call and fingered an aching throat.

Staring morosely at the mass of notes he wondered if his instinct was serving him wrong. Praeger was a man from the shadows; a man accustomed to concealing details from subordinates while at the same time expecting unquestioning obedience because only he knew the complete picture. Why shouldn't he issue commands which seemingly defied logic. And what justification could he, Bellman, a drunk and a nobody, have in deciding that Praeger was sailing under false colours?

The deep-down gut certainty that he was right. *That* was what.

But he needed more. There had to be a link. A man in Praeger's position could not expose himself to any kind of publicity, therefore there had to be someone on the outside to look after his interests.

He made an alphabetical list of the directors' names, then marked off those with more than one directorship. There were seven. It was a drastic method of cutting down the list, but one he felt justified in using; the name he was searching for was bound to hold more than a token position, surely.

He was sitting with his head in his hands when Jo came through from the bedroom.

'You going out?' he said.

She pulled a face at him. 'That means you want me to. Anyway – yes – hairdresser's.'

He stayed in the same position until she had gone.

Pulling a piece of paper towards him he doodled for a time then, with increasing purpose, copied the total Pool enterprises down one side of the sheet and wrote the names of the seven dual-directors on the other. Then he connected the names to the separate holdings with straight strokes of the ball-point. The result told him nothing.

The companies which interested him most, the so-called leisure activities: sauna clubs, massage parlours, the betting-shop chain, the obvious fringe-of-crime businesses, did not throw up a single dual-director. Except for Pool himself. Apart from him the boards were seemingly unconnected.

He lit a cigarette and blew smoke at the jumble of names as though an answer would appear with the clearing of the fumes. Nothing.

He had been sitting with head raised, eyes on the ceiling when he straightened suddenly and re-read the seven names. There were three who were entitled to sit in the House of Lords, two Members of Parliament, and two who could claim nothing more illustrious than personal initials before their names. One of the Parliamentarians was a woman.

Then it hit him.

Their Lordships were in no position to influence political decisions at inception, so count them out. He crossed the names off, together with the two who had no political pull whatsoever.

Females who captured a seat in the Commons, to Bellman's mind, were too career-orientated to allow themselves to be involved in anything shady, as well as being hampered by an overdose of honesty. He eliminated the name of the woman MP.

Edward M. Mansley was the only name that remained.

Bellman traced the lines from Mansley's name to the directorships he held. There were two: a wholesale trading company and an innocuous-looking hotel chain. Perfect. Mansley's absence from the boards of companies subject to criminal influence served to confirm rather than deny that he could be in Pool's pocket. The quandary of how to reward someone for betraying their position was always difficult to solve if the reward was to be a large one. A cash payment was convenient, but it could be embarrassing if the receiver was ever called upon to reveal where it came from. A seat on a board was far more acceptable, and the fee that went with the position caused no raised eyebrows. And it was an obvious step to locate the name where it would be free of any link with questionable activities – the trap that could not be avoided.

The certainty that coursed through Bellman reminded him of other times, other cases, when viewing a problem negatively had produced the right answer.

He celebrated with a whisky, returning the bottle without a single regret, then stretched luxuriously. The easy part was over.

A recollection sent him delving amongst the pile of newspapers and magazines he had accumulated. Because of his haste the article he was searching for eluded him, necessitating a second hunt before he found it between the covers of a Sunday supplement.

Edward Mansley, Member of Parliament for Orsly West, stared at him in living colour.

The photograph showed a youthful-looking forty-nine-year-old and his obligatory tweed-suited wife, standing before a house of medium size. On the lawn beside the smiling couple there was a tongue-lolling Labrador. There was always a Labrador. 'EDWARD MANSLEY AND HIS WIFE JEMMA IN THE GROUNDS OF THEIR SUSSEX HOME ...'

The caption did not mention the dog.

Staring at the photograph, Bellman was visited by a brief

doubt, but he thrust it away, telling himself that if he was wrong – so much the better.

'Did we have to meet here?' Kitholm said, eyeing the expanse of Hyde Park with undisguised distaste.

'I thought the fresh air would be good for us,' Bellman said.

It was nearly twenty-four hours since his enquiries and ruminations had ended with the discovery of Mansley's photograph. He had called Kitholm in the late afternoon of the previous day, asking him to deliver the money he had requested. The need to speak to Kitholm was more urgent than the receipt of the three thousand.

'So?' Kitholm pushed his hands into his pockets and wriggled on the bench, the collar of his coat rising until it almost obscured his face. 'What are you going to do?'

Bellman snorted disgustedly. 'You never tire of asking, do you? I've never given you prior knowledge of my intentions and I don't plan to start now.'

'Three thousand pounds is a lot of money.'

'Briller is different – as I told Praeger. It's still cheap.'

'You've made your plan?'

'Yes,' Bellman lied happily.

Kitholm wrestled at his pocket. When the package came free he handed it to Bellman. 'Do you want to count it?' The parcel looked like a packet of sandwiches.

'No need,' Bellman said. 'If it's not all there I'll only kill half of him ... This wasn't the only reason I asked to meet you. There're a few questions I'd like to put to you. Will you answer them?'

Kitholm's head turned slowly. 'It depends what they are.'

'Nothing very deep, but I want you to do something for me: keep them to yourself. Don't mention them to Praeger.'

'Why ever not? Praeger's my superior.'

'Keep it between us. It could be to your advantage.'

'Bellman, you're a devious man. If you think you can attract me by offering to further my . . .' Kitholm broke off as Bellman grinned and nodded. 'Just what have you in mind? I make no promises. If I think anything you say might affect Decimate L then I will inform Praeger.'

Bellman did not begin immediately, pursing his lips in a soundless whistle he stared at the distant traffic on Bayswater. 'I'll ask you anyway, Kitholm, but before repeating the conversation to Praeger – give yourself time to think. Reason out *why* I'm asking.'

Kitholm did not comment but watched Bellman with eyes full of concern. There were no rules covering the event.

'The obvious ones first,' Bellman said. 'On one of the earlier briefings – after I'd dealt with Toper and Datchett – do you recall telling me that the attacks had caused the required dissension between two camps.'

'Yes, the reaction was apparent to everyone. After that wild-west show in the streets, things haven't been the same.'

'But it didn't affect Cliveson or Pool, did it? They weren't the men you meant.'

'Of course not. Their lives were made easier, in fact.'

'Right,' Bellman said, satisfied. 'Let me leave that for a moment . . . Cliveson – earlier you said he was a club man. How come I haven't seen him on the circuit?'

Kitholm nodded understandingly. 'Cliveson has purposely stayed away from the places where Elson *was* operating. He didn't want to risk the possibility of anyone making the connection. He owns several, smaller night spots. They are where he's been spending most of his time recently.'

'I see. Now – to get back to the previous tack. Why was I given the names of the principals – Pool and Cliveson? With Toper and Datchett I was just told what to do.'

Kitholm sighed heavily. 'This was explained when you were first given the task of interfering with them. It was felt that you would probably find out their names in any case. To pre-arm you, we thought, would help you to do a good job.' He glanced uncomfortably at Bellman. 'To be honest, it was mainly my doing. I have always believed that men work better when in possession of the facts.'

'Very commendable,' Bellman said, 'but the revelation does not surprise me. Now. This may seem very obvious, but who would you think suffered most from Elson's death? Discounting the dear departed, that is.'

'It's obvious – Cliveson – for the moment. He lost what he considered to be a good man and I understand that Elson had made many contacts. Briller will take them up, but it has meant a break in continuity – it's been disruptive. But in the long run, Pool will suffer too.'

'And Cliveson's firm hasn't retaliated in any way?'

'Against Pool? – No, but that is because they are not absolutely sure who killed Elson. It will be different when Briller goes.'

Bellman chewed a lip. 'How can you be sure? They still won't have proof. On one occasion you said both Pool and Cliveson were careful not to make waves. Perhaps Cliveson will swallow it and confine himself to what he has.'

'That would mean we have been successful. We could concentrate on Pool.'

Bellman slapped his knee aggressively. 'Why not do that immediately – as I suggested? Brantner – Pool's man – is getting more time to establish himself.'

'Praeger doesn't want it that way.'

'That's right – he doesn't. What is Praeger?'

Kitholm's eyes widened at the question. 'How do you mean?'

'What is he? Civil servant or what?'

Kitholm fingered his chin. 'This is an area where your questions become too probing.'

'Surely you can give me an indication.'

'Why should I? You seem to be losing ...' His voice

trailed away but picked up again immediately, the new tone slightly conciliatory. 'Speaking of obvious answers, I would have thought.... As I told you, he's responsible only to a Government Minister. He's not a civil servant – in the accepted sense.'

Bellman snorted derisively. 'One of the shadowy few.'

'He's important.' The statement emphasised the fact by its simplicity.

Bellman tried to keep his voice normal. 'His proper name is Rolland, isn't it?'

Kitholm twitched violently. 'How did you ...?' He stopped, staring worriedly at Bellman.

Bellman was satisfied. 'Okay. Now, I won't attempt to pry too deep but you've said your facilities are comprehensive. Who keeps the file on Decimate L?'

'I do.'

'All of it?'

'How do you mean?'

'Is it the full record? You know, copies of intercept tapes – the works?'

Kitholm wriggled uncomfortably. 'I record the overall picture.'

'The tapes, Kitholm?'

'I didn't say there were any.'

Bellman made a disgusted movement with his hand. 'Come *on*, Kitholm.'

Kitholm's face took on a petulant expression.

'Intercepts – if there are any – would not be conducted from Selgo. The technicalities prevent it. Praeger brings in any documentation that is not sent directly to the office in ...' He bit off the last few words, glaring savagely at Bellman.

Bellman had trouble in preventing his voice from rising. 'You have to work on what he tells you?'

'To some extent – yes. I think it's now time to ...'

'And Praeger keeps all the original records?'

'Yes.'

'Including those relating to Pool?'

Kitholm bounced to his feet. 'You're overstepping the mark, Bellman, and I don't see what ...'

Bellman had risen with him. 'One last question. Have you noticed that recent information concerning Pool has been on the sparse side. Almost non-existent, in fact?'

Kitholm made two quick strides then turned. 'I've said you're overstepping. Now that's enough.'

'So I'm right?'

'Not at all. Praeger *runs* the show.'

Bellman swung his feet at the leaf mould underfoot. 'And you're only told as much as he considers necessary,' he said bitingly. Kitholm began to move away but Bellman remained where he was, raising his voice, causing Kitholm to hurriedly retrace his steps. 'Which Minister is Praeger responsible to?'

'Bellman, I'm warning you ...' Kitholm's face was suffused. He stood facing Bellman in an attitude of aggression.

'Home Office?' Bellman said.

Kitholm turned abruptly and stalked away.

Bellman followed him more slowly, eyes on the ground. Finally he lengthened his stride and drew level with the affronted figure. 'Are you going to tell Praeger?'

'About your questions?'

'Yes.'

Kitholm continued walking, his stride gradually firming as Bellman waited for a reply. 'Apart from confirming Praeger's real name I don't think you've learned much.' The words were self-assuring as much as an answer. 'It is normal procedure for a man in Praeger's position to assume ... incidentally, how did you ...?'

'Good,' Bellman said, halting in his tracks. 'Let me remind you of what I said. Ask yourself *why* I asked the questions I did.' He lifted his hand and turned away.

Kitholm watched his progress, shaking his head sadly, then pivoted on his heel and marched towards Park Lane.

Before he reached the road his head dropped slightly as he began thinking about the interview.

Just as Bellman had advised.

Bellman toured the flat looking for somewhere to hide the money. He had broken open one side of the packet, checking that the notes were genuine.

After discarding several possibilities he decided on the oldest piece of furniture which stood in a corner of the living-room. It was the only intruder on a contemporary scene, a squat cupboard in heavy wood with short, stubby legs just visible below an ornamental frieze.

He ran his fingers under the decoration then tilted the cupboard on its side. There was a four-inch clearance between the bottom of the frieze and the floor of the compartment, ample space to tape the packet so it was not visible when the cupboard was upright again.

He was relieved when the money was out of sight.

After setting the inevitable mug of coffee on the low table, he went to the bedroom and fetched the papers where he had recorded his previous assessments. Drawing a new sheet towards him he wrote down the three names which were beginning to dominate his every thought, sketching a brief review of collected information below each heading.

Vincent Rolland/Praeger

Controller of group formed to counter criminal developments. Actual department not known. Answerable only to HS.

Warwick Dunn Pool

Old family background. Wide-ranging interests. Known to be planning massive take-over of criminal activities. Figurehead in many enterprises endorsed by well-known individuals. One such: Edward Mansley, MP.

Edward Mansley MP

Member of Parliament for last nine years. Holder of safe seat. Not a member of Cabinet, but active in many political spheres. Was invited to sit on committee investigating criminal growth. Director of two companies presently headed by Pool.

Bellman read the notes with satisfaction. His morning search in the library had revealed the fact that Mansley had sat on the committee investigating crime, and that just *had* to be significant.

He knew he was guilty of reaching a conclusion without possessing real evidence and trained caution clawed at the foundations of his convictions, especially when he thought of the extraordinary coincidences he had known.

He began to write again, the words sprawling across the page this time, attempting to convince by their size and number.

1. Pool and Mansley are known to each other – fact. Mansley in position to advise Pool on official policies re crime-fighting and be repaid by directorship(s).

2. Praeger. Key figure. Heads Decimate L. Answerable only to HS. Could easily divert attention from Pool allowing construction of unbreachable criminal organisation.

3. Reasonable to assume Praeger and Mansley met when latter engaged on committee – if not before. Mansley could be vehicle for collusion between Pool and Praeger – or at least introductory factor.

4. Praeger undoubtedly favouring action against Pool's rivals. Also controlling evidence detrimental to Pool.

The précis still failed to completely clear Bellman's doubts. There were too many assumptions and too few facts. But if Praeger *was* shielding Pool then there was bound to be a shortage of facts.

What of the others involved? Kitholm and the rest of the staff?

Kitholm would be ideal for a man like Praeger. Once convinced that Decimate L was the only answer, he would obey any directive concerning its success. He probably gave Praeger some nasty moments when he persisted in disclosing the names and intentions of Pool and Cliveson to Bellman. So what? There was little doubt that a man like himself who had been the tool of destruction would never find himself in a position where he could use the information he had gained. In fact, was that not now the case? 'Dear Sir, a respected member of the establishment, a Member of Parliament, and a Government employee are conspiring to ...' Wonderful stuff.

Other staff would be controlled by Kitholm who in all innocence would carry out Praeger's policies.

But if this was a take-over of crime, how could Praeger and the others possibly hope to keep it concealed? – easily, once it was an established fact. Or would it be?

Bellman shook his head violently, like a dog freeing itself of water.

There was only one certainty. If his reasoning was right, of all the expendables in the operation, he was by far the most dangerous to Praeger. And he *was* expendable. That had been emphasised often enough. So how near was the time when Praeger would make a decision about him? What could he do about it? Why did he *want* to do something about it?

Bellman began to sweat. He knew it was not fear – at least, not for himself. Balls! All fear was basic to oneself, even when it concerned another. So something had to be done.

Suddenly he anticipated a return of the nightmare which had attacked him before. In that very room. The move to the whisky bottle was panic-driven, his feet colliding with each other. There was no time for a glass. He tilted the bottle and drank deeply, closing his eyes as the liquid burnt its way down his throat.

He was in the act of raising the bottle again, troubled by what he knew he must do, when she said, 'Caught ya, ya bum.'

He had not heard her come in. She was standing by the door, arm outstretched, index finger pointing at his head. She closed the door and moved quickly across the room to lift a glass and hold it beneath the bottle.

'You want one?' he asked in surprise.

She looked at the glass she held and then at him. 'Not really,' she said and walked towards the bedroom, shaking her coat free as she walked.

'Hey!' he called after her. 'Want some coffee, then?'

'Please.'

When she came out of the bedroom she indicated the re-capped bottle. 'You don't have to desert the ...'

'That?' he said in mock disgust. 'Filthy stuff.'

He poured her a coffee and watched as she drank. The colour of her eyes baffled him again. Now they were a deep pit of green with the flecks a darker brown than normal. Even unspoken 'sea-green' was trite, but there was no other comparison. His eyes moved to the teeth that showed above the coffee mug. They were beautifully white and slightly too large.

With Jo everything was either too large or too small.

He slid along the couch and deprived her of the mug, causing her to yelp with surprise which changed to delight as he bore her down. He kissed her and slid his hand under her skirt.

They both attempted to undress and retain a hold of each other. Neither cared that they did not fully succeed. The act was fierce, brutal almost.

Afterwards they laughed at the tangle of clothes.

She lay back and said, 'Ker-*pow*.'

Bellman kissed her on the neck. 'It makes a change from "Wow".'

Chapter Twenty

Bellman waited in the club for an hour before the little man appeared, blundering past the table where he sat, peering myopically in the dim lighting.

He jumped fearfully when Bellman grasped his arm.

'Cor, guv. I didn't recognise you with the brush.' His fingers painted his own upper lip. 'How was the ... thing I sold you?' The question was desperate for the assurance that he was not facing a customer complaint.

'It was all right,' Bellman said. 'I want to do more business. Order a drink first – on me.'

The sparse body hurried to obey, chivvying the waiter fearlessly but looking to Bellman for support if the other took exception to the hurrying.

When they were settled with drinks before them, Bellman said, 'Can you get me another shooter – two, in fact?'

''Course. Whatever you like.'

'Sounds as though you've got a bloody armoury.'

Caution quietened the small boast. 'Not me, guv. But I know somebody who has. I'm only a runner – on commission. You name it – I'll get it for you.' The words were issued with a touch of pride.

'I want two. At least one of them must be a revolver.'

'What sort?'

'Christ! A Webley?'

'Easy – thirty-eight. What about the other one?'

Bellman shrugged. 'Whatever comes.'

'Automatic?'

'Fine.'

'When?'

'Now.'

'Okay. One-and-a-half for the two – and ammo'.'

'Why the uppers? I'll pay one.'

'Guv, guv, now . . .'

'Discount for quantity. One two five.'

'Done.'

'The revolver's got to be perfect.'

'It will be.' And he had gone.

Less than an hour afterwards, Bellman was in the flat, checking the hand-guns in the bedroom. The automatic was a Beretta, in good condition. The Webley seemed brand new, the original oil and packing not faked. The serial number had been neatly erased. Beautiful.

Careful. What had someone once said to him? The feel of your favourite gun adds twelve inches to your height?

There were twelve rounds to each weapon. Not over-generous. Little bastard. He should have checked.

He wrapped the guns and put them in the bottom of the wardrobe on 'his' side. The division had been achieved after much wrangling. Jo had won a seventy percent share. But each territory was sovereign. He spread the Lexington Street dust-coat over the weapons.

Jo glanced enquiringly at him when he entered the room, but said nothing when he avoided her eyes. Bellman paced the floor for a time, whistling under his breath, oblivious of her agitation.

When he spoke, his voice was taut with decision. 'Get ready, we're going out.'

'Now? It's ten o'clock. Where're we going?'

'Round the joints.'

'Working?'

Bellman looked at her. 'No, kid. You're not working again – at least, not in the same capacity.'

'How do you mean?'

'You've finished brassing, Jo.'

'Finished?' She stood with hands on hips. 'Mike, aren't you losing sight of . . .'

'No arguing.'

'What's my work now, then?'

'Window dressing. Come on. Time's wasting.'

The Loom was unusually quiet.

Bellman and Jo ate unhurriedly. They turned their attention to the cabaret only to be interrupted by a waiter stopping by the table and murmuring softly in Bellman's ear.

'Mr Briller is at the bar, sir. He would like a word with you.'

Bellman thanked him. 'Tell him I'll be there shortly.'

Jo was watching him steadily.

He winked at her and smiled. 'Earlier than I thought – the call from above. I want you to collect your coat and take a taxi back to the flat.'

'I want to stay,' she said defiantly. 'I know something is ...'

'Please, Jo.'

It was unlike him to beg.

She lowered her eyes. 'All right. I'd rather stay but if you really want me to ...'

'I do.'

When she stood up he said, 'Good girl, don't worry,' and punched her lightly on the arm.

'Now I *am* worried,' she said. 'If that bastard ...'

Bellman halted her by laughing. 'What would you do? Tear his eyes out?'

'No. Kick him in the ...'

He ushered her away quickly. 'Make sure no-one overhears your instructions to the cabby. It's only a precaution,' he added hurriedly when she faltered. 'If you do think you're being followed – come back here.'

'You'll be here?'

'As far as I know. Look, perhaps I shouldn't have said that about being followed.' He took her arm. 'I was just trying to cover the possibilities. The main thing is that they should not be allowed to discover where we live. In this game, that information is important.'

There were two others at the bar with Briller. Bellman recognised one as the nondescript type who had been with Briller when they were first introduced. The other was a squat gorilla of a man who carried the bewildered air of one not used to lush surroundings.

Briller nodded as Bellman approached. 'Wanna drink?'

Bellman said, 'Scotch,' and sat down.

Briller studied him arrogantly. Bellman fidgeted under the psyching examination, avoiding the dull eyes which silently challenged him, his evasion placing him on the proper rung of the ladder.

'I wanted a word about her.' Briller hooked a thumb in the direction of Jo's departure.

'Oh, yes?' Bellman's tone was carefully neutral.

'Where's she gone, anyway?' Briller lumbered round to search.

'She's gone home – not feeling too good.'

Briller turned, snarling. 'What's your game, Cater? I wanted her here.'

Bellman appealed with his hands. 'She's ... they can't work all the time ... you know?'

Briller's eyes covered him accusingly. 'You're not trying to be clever, are you?'

'No,' Bellman assured. 'I'm here, aren't I?'

Briller wiped his mouth. 'Right – let's go.'

'I thought you wanted to talk,' Bellman said.

'I do, but not in here,' Briller said and ambled away. The other two followed him. Bellman tagged obediently behind.

They stood in a group at the door until a car-jock delivered a Vauxhall to the short man who slid behind the wheel with the relief of one pleased to be back in his own, specialised world.

Briller climbed into the rear seat saying, 'In here,' to Bellman.

Bellman followed Briller's blundering entrance while the anonymous type swung into place beside the driver.

There were no preliminaries. 'From now on the bird works for us,' Briller said, clicking his lighter at a cigar.

'Come *on* now,' Bellman peered anxiously at the shape beside him.

Briller ignored the plea and addressed the driver as the car moved off. 'Keep to the back-doubles.' The head in front moved in a hurried nod and Briller turned back to Bellman. 'You heard. She works for us.'

'Look,' Bellman protested, 'I know something's going on – something big, but surely I can have a slice of the action. I've laid out quite a bit of . . .'

Briller's movement was surprisingly quick. He grasped Bellman by his tie. 'Listen, cunt. She's with us.' He twisted the tie and forced Bellman's head backwards. 'Understand? Ponce!' The words were spat through gritted teeth.

Bellman flicked his eyes in answer, the only movement he could make without fear of misinterpretation.

Briller released him reluctantly. As Bellman eased a tentative finger into his constricted collar, Briller crashed a great open-handed slap onto his cheek. The final contemptuous insult.

Bellman recoiled and lay sprawled in the corner of the seat.

Briller looked down at him in disgust. 'Like all ponces – not two pennorth of arsehole. You're finished, Cater. Hear that?' He listened to the appreciative chuckles from the front seat, then said, 'Mind you, if you can produce another bird like her, well, you might be allowed a cut in the new one's earnings.'

There were more sniggers as Bellman rubbed his cheek.

'I won't be around,' he said.

Briller roared his delight. 'See what I mean about these bastards? Show 'em a fist and they shit themselves.'

The two heads in the front seat nodded in agreement.

'Shall I tell him how I initiate the new talent, Bernie?'

Briller choked. He poked Bellman in the ribs. 'I have to try the goods, see? And she'll have to perform to please. I'm going to fuck the arse off your bird, Cater.'

He waited for Bellman's reaction, disappointed when he remained in the slumped position. He tapped the driver on the shoulder. 'Find a place to pull up, we'll drop this prick off.'

When the car was stationary Briller grasped Bellman's arm. 'Bring her to the Loom the day after tomorrow. Understand?' The fingers tightened with the query. 'And don't fuck me about. If you have it on your toes with that bird – I'll find you.'

Bellman whimpered and tried to free his arm. 'All right. She'll be there.'

Briller gave him a contemptuous push. 'Piss off.'

Bellman opened the door and climbed out. 'What about the other fellow?' he asked, head bent low.

Briller turned the bored, hooded eyes towards him. 'What other fellow?'

'You know, I had another approach ... Brantner or some such name ...'

'Don't worry,' Briller slurred. 'Friend Brantner's been told. He won't bother you – or anyone else. If he tries to ...' he broke off and reached towards the door. 'Piss off and leave that to men who can handle it.'

Bellman stood by the roadside watching the retreating car, controlling his breathing with deep, sucking intakes. It had been a long time since he had needed to use such restraint.

When he opened the door of the flat Jo was perched on an upright chair. She still wore her coat. Her eyes searched his face.

He said, 'I told you not to worry.'

In the morning it took Bellman an hour to telephone the clubs he thought might be owned by Cliveson. Many of his calls went unanswered. Replies from those which did respond varied from polite denial to terse rebuttal when he asked if they belonged to the Cliveson group.

Just two gave an affirmative reply.

In the afternoon he rang both clubs again. The first call was answered by a female whose voice lacked the usual modulated tones of classy receptionists. When Bellman asked for Briller, she said, 'Who, love? Aow, yeah, I know who you mean. No he don't come in here very often. Try the Night Owl. He goes there most nights.'

The man who answered the phone at the Night Owl sounded surly. 'It's too early for him. He'll be here about eight – usually has a chat with Mr Cliveson then goes out again.'

It was still light when he stole the Vauxhall, finding the choice of vehicle ironic, though it was not the same colour as Briller's machine. He abandoned finesse for the need to move the car quickly out of the tree-lined avenue beside the cemetery. He parked it half a mile from Fortis Crescent.

Jo asked for no explanation when he barred her from the bedroom while he disinterred the automatic.

On the way out he said, 'Don't wait up.'

She grinned and waved.

The Night Owl was in Bermondsey, set beneath one of the myriad arches of the railway skeins. The outside of the club had been deliberately left in its original state of crumbling brickwork. The doorway and interior view of a jazzy reception area spoke of better things inside while high above the entrance a neon owl gave a three-second wink of its purple eye.

Bellman parked directly beneath a street lamp, the illumination hitting the roof of the car, leaving the inside comparatively dark.

Satisfied with his view of the club, Bellman waited. He found it difficult to light a cigarette with his gloved hands, even though the leather was thin and tight. He finally gave it up.

There were few people in the street. Less entering the club. The few who did visit, disappeared quietly into the confines, not yet injected with the alcoholic promise of a better tomorrow. Bellman viewed the area with a jaundiced eye. It was so like other times. But then the stakes had not been so high.

The thought made him move suddenly in the seat. Why this feeling of invulnerability? It was stupidity. Stealing a car and using it without changing the plates was an acceptable risk if it was only to be used for a short time, or after it had been housed, but to sit outside a place like the Night Owl in a hot vehicle *and* carrying an untried gun with the intention of killing a man.

He rubbed a hand tiredly over his eyes. When his vision was clear again he was presented with a sight which reinforced his self-condemnation: a patrol-car cruised along the street; a mechanical night-hunter. But the occupants' heads were turned, observing the entrance of the club.

When a Daimler deposited a man outside the club, Bellman guessed it was Cliveson by the way he surveyed the outside of the premises, standing back to look for possible defects in the manner of a critical owner.

He was a spare man, totally unlike Bellman's mental picture, dressed in a dark coat which accentuated the silver hair resting on the collar. There was a brief glint of purple on the thin features as the neon caught the steel of narrow-framed spectacles.

He was already unbuttoning his coat as he went inside.

Briller's arrival took Bellman by surprise.

He had expected him to drive to the club. Instead he appeared from behind the Vauxhall, swaggering as he walked.

Bellman dropped his hand to the side pocket and pulled at the automatic, tapping the chrome ring inside the steering wheel with his other hand, sounding off the short, friendly 'paps' which begged attention.

Briller turned as Bellman climbed from the car. There

were still three yards separating them when Briller started in recognition.

'What are you doing here?' The tone still carried contempt.

Bellman took one step closer. 'Who were you going to fuck the arse off, Briller?' He raised the gun slowly, allowing time for the words to be associated with the threat from the weapon.

In the second before Briller began to turn away, his whole frame showed he understood his miscalculation. The large head dipped nervously as the shoulders hunched in a futile gesture of protection.

Bellman shot him.

The bullet entered Briller's body at the side, tearing into the stomach. The impact knocked him sideways but he kept his feet, holding out the hand that did not clutch his stomach, in supplication. His collapse to the pavement was not a gradual thing but a sudden convulsion which drew his legs upwards, dumping the body to the ground like a dropped sack.

Bellman stepped alongside him and shot him again. In the head.

As he sent the Vauxhall roaring away, Bellman caught a glimpse of enquiring faces at the club entrance. He ducked his head and deliberately skitted the car through the corner, tyres juddering and protesting.

He slowed soon afterwards and drove to the Pill Box pub on the south side of Vauxhall Bridge.

Before transferring to the Toyota he allowed a laughing group of youngsters to enter the bar.

Ten minutes later he was outside Brantner's flat. The sports car was not there.

He debated the wisdom of leaving the scene and returning later, but rejected the thought, then his eye caught the message 'Saloon Bar' and he was out of the car and walking.

After two whiskies he realised he did not want, or need, more alcohol. He thought of ordering another just to see if the decision was genuine and not the child of hope. He could not even bring himself to do that.

So what was the substitute? The act of violence? Death?

When he returned to the car he climbed into the rear, sitting back with his head in the corner.

He dozed periodically, coming awake with sudden jerks to peer out like an exposed seal.

Brantner was out of the car and half way to the entrance of the apartment block before the noise from the dying engine filtered through to Bellman's brain.

He waited until Brantner had been gone for ten minutes before moving, stepping cautiously from the car and easing his cramped limbs. His approach to the low-slung vehicle was cautious, eyes alert for any witness who would spoil the effect.

Spurred by the need for perfection his fingers regained the expertise which they had lost recently. He had the door of the car open in less than a minute. Thirty seconds later the vehicle was secure again – with the automatic pistol resting beneath the passenger seat.

Chapter Twenty-one

Bellman was lying on the couch fully dressed except for his shoes when Jo emerged from the bedroom.

She made tea and they drank it together. There was no interchange; no questions or explanations.

On the hour Bellman said, 'Turn the radio on – the news ...'

She moved across the room and complied, a slight lift of the eyebrows the only indication of surprise.

The newscaster's voice was already relaying the dismal catalogue of world events. Bellman did not move as there was a pause and the voice changed key: 'In London last night there was another murder by shooting. It happened in the early evening outside a club on the south side of the river where a mystery gunman shot and killed a Mr John Briller of Paddow Drive, Kennington. Police are requesting that anyone who saw the killing or have information which ...'

The voice was cut by the click of the radio switch. Jo stood by the receiver, her face averted from Bellman.

'You killed him, Mike,' her voice was almost a whisper.

Bellman lit a cigarette. 'Yes.' His hands were surprisingly steady.

She began to move about the room with dream-like steps. 'And Terry Elson?'

'Yes.'

It was a long time before she stood in front of him. 'Mike. Are you a villain? A real gangster?'

'No.'

'And you're not still a policeman? A sort of ...'

'No.' There were inner convulsions tearing at his stomach but he still could not say more.

She travelled the room again. He watched each step with a new agony.

Her next question astounded him. 'It was necessary?'

He opened his mouth several times before any sound emerged. Finally. 'Yes. It was.'

'Because they were trying to take me over?'

'No – at least, that's not the real reason why I killed them.'

'Would I understand if you explained?'

'You might. But I can't.'

She stood before him again. 'Okay. Okay.' Twice. Very quietly.

'Okay?' he echoed, desperate at his own inability to say more.

'What I mean is – I'm with you.'

'Why?'

'I love you.'

When he made to protest she put her hand across his mouth and dropped to her knees beside him. 'I can think of all the arguments – and the possible trouble. I love you.'

The simple explanation, incredibly, ended the discussion.

She cooked breakfast and they ate it together. When he had finished, Bellman moved round the table and drew her to her feet.

'I don't know what I have to offer – probably very little. I need a few days to complete some business. Afterwards perhaps we can have some time together. If not, well, I have some money which I'll give to you. At least you'll have that.'

She put her head on his chest. 'Forget the money. Let me have you for a time – as long as possible.'

He pushed her gently away, lost for words, realising he was in awe of her feeling – her faith.

'If I can ever explain – I will.' It sounded very inadequate.

She clapped her hands to change the mood. 'What now? Do you want me out of the way?'

Bellman managed a weak smile. 'Yes. I have to use the telephone . . .' he had to say more. 'Jo, if it would help you could listen but . . .'

She stood ridiculously at attention, one hand raised in a parody of a policeman's 'halt' signal.

This time he laughed. 'Go out and amuse yourself for a few hours. When you come back I'll know what my next move will be – or yours. You may have to go it alone for a time.'

The prospect drowned her mood but she nodded and went to dress.

Before she left she kissed him on the lips firmly; without passion. The touch negated further words.

As though her exit was a signal, the telephone rang.

Praeger said, 'And that cost an extra three thousand?'

'He's dead isn't he? Anyway, that's only part of the job. The best is to come.'

'I don't see what else there can be. I only wanted Briller removed.'

Bellman spoke with his eyes closed. 'Wait until midday or thereabouts. The rest will be clear then.'

Praeger looked enquiringly at Kitholm. 'At least he did as he was told.'

Kitholm said nothing, recognising Praeger's satisfaction, unwilling to spoil it by voicing his own doubts.

Bellman pondered deeply before taking the irreversible step, but the examination stopped when he considered the position he had been forced into.

At ten he lifted the telephone receiver and checked the line again. He was more certain since his talk with Kitholm. Even though Praeger controlled the intercept tapes the contents would still be known to the operators. The information relating to Pool would be only part of the total, easily concealed, but if his own line was tapped, the recorded conversations would indicate an authorised killer and he did not think Praeger would risk that. Even with a security-cleared operator.

The line still buzzed innocently, anyway.

The Detective Sergeant at the station on the outskirts of the Metropolitan area was very sceptical that a man named Brantner was responsible for the death of John Briller. But he promised to pass on the information about the contents of the sports car.

When he began to question Bellman he was left with only a purring line and the puzzle of why he, of all people, had been selected to receive the information. Anonymous calls were not his favourite method of obtaining the snippets of enlightenment which made the work that bit easier.

When the telephone rang at one-thirty Bellman was waiting, lifting the handset before it had a chance to ring a second time.

'Why did you do it, Bellman?' Praeger said.

'Do what?'

'Frame Brantner.'

'I thought it was perfect. Maximum dissension ...'

'I told you to take out Briller. Nothing more.'

'You gave me a job to do. I'm doing it.'

'Kitholm explained that this time you were restricted to ...'

'Why, Praeger?' Bellman shouted. '*Why* don't you want Pool's men touched? You'd better explain because I have further plans to ...'

'*Bellman!*' Praeger's voice was unlike any other time. 'You are to stay where you are. Someone will ...'

'Too late, Praeger. I'm out and running ...'

The click on the line was like a knell.

Praeger stayed where he was, one hand still resting on the

telephone. 'I want all operatives in the office within an hour. I don't care where they are. Bring them here.'

'Bellman's overrun his responsibility,' Kitholm pleaded, 'but surely there's no need to ...'

'Within the hour,' Praeger repeated.

When Bellman telephoned the Night Owl and asked for Cliveson there was a long delay before he came on the line.

'Who are you? Why wouldn't you give a name?' The voice carried the tired tones of a man who would normally have been asleep but there was wariness too. The caution which was a result of murder-squad questioning.

'There's no point in telling you who I am,' Bellman said. 'Just listen to what I have to say. First – are the police listening-in to this call?'

There was a pause then, quietly, 'No.'

'You know a man's been picked up for Briller's murder?'

'I didn't. There was an indication some time ago that something was happening but ...'

'They've nicked a man named Brantner. He'll probably wriggle out of it but he's the one ... he works for a man named Pool.'

'I see.'

Bellman admired Cliveson's coolness as he let the receiver clatter onto the cradle.

The bad time was on the way. He cursed himself for letting Jo leave – making her leave. He could have been out and running. Just as he had promised Praeger he was.

He began a patrol of the windows, front and rear, staying well back, waiting for the result of the catalyst he had thrown into the mixture of events.

For all his alertness he nearly missed the first action. He had failed to notice the appearance of the dark-blue car higher up the crescent. Only the upper half was visible, its body dissected by the swell of rising ground. It was the movement above the roof of the vehicle which caught his attention. The movement of a head. A head with outsize eyes which were fixed on him. He realised then that the binoculars were resting on the roof of the car, the large lenses giving the illusion of a larger face behind.

Certain that the net curtains and his own caution had prevented him from being seen he moved into the living-room and scrutinised the gardens at the rear.

The only sign of life was a lone figure, standing where the gardens joined the road.

Twenty minutes later the doorbell sounded. Twice.

After a period of silence Bellman heard voices on the stairs, one unmistakably that of Mrs Anstey. The other was deeper, questioning.

Clearly he heard her say, 'But if you rang his bell he would have answered.'

The reply was unintelligible. It was followed by a heavy knock on the door at the head of the stairs.

Bellman sat on the couch, eyes on the door. There was another murmur then Mrs Anstey's voice, raised in in-dignation, 'Certainly not. Yes. I have a key but I have no intention of using it. Even if Mr Bellman is a friend of yours it gives you no right to ...' The words faded with the retreating footsteps.

Bellman began to worry about Jo as the light failed, blaming himself for not giving more specific instructions – for not keeping her by his side. Then he changed that too. He should have sent her away before goading Praeger.

But that did not explain why she was away for so long. She was often absent for long periods. But today? When she knew something was amiss? What if Praeger's men had seized her? Bellman took an involuntary step towards the telephone.

What if they had? Praeger was hardly likely to complicate the issue. And how much was known of his and Jo's rela-tionship? Very little apart from the working arrangement.

He was not even sure if it was known that Jo was living

at the flat. She had answered the telephone on at least one occasion, but that was not proof.

He squeezed his eyes tight-shut. Reasoning was pointless. Praeger was capable of using her as a lever if he thought it stood the slightest chance of success.

Where was the bloody girl?

With the curtains still open the rooms were slowly invaded by the outside lights: amber sections from the street lamps coupled with the brighter, intermittent flashes from the traffic on the road.

He desperately needed a cigarette but was afraid that the flash of lighting it would be seen on the outside.

The car in the crescent was now only a dim shape but twice he had seen movement in the rear gardens. Once the distinctive shape of a man's upper half. The second an indistinct moving shadow that could have been an illusion.

He beat a fist into the opposite palm in frustration, but then calmed himself and disciplined his mind. If Praeger's men were anything to do with Jo's absence then precipitate action on his part could be what they wanted. On the other hand, as far as he could tell, they had accepted that he was not at the flat and the present observation was merely a precaution. . . .

His head began to spin.

He decided to wait until eleven o'clock before doing anything about Jo. He was not sure what he *could* do but the deadline gave him comfort.

At twenty minutes to eleven he heard the lower door open. He listened for an accompanying voice but the only noise was the metallic click of the lock followed by the sound of her feet on the stairs.

As the key scraped in the door of the apartment he scuttled for the bedroom, crabbing across the floor, keeping below the window level.

He crouched in the corner by the window, the Webley in a two-handed grip, forearms on knees.

The light from the living-room partly illuminated the spot where he waited, when Jo switched it on.

He heard the swish of curtains then, tentatively, 'Mike?'

He did not reply immediately, waiting until the pad of her feet came nearer. Then, very quietly, he said, 'In here, Jo.'

There was an audible gasp, followed by a sob. She said, 'Mike' again.

'Act normal,' he ordered. 'This room is being watched from the outside. Come in, cross to the window and draw the curtains. Don't be startled by me. I'm sitting on the floor – with a gun.'

She moved swiftly, doing as he said. When she turned and saw the gun in his hand her eyes widened. Then she was on the floor beside him.

'Mike. Are you all right? Oh God, I've been so scared.'

Before her face disappeared into his shirt front he saw that it was strained. Streaks of make-up lined her cheeks. She sobbed quietly, gripping him painfully with her fingers.

Bellman said, 'It's all right, Jo. It's all right.' His hand stroked her hair then travelled over her back as he tried to smooth away the fear. She flinched, arching her spine to avoid his touch.

'What's the matter?' He held her from him so he could see the wreckage of her face.

She threw her head back and let the tears fall. 'They picked me up, Mike – took me away . . . they . . . they wanted to know where you were.' The words were punctuated by convulsive, part-smothered sobs.

Bellman stood up, taking care that his shadow cleared the curtains, and led her to the bed. He unbuttoned her blouse and carefully removed it before insisting she lay on her stomach.

She did as he said but reluctantly. He looked down at her.

The fury spread through his body as he saw the single, inch-wide weal that crossed her back, beginning at her left shoulder then travelling diagonally until it ended near her

211

waist. The skin of the wound was raised and suffused. In places there were pin-points of blood where the flesh had ruptured.

He said, 'Tell me what happened.' The words were barely audible.

She pushed herself upright, swinging round to sit on the edge of the bed.

She had quietened. The tears still came but they were controlled, shaking her body with diminishing force.

'I was on the way back – about four o'clock – when a man stopped me on the corner of the crescent. He said he wanted to talk about you. I tried to walk on but a car pulled up and he pushed me inside ... well, he didn't push me exactly, but he ...' she stopped and looked at him appealingly.

'He made it clear that you were to do as he said?'

She nodded vigorously at the words that had eluded her. 'Yes.'

'This man. What did he look like?'

She pushed her hair back, then shuddered. 'He was tallish, not heavy ... Oh, Mike he was ...'

Bellman held her again until the paroxysm was over.

'Light me a cigarette, please Mike.'

He lit two, passing one to her, hardly noticing his own deep intake.

'He was posh,' she said suddenly. 'Well-spoken, I mean.'

'What colour was his hair?' Bellman asked, remembering the voice of the man who had first picked him up; and the head as the metal of the van door trapped it a century ago.

'Fair-haired – nearly white,' she said.

Bellman's eyes closed slowly. He dipped his head, urging her to continue.

She took another deep draw at her cigarette and put a hand on his arm. 'Mike, that man was frightening. More. He terrified me. And that was before he did ...' her head gave a backward toss.

Bellman's eyes were an inferno. 'He did that to you?'

She nodded. 'There were two other men in the car. One was driving, of course, the other just sat in the passenger seat at the front; he was small and fat. The blond chap sat in the back with me. He was asking questions about you. Where I thought you might be. Had you mentioned that you were leaving before I left. Where did you go when you were drinking. I didn't tell him anything – just that I worked for you. Then we got to the place.'

'The place?'

'It was a sort of big house, but I don't know where. He made me duck my head down for the last ten minutes of the journey. When we stopped the car was in a garage. They took me through to the house and into an upstairs room. The house was funny ... I don't know if I can explain ... it was, well, it had a smell about it. Like a hospital. Do you know what I mean?'

He knew.

'Then what happened?' he said.

She pulled a wry face. 'There was a lot of coming and going. I heard telephones ringing in another room and one of them would go to answer. I stuck to the truth – or near to it. Anyway, I don't know much about you – apart from what we've done together. Working, I mean. They didn't seem very interested in that. I didn't let them know how I feel about you, in fact, I tried to give the impression that you were a bastard – keeping me short of money and so on.' Her eyes were on him, anxious.

He put the back of his hand on her cheek and moved it slowly back and forth. 'You did right.'

She gave a decisive nod. 'Yes. When they thought I would help them, their attitude changed. I think I had only been recognised by a stroke of luck and they seemed anxious to soothe me – leastways, two of them did. That tall ...'

'Why were you so long? And how this?' he said, pointing at the mark on her back.

She flinched again at the memory. 'Well, there was a lot

of talking between them. It seemed to go on for hours. I think they were getting instructions over the telephone. Anyway, I agreed to cooperate – help find you. I was to ring them if you got in touch with me. They gave me a number. They seemed pretty sure that you'd gone from here but in case you hadn't I was to move the bedroom curtain backwards and forwards twice when I got in. They wanted to come back with me really but I told them the landlady was a cow and that she would want to know who they were.' She picked up her blouse and took a scrap of paper from the small pocket. She handed it to Bellman. 'That's the telephone number they gave me.'

The number meant nothing to him. He stood and marvelled as she slipped into the blouse. How many women would be capable of dealing with the men Praeger employed? Come to that, how many men?

'Hey,' he said, realising he had been side-tracked. 'I asked about your wound.'

She shook her head sadly because he had remembered. 'It was the blond chap – I think I heard one of them call him Swingler. Even when they were friendly – after I said I'd help – he was looking at me strangely, you know, like some men do. Anyway, when they'd given me instructions on what I was to do, the others lost interest in me – left me with him for long stretches. Just before I was brought back he said he was going to show me that they weren't all sweetness – that they could be rough.' She stood up. 'He gave me a whack . . . I'm going to make a drink – coffee.'

His hand stayed her as she edged away. 'It wasn't as simple as that. Tell me.'

'Mike. It hurt but now it . . .'

'*Tell* me.'

She recoiled slightly at his vehemence. 'He made me lie on the bed and pull my skirt up to my waist, then he told me to roll over. When I did he hit me with a strap.'

Bellman raised his head. A strangled groan rose from deep in his body.

Jo rushed to him and put her arms around his neck. 'Mike, Mike, don't think about it. He was a kink – that's all. The others heard me scream. They went off at him.'

'And what did he do?' Bellman gritted.

'He laughed at them,' she admitted.

Bellman made a silent promise to himself but only said, 'Okay.'

While she was making the drink Bellman searched for a salve for her wound. When she realised what he was looking for she stopped him. 'No, Mike. I want to feel it. It's ... well ... it's for you.'

'Now who's a bloody kink?' he said roughly.

She tried a small grind of her hips. 'Corr!'

He kissed her and insisted that she sat down while he thought.

He was staring into the distance when he suddenly shook himself. 'I'm sorry you got involved in this, Jo. If I'd known how it was going to turn out ...'

'Don't take it away from me, Mike,' she pleaded. 'Don't you see? I love you. Up to now I haven't had much feeling for anyone – it's great for me that I *am* involved.' The accusatory finger was out again. 'And that's another thing – Michael *Bellman*! Do you realise I've been sleeping with a fellow under the wrong name.'

Bellman grinned. 'Does it make a difference?'

'No. I like Bellman better than Cater, anyway.' She was serious again. 'Those men – Swingler and the others – they weren't villains. More like policemen, but they weren't that either ...' she shook her head. 'I don't know what's happening but I think that what you're doing is right – or you believe it to be – and that can be just as important.'

Bellman nodded seriously. 'I believe I am doing the right thing – now.'

She said, 'Good. I'll do whatever you want. When it's all over you can tell me – if you want to, that is.'

'I have something to do, Jo. It means leaving here and I can't take you with me.'

'I expected something like that. Will it take long, what-ever it is?'

'I don't know. First I have to shake off those bastards outside.'

'What will they do if they catch you?'

He tried to think of a simple, unmelodramatic way of telling her. He did not mind lying if he thought it would help but somehow he knew the truth was important. 'I think they will kill me.'

She accepted it coolly. 'I'm glad you told me.'

'I've been thinking,' he said. 'Providing I can leave here without their knowing, you should be safe.'

She shook her head decisively. 'No. I am leaving with you. That way they will know I never intended to help them.'

'It's pointless. And dangerous.'

'Perhaps,' she said, Then, 'What sort of future do we have?' She smiled at his stricken face. 'There – no future. Right? So, let me hurt a little.'

'You already are.'

She blew a disparaging raspberry. 'That? It would take more than that long streak to hurt me.'

She had already proved herself to him. He knew how he felt. So he said it. 'I love you, Jo.'

The tears sprang to her eyes as though commanded. She lowered her head. 'I never thought you would say ... I never ... I ... Oh shit!' she said, laughing at her own embarrassment.

He went over to her and kissed her. She patted his arm to show she understood when he broke away.

'We have to leave here unseen,' he said. 'Then I have to find somewhere for you to stay. When I've finished my business I want to know where to find you – that's provid-ing everything works out.'

She just said, 'Yep.'

'It may be some time ... a month, more. If you haven't seen anything of me by then ...'

'Don't let's talk about time limits. If I don't see you again it will take longer than a month for me to recover.' She clapped her hands as she always did when an idea struck her. 'Now! I've thought about a place where I can stay.' She paused. 'It's not in London. I wouldn't be near you.'

'That doesn't matter. Chances are I won't be in London permanently.'

'This place is off the beaten track, you might say. It's a village called Durnston – near Yarmouth. I used to go there as a child and stay on a smallholding which belongs to relatives of my father – distant cousins or something. If you could join me up there, no-one would find us.'

'In a village? Don't be so sure.'

'You don't understand. The locals are used to strangers. People stay on the smallholdings for their holidays.'

'It still doesn't mean ...'

'It's lovely up there, Mike.' She was completely carried away. 'It has a river and on the smallholding there're chickens and ...'

'Hold on,' he laughed. 'We don't know that your relatives are still there – or if they'd take us in, if they are.'

She gave him a sheepish smile. 'They are. I visited them once – over a year ago and I've kept in touch, well, as much as I could when I was on the road. The couple who own the place ... they like me. Mr and Mrs Hampson's their name.'

'I suppose we could phone them,' he said doubtfully.

'No need. I'll just turn up. They'll take me in. And you when you come. They are quite old but they like young company. The last time I was up there they were asking if I had a boy friend and so on.' She broke off to roll her eyes. 'Christ! If they'd only known.'

'Okay. You'd better give me the details of the place.'

'It's named Crosslea – just outside the village.'

'The village was Durnston?'

'Yes.'

'I'll find it.'

'I hope so,' she said feelingly.

'Which is the best way for you to get there? Train?'

'Yes – Kings Cross.'

'That's settled, then. Now we have to get out of here. You any good at climbing?'

'Climbing?'

He pointed to the window. 'Out there, down the drain-pipe and through the gardens to the main road. They're watching the door in the crescent.'

'Won't they be standing guard in the gardens too?'

'Yes, but there's only one out there – I think. I have to deal with him first. I want you to pack a suitcase, take the minimum you can manage with, then dress in something sensible – trousers or jeans. After that we'll make as though you're going to bed, you know, douse the lights and so on.'

She headed towards the bedroom with a new spring in her step, the prospect of excitement overcoming fear.

Bellman recovered the money from below the cupboard and followed her. Her eyes widened when he undid the parcel and counted out five hundred pounds, giving what remained to her. 'There, kid.'

She looked at the packet dumbfounded. 'Mike, I don't need all this. I have ...'

'Keep it – for both of us. Maybe we'll be able to begin some sort of life with it. You can always use it if we don't meet again.'

She was crying then, the money held away from her body as though it was the cause of the separation. Bellman did not try to comfort her, pushing the post office book into her hand with the notes. 'The rest of your earnings.'

He left her and packed some clothes into a holdall. The Webley fitted into his outer pocket where it was awkwardly prominent but easy to reach. When he was ready he said, 'Come on. Finish whatever you have to do and stop crying. I need help.'

It was the right thing to say. She immediately quietened and finished her task with the suitcase.

They turned off the living-room light then, after a pause, darkened the bedroom.

Bellman waited for twenty minutes before venturing to peer through the curtains of the living-room. The lights from neighbouring houses and the distant lofty brilliance of the street lamps threw odd-shaped shadows over the garden area. Shiny-leafed shrubs reflected pin-prick spangles, adding to the subdued, fairy-land aspect.

It took five minutes of careful searching for Bellman to locate the watcher. He was sitting on a bench, well away from the house, blending into the background of a large bush. He appeared to be alone. The movement which attracted Bellman's attention, a gentle shift of position, was gone again. Whoever it was down there, he knew the basic principles of careful observation.

Bellman turned to Jo and indicated the luggage. The case had a length of cord he had found in the bathroom tied to the handle. 'You can throw the holdall down to me but you'll have to lower the case.'

'Are you going now?' She sounded breathless.

'Not yet. There's someone down there. I'll wait until he moves. He mustn't see me leave the window or he'll call out the pack.'

'What will you do?'

He smiled and winked reassuringly. 'Don't worry. When I leave, pull the window to and close the curtains. I'll toss something at the window when it's safe for you to appear. Do you think you can manage the climb?'

She nodded and Bellman returned to the curtains.

It was forty minutes before the watcher showed signs of restlessness, standing to stretch and look around, then sitting again. Five minutes later he was on his feet, staring up at the window where Bellman waited then turning to walk slowly down the slope, his back to the house.

Bellman gave a quick thumbs-up to Jo and slipped

behind the curtains. He had the window open and a grip on the drain-pipe before the man had covered thirty yards.

The descent was easy, large brackets and joining pipes made adequate hand- or foot-holds. He heard the window close quietly as his head disappeared below the transom.

At the bottom he breathed a silent prayer of thanks when he saw that the light in Mrs Anstey's day room was out.

The ground was damp and slippery but the moisture-filled mulch made no sound. Bellman swung his leg over the small fence at the bottom of the garden and skirted the paths leading to the bench where the watcher had sat. Once he banged his knee on the low, iron fencing which policed the pathway, setting up a chain of rattles which had him crouching tensely. The man gave no sign that he had heard, continuing his slow progress towards the end of the gardens.

Bellman positioned himself behind the bench, his outline merging with the branches of the overhanging bush.

From where he was it was difficult to observe the progress of the watcher, his view obscured by intervening shrubs which hid the dwindling figure for long, anxious seconds. Soon he could see nothing more of him.

He heard the man return before he saw him, the scrape of a foot on the surface of the path, the snapping of a twig.

In spite of the warning he was surprised by the nearness of the man when he did appear, the figure looming from the shadows to stand silently by the bench. The outline of the face was just visible, tilted to look up at the house. After some preliminary shuffling the man turned and lowered himself to the seat.

Bellman moved as the trunk straightened from the action of sitting. Branches from the bush caught at his shoulders, giving sibilant warning of his move, causing the watcher's head to turn in enquiry. But Bellman was now directly behind him. He struck the enquiring head with the heel of his hand, a blow which carried the weight of his body, hitting the skull above and behind the ear.

The man fell forward, tumbling off the seat with limp arms.

Bellman knew the effect the blow would have – a temporary void of blackness inside the head but senses quickly recovering from the brain-addling jolt. He vaulted the bench and turned the man over, grasping the lapels to lift the upper half of the body then crashing the head to the ground, once, twice.

As he searched the pockets of the unconscious form he had time to think of the army sergeant who had demonstrated the hand-strike, insisting that each pupil should experience a modified version, the modification depending entirely on the sergeant's judgment.

There was a small, two-way radio in the outer pocket of the light raincoat and an automatic in a leather shoulder-holster. Bellman put them on the ground, then felt the man's neck pulse. It was noticeable but weak. He dragged the body into the cover of the bush, leaving it face down, before collecting the radio and gun and trotting towards the house.

He hid the weapon and walkie-talkie beneath the glistening leaves of a laurel before reaching the patio, bending to feel for gravel at his feet.

The curtains twitched as soon as the first of the small stones spattered against the glass.

'The holdall first,' he called quietly when Jo's face appeared at the open window.

He caught the bag, grunting as the weight hit his chest, then watched anxiously as she struggled with the suitcase. For the first three feet it travelled swiftly then stopped with a suddenness which he knew must have burned her hands.

As soon as the case was on the ground she threw the remainder of the cord outwards and swung towards the pipe. Incredibly she pushed the window closed as she lowered herself downwards. Bellman climbed up and guided her feet to the safety of the lower abutments.

'Are you all right?' he said when she stood beside him.

She peered at her hands in the poor light and whispered, 'Yes.'

He untied the rope then lifted the case. 'Come on,' he motioned her to carry the holdall.

'Where is he?' she asked when they were away from the house.

'Sleeping,' Bellman said tersely.

They emerged cautiously from the small lane into the main road. He knew the only danger now was from a back-up patrol circling the area.

He insisted on crossing over and walking up the hill, continually looking over his shoulder for sight of a taxi. The traffic was very thin and they were nearly at the top before a cab appeared, the driver eyeing the luggage suspiciously but nodding abruptly when Bellman told him to take them to Victoria station.

'He thinks we're doing a moonlight,' Jo giggled, holding tightly to his arm.

Bellman smiled in the darkness. She never failed to amaze him. The relief at the apparently unseen escape had left him feeling weak after the tension of the last half hour so he understood her exorcising fear with a joke.

At Victoria he waited until the taxi they had used collected a new fare then led Jo to another one and ordered it to King's Cross.

Bellman chose a small hotel not far from the station, ignoring the forced cheerfulness of the night porter-cum-receptionist.

The room they were shown to had a well-used look but it was clean.

They slept close-locked. Jo murmured in her sleep when a movement brought contact with the wound on her back.

They had no alarm clock with them but Bellman's own internal warning had them up and checked out by eight o'clock. They ate in a café crowded with early workers.

Bellman was anxious to get Jo on the train but was unsure as to the extent Praeger's search would reach. He was certain that the man he had disabled would have been found so it would be known that Jo had double-crossed them and that he himself was in the area.

Without knowing the number of staff Praeger could call in it was impossible to forecast what search-policy would be implemented. It was reasonable to assume there would be insufficient operatives to cover all the stations, rail and coach, together with the motorway exits and the airports. The pertinent question was whether or not Praeger would be able to call in the extensive machinery of conventional police.

On balance, Bellman thought he could not. Praeger was hardly likely to risk involving outside forces for fear they might learn more than he wished them to.

Despite the reassurance of his thoughts, Bellman insisted that Jo should follow some way behind when they approached the station. He checked the area while ascertaining the most suitable train for her to use and buying the ticket. There was no activity to trouble him.

With twenty minutes to wait they stood well back from the platform entrance. 'Is the money safe?' he asked.

She patted her pockets, then pointed in turn to her handbag and suitcase. 'I've split it up. Most is near to me, though.'

He nodded an endorsement of her caution.

When it was time he turned and faced her, ''Bye, kid. Take care.' He bent slightly and kissed her.

She said, 'I love you,' and squeezed his arm.

The simplicity touched Bellman more than wait-for-ever vows would have done.

She boarded the train, returning only once to the door to wave and blow a kiss.

He watched the train out of sight then turned and headed for the Underground.

Chapter Twenty-two

Bellman got off the train at Tottenham Court Road. The mass of Centre Point towered over him when he emerged into the daylight and turned towards the nearby Y Hotel, rearing into the sky like an upstart offspring of the bigger glass and concrete monster.

The foyer was resting from the high-summer influx of visitors. He found it easy to book a room, paying for two weeks. He gave his name as Johnson. The three o'clock rule of residence was waived because the room had been unused the day before.

He took the lift to the eighth floor and thankfully closed the door of the room. There was a single bed, a toilet and shower and a chair tucked into the recess of a fixed writing top. The window faced south. He stood for a few minutes watching the foreshortened midgets walking along Great Russell Street.

When he turned to check his security, he was pleased. The door was heavy, fireproof, faced with wood. It was secured by a lock incorporated in the circular handle. An extra 'in residence' lock was operated by a centre pin. Once inside there was no chance of being surprised.

He unpacked the skimpy holdall and went under the shower, banishing the tension from his body with the hot water. Afterwards he lay on the bed, cigarettes at hand, to contemplate his next move. He had been so occupied with Jo's safe departure he had given no thought to his future since the day before.

Praeger had obviously given orders which would prevent any further interference in his scheme – if Bellman's own theories were right. And it was certain that the preventive action was in the drastic category. But what would he do now? What *could* he do? Search for him – obviously. And if that failed?

He blew a stream of smoke towards the ceiling. The only thing that could be done was to cover the vulnerable positions, and they would depend on how much Praeger thought he knew.

Would Kitholm disclose what had passed between them that day in Hyde Park? If he did, Praeger probably realised by now that he had made the connection between Pool and himself and not merely guessed Praeger's intention to raise him as a high-priest of modern crime.

Mansley? Would Praeger have assumed Bellman knew of the honourable member's involvement. Possibly not, but . . .

Ten minutes later he still did not know many of the answers – or any of them for certain. He hoped Praeger was in the same position.

And there, suddenly, *was* the answer.

Everything he had done for Praeger carried an individual touch, so it would be difficult to forecast with any certainty what he would do. Which left him in the driving seat. Praeger must defend.

The thought gave him comfort. Once convinced that it was a reasoned assumption he began to plan ahead. It did not take long. There was no definite sequence but he believed he had all the ingredients.

He made a list of his needs and began a round of the nearby stores to purchase them.

The portable typewriter and stationery he carried straight back to the hotel, setting off again immediately.

In a large store in Oxford Street he rigged himself out in outdoor kit: track suit; two-piece waterproof outer clothing and a pair of high-sided mountain boots. From the same department he chose a frame-pack to carry the rest of the equipment he intended buying. The binoculars were easy – the most powerful of the smaller models – these from a small shop whose owner appeared to part with the glasses reluctantly. The special sleeping bag he got from a keener salesman.

He added some thick socks to the rolled-neck sweater and T shirts at the outfitters and carried them all back to the Y.

Before entering the supermarket on his last trip he tested and bought the tiny transistor radio which the makers claimed could do everything but broadcast to the Moon.

He chose his food bearing in mind that he did not intend to carry a portable stove. The selection consisted of sustaining foods which took up little space.

When he had finally decanted the last of his buys into his room he went down and ate a meal in the adjoining restaurant before returning to discover the workings of the typewriter.

It was some time since he had compiled a report, but he found the habit returned easily enough. After roughing out a draft he sat down to type the final article.

It was difficult to be convincing without disclosing his own part in the events he wrote about. To accuse was simple, but to convince was another matter. Unless he could produce the evidence. And he could not. Yet.

He made three copies.

Reading it through, the accusation of a massive conspiracy looked anything but water-tight, lacking the intuition leading to his own belief. But at least, without that, the report was fair. The facts, though incomplete, were presented. A defence or explanation could be entered – if the data were ever to be seriously considered.

He folded the reports and put them in separate envelopes, addressing the original to the Home Secretary. The first of the copies he marked out for the attention of the Commissioner, Metropolitan Police, while the second carried the same address but was for Kitholm's eyes.

The Commissioner's copy, he knew, would eventually settle at the Home Office but at least it would have had one stop on its journey, avoiding interference from Praeger.

Kitholm's copy should also avoid interception – providing he still remained in contact with the Yard. Bellman thought he probably did. It was hardly likely that the Selgo office claimed his exclusive attention.

When he wrote the name of Peter Say on the fourth enclosure he wondered if the journalist would consider it a fair return for the information he had provided. And what he would be able to do about it? The ever-present threat of a 'D' notice had Fleet Street neatly tied down.

Bellman rubbed his tired eyes, briefly troubled by the thought that he was wasting his time. Anonymous allegations, rightly, were treated with scepticism, but they could also cause the biggest upheavals. The thought helped.

After retaining the envelope addressed to Kitholm he stowed the others in the pack.

Out in the street he told himself he was right. It was not yet time to send out every report – just the one to Kitholm who, if he found the courage, could do most damage from his position in the heart of Praeger's organisation.

It was certainly too early to alert the Fleet Street bloodhounds and if Praeger was notified of the allegations too soon by the disclosure of the reports directed at the Commissioner and Home Secretary, he could use his position and influence to discredit the charge.

Perhaps by the nature of his defence Praeger would find himself less credible but he was clever enough to ride the storm and successfully complete his long-term plan. And that would only be necessary if the report was given any sort of serious consideration. An unlikely event as things stood. It was one thing to get the contents of the envelopes to their destinations without interference, but something else to hope to start an investigation by means of an unconfirmed allegation.

Bellman posted the single copy then entered a pub, calling for and drinking two pints and the same number of whiskies in less than ten minutes. There was no urge for more.

Crossing the road to the Y Bellman laughed out loud. What a hell of a way to get cured.

In the morning Bellman left the hotel and purchased as many different newspapers as were available, taking them back to his room and reading them stretched out on the bed. The updating was essential if his next move was to be the right one.

Brantner had been released. There had obviously been witnesses to prove he was somewhere other than Bermondsey when Briller met his death.

That was unimportant so long as Cliveson still believed he was guilty.

The investigation was gathering way again after the inevitable slowing down caused by the production of a live suspect. Bellman stopped reading for a few moments to enjoy the dilemma Praeger must have been in when hearing of Brantner's arrest. But that was in the past. Praeger was unlikely to remain unbalanced for long.

Bellman sought the Underground again and travelled to the East End. From a call-box which stank of urine and tobacco smoke he tied up the loose ends; informing the car-hire company where they could find the Toyota, then ringing Mrs Anstey to say he had been called away suddenly. She sounded genuinely sorry.

'There have been a lot of friends asking after you, Mr Bellman.'

'I'll see them some other time,' he said.

Friends.

Well, trace this call, Praeger and send your men running down east.

He felt very isolated when he left the call-box. Even the simple act of severing connection with the Toyota and the apartment gave him a feeling of loneliness too reminiscent of a few months before to be comfortable.

He knew it was not the wisest thing to approach the attendant at the Turkish Baths and ask him to get a driving licence – for a price. But it was the quickest.

The twenty-pound note failed to convince completely.

'Who told you I did things like that?' the fat man said suspiciously.

'No-one,' Bellman soothed. 'I'm taking a chance. You might report me.' He stood quietly under the other's scrutiny.

Finally the note was whisked from his fingers. 'Wait here.'

He returned very quickly, holding a driving licence by the edge of its plastic cover. 'Here, that bloke's pissed. He might remember to check his money when he leaves, but that's all.'

Bellman travelled over the river by bus, alighting at Kennington and using the licence to hire a Ford.

Ignoring the parking facility at the hotel he left the car in a nearby square.

In his room he fitted the Webley into the cloth shoulder-holster he had fashioned, then changed into the track suit before harnessing the gun to his armpit. The waterproof outfit covered the protrusion easily. When he levered his feet into the mountain-boots and stamped around in them, they felt heavy and strange, his feet accustomed to town walking. But he was pleased that, despite the newness, there was no immediate threat of pinching toes.

He humped the loaded pack to his shoulders and went down to the reception desk. The girl who took his key was used to YMCA members dressed as he was and found nothing strange in his explanation of an absence that would be taken up with hiking.

Satisfied that he had covered as many contingencies as possible, he made his way to the car. In his experience it was often innocent mistakes, like failing to return a hired car or an unexplained absence from a hotel room, which caused most problems.

He swung the pack into the rear of the Ford, settled behind the wheel and drove unhurriedly out of London.

With the route south fresh in his mind the drive was easy but now he was actually venturing towards the opposition, his spirits sank.

His scheme was plausible but he had no idea what he might encounter. What if his efforts met with nothing? Or worse – indifference.

Suppose Praeger called off the hunt, relying on the police to discover his part in the murders, or leaking the information to them. But would he dare?

His thrusts at the Pool empire had revealed that he knew Praeger's true intentions which meant that his death was a priority if he was to be prevented from disclosing the information to any authoritative ear that might care to listen, unlikely though he was to be believed.

He turned off the main road and headed for Bailey Fall. To shake the mood he sent the Ford into a corner imprudently, rocking the body as the wheels lifted. He had nothing to lose. He was a target – expendable.

A few weeks ago he would not have cared, but now he did.

So why not run? What did he think he was – a modern avenger?

No. But he was not prepared to wait for the inevitable. With the Praegers of the world you did something – anything. Blindly, perhaps, but something.

He kicked the accelerator savagely, the frustration easing slightly as he struggled to control the bucking Ford.

He waited for twenty minutes on the outskirts of the village before a suitable vehicle passed – a lorry, loaded with bales of straw.

Bellman nosed the car out and closed with the lorry as the driver dropped down the gears on the hill leading to Tetham Lodge. Tucked in close to the swaying mass he had a chance of going unnoticed by any observer at the gates of the house.

The Ford juddered a protest at being restricted to the lorry's speed but he rode the clutch and hung in, watching for vehicles in the driveway. There were none.

At the top of the hill he slowed and let the lorry pull away. The light was fading but he continued until he was hidden from the woods surrounding Pool's home by a fold of the land.

He waited in the car until it was fully dark, then opened the door and set off towards the trees.

The boundary fence loomed out of the darkness suddenly, causing him to stumble as he broke his stride to avoid contact. Using the fence as a guide he moved towards the gateway which stood before the little-used drive at the rear of the house, pausing to listen every few yards. If there were men posted around the house, which there could be after his threats to Praeger over the telephone, they would certainly cover the rear but, unless they were country born or jungle trained, they were unlikely to stray far from the order of pathways or roads.

He slipped his hand inside the waterproof coat and tested the accessibility of the Webley. The holster was not as efficient as a leather one but the gun came clear with a minimum amount of snagging. He pushed it back into place and edged forward again.

It was strange how quickly the senses re-learned to attune to the night sounds. His had been trained in a country thousands of miles away, in a jungle much different to an English wood, but many of the noises were similar: an unidentifiable rustle in undergrowth; faint, hard sounds like wood on wood; a span of silence ended by the crack of a twig.

Occasionally there were living sounds: a brief twitter of indignation from a roosting bird or a distant yap which might be a fox.

But there the similarity ended. There were no subdued trills of living creatures and the incessant, whirring chorus of the jungle was missing. So was the moisture. The steady drip and plonk which could drive you to distraction.

Perhaps there was another similarity: that of men, waiting. If there were it was certain they would not be dressed in scraggy shorts and shirts and they would not have the slant eyes of semi-starved fanatics whose patience made them so dangerous.

These would more likely be dressed in expensive city suits with, perhaps – the concession to local conditions – a pair of rubber boots.

Bellman stopped and listened again. A bullet was a bullet no matter who fired it.

As he moved on again it occurred to him that it was not beyond the bounds of possibility to meet a jungle-trained veteran. Plenty had found work with various security forces. On the other hand it was unlikely that Praeger would dare to use department men to guard a man who was, to all intents, the object of the department's attention. No. These would be men from the ranks of Pool's army. And not the legitimate side.

For all his caution, Bellman nearly blundered into the man by the gate.

He had estimated that the avenue through the trees was at least forty yards further on, but the quiet cough seemed to sound in his ear. He stopped, one foot raised, eyes straining. His supporting leg began to ache before another sound indicated the direction and distance of the man nearby. It was a dull thump, the sort of sound made by someone shifting position. Identifying the possible cause reminded Bellman of his own discomfort and he lowered his foot to the ground.

The fence by Bellman's side creaked and he faintly discerned movement ahead of him. Whoever was there had climbed on to the gate, the action recorded by the adjoining fence. He estimated the man was twenty yards away.

Bellman lowered himself to the grass and began to inch forward, each yard of progress preceded by a hand search to remove material which might disclose his presence. Ten yards from the gate he paused and edged towards the fence and the clumps of grass which grew longer near the protective posts.

Nothing happened for fifteen minutes, a period of emptiness punctuated only by occasional small sounds as the man on the gate changed position.

Bellman considered moving off and approaching the house through the woods; an idea he quickly discarded. Even a top woodsman would find it impossible to make a silent journey through the dry and congested undergrowth. But he was impatient with the lack of action.

The sound of sudden movement quelled his frustration. He was just able to make out the man's outline as he turned to look over his shoulder.

A voice said, 'That you, Mich?' The question was spoken quietly but sounded like a shout after the previous silence.

Another voice said, 'Yeah.'

The fence relayed the clatter as the man jumped to the ground and the two shadows joined. They began to talk in low tones, the conversation reaching Bellman indistinctly.

'Anything?'

A negative murmur, then, 'Think the bastard'll come?'

The other must have shrugged for there was no answer but then Bellman caught something which made him strain his ears. '. . . long are we going to be stuck here?'

'Don't know. Maybe . . .'

'. . . fuck . . .'

'Yeah.'

'. . . supposed to . . . been . . . in the jungle . . . he?'

Another sharp laugh. '. . . apparently. Look after yourself, then.'

There was the sound of muffled footsteps as one of the men moved off. The newcomer had either been a relief guard or a roving patrol.

Bellman waited for another ten minutes, then retreated, carefully sliding away until he was fifty yards from the gate before getting to his feet and walking across the grassland towards the car.

The half-mile walk to the Ford gave him time to think about the brief snatches of conversation he had overheard.

It told him little except that Praeger had anticipated that he might visit Tetham Lodge – and had told Pool so. It did serve to confirm that Praeger/Pool link but that was all. And it was not evidence as such.

He took the Ford away very quietly, heading south then west, finally stopping in a lay-by where he settled down to sleep, a traveller overtaken by weariness.

The roar from the engines of steadily increasing traffic roused him. He was stiff and cold. His neck ached from the unnatural position it had been forced into at the corner of the seat.

It was light.

He got out of the car and stretched, stamping his feet to counter the early morning snap.

A lone transport café reminded him briefly of Jo. The breakfast was large, if greasy, but after that and two mugs of tea he felt human again.

It took him two hours to reach the vicinity of Praeger's house and reconnoitre the countryside, using the small country roads to circle the home from a distance.

There were no hills overlooking the area but a road running parallel to Rawl House Lane crested a slight rise which he thought might be enough. It was not, but the sight of stacked straw bales near the low summit made him turn the Ford into the narrow opening and drive it over the mushy, waste-straw until it was out of sight of the road.

He climbed to the top of the stack and began quartering the country with the binoculars.

Praeger's house appeared deserted. The windows were tight-closed as were the garage doors. Bellman traversed the glasses over features which looked capable of hiding an observer. Nothing.

Conceit on Praeger's part? Not believing his home was discovered. Or a trap?

At midday a small van stopped outside the house and the driver approached the front door with a parcel in his arms.

Bellman centred his focus on the doorway. The man reached out to the side of the door then, after a short pause, raised his fist and banged on the woodwork. After successively using his fist and the doorbell to try and rouse someone, he turned and carried the parcel back to the van.

Bellman waited for another hour then climbed down from his position and drove the car on to the road.

The drive to Sevenoaks was a bore but it was near Pool's home and necessary.

He telephoned the Selgo number from a call-box in the centre of the town, identified himself to the woman who answered and asked for Kitholm.

He knew immediately that she had been given specific instructions in the event of a call from him. She said, 'One moment.' Words of normality but the timbre was fractionally high as she tried to conceal her excitement.

He waited for thirty seconds then jiggled the cut-out and said, 'Hello, hello ...'

'I am trying to locate him, sir,' she broke in at once. The effort to create an impression of a vast office complex was ruined by the fact that he had seen the cramped premises in Lexington Street. The 'sir' was also wrong.

Bellman heard the first, faint click a few seconds later. It was a creditable effort, especially as inter-location hook-ups had to be used.

The woman's voice sounded in his ear a second after the next tracing click. 'I'm sorry, Mr Kitholm doesn't appear to be on the premises. Would you like to speak to anyone else?'

He had no intention of ringing off too soon so he made her job easier. 'Is Praeger there? No, wait ... forget that. When will Kitholm be ...' He simulated strain. 'Here! are you bastards trying to trace ...' He slammed the receiver on to the cradle.

He estimated there had been ample time for the engineers to make the trace. Delaying longer could have made the effort counter-productive by rousing Praeger's suspicions.

He wasted no time in leaving the town.

Once clear of the danger area, as he considered it, he stopped and filled the Ford's tank with petrol then drove steadily westward. When the road began a twist of agony as it mounted the Sussex Downs he kept an eye open for somewhere to stay overnight. His adopted appearance limited his choice but his clothes were respectable enough to stay in any small guest-house. The thought of another night in the car did not worry him but old instincts were returning. The proper preparation for an extended stay in the field was a comfortable night's rest and, if possible, a bath and clean clothing. Sweat-soaked under garments were not anathema because of their possible offensiveness but because they seemed to attract the cold like some atmospheric magnet.

The Sussex Downs did not lend themselves to cheap or prolific lodgings for overnight travellers.

Eventually he saw a weathered sign tacked to a tree. Originally it had carried the message 'B & B' but one of the letters had fallen off and the house that skulked in the trees behind the entrance drive looked almost derelict.

He decided to give it a try. The old man who answered his knock left no doubt that the sign was out of date. 'That was when the missus was alive.'

Bellman intimated that his wants were simple and eventually gained grudging admittance. He was given bedding from a cupboard and shown the bathroom with the minimum amount of words and gestures. He paid the old man the amount he asked for without argument and told him he would be leaving early, not waiting for breakfast.

From the look in the rheumy eyes he gathered that he was not going to be provided with anything so sophisticated, in any case.

After a tepid bath and an entry into a bed which carried the promise of dampness he wondered if he would not have been better off with a night in the car.

Chapter Twenty-three

Bellman's watch showed it was seven-thirty when he woke. He drove away from the house with a sense of relief.

The article about Mansley in the newspaper supplement was his only source of information concerning the politician's address. And it only stated that the residence was 'a converted farmhouse situated near the picturesque village of Barhurst' but he considered there was enough detail in the photograph to enable him to recognise it.

He had memorised a route to Barhurst which took him short of Chichester on the western run, then dog-legging north and over the Downs.

He stopped to eat at another café by the roadside, stacking himself with more food than he really needed, but determinedly so. Before he left he filled his polythene container with water from the drinking tap in the toilet.

At any other time the drive would have been a pleasure. The late summer sunshine still carried enough heat to warm the interior of the Ford and he drove with the window wound down. When he struck off towards the Downs the road twisted up the seaward slopes in a series of wide swings affording him broad views of rolling country, censored intermittently by overhanging trees.

It took five minutes of trial-and-error positioning before he found a spot on the northern slopes of the Downs which overlooked Barhurst.

He sat beside the car, sheltered from the road, searching the area with the binoculars. The village was small, forty or so houses. Several farms stood off from the clustered dwellings but none resembled the picture of Mansley's home. Bellman was about to move when he saw it, tucked at the bottom of the hill where he sat, a mile to the east.

He got in the Ford and drove towards the farmhouse, hoping the road would continue in the right direction and not drop its altitude. In fact, it led higher, but turned sharply to disappear over the crest when still half a mile short of the house.

Bellman parked beyond the bend, on a wider section of the road, then walked back until the house appeared again. He used the glasses to search from the extreme limits to the confines of the Mansley homestead, scrutinising every feature which could conceal a man guarding the holding. Nothing. As far as he could see.

Afterwards he studied the domestic area, learning and memorising the geography with each new movement of the glasses.

The house was stone, long and inefficient in design, but there had been improvements. The roof was newly-tiled and wooden, bay windows stared towards the village, brilliant in their whiteness. A small cluster of buildings stood at the rear. The total was surrounded by a low wall which circled at an irregular fifty yards. By some structural chemistry the buildings seemed to snarl a defiance at the dominance of the hills where Bellman stood.

He wondered if it was an omen.

When he swung the glasses away from the house and over the ground beneath his feet he saw that it dropped steeply, merging with the level terrain some four hundred yards from the house. The high ground was covered with long, drying grass and the waving stalks of bracken fronds, broken occasionally by outcrops of chalk which mantled the foliage with a fine, white dust.

Bellman pursed his lips and lifted the glasses to study the rear of the house but the ground there was level, not rising until it met a thatch of trees two or three miles away. At the front of the building there was a narrow paddock next to the wall, then the ground broke up into rough country which had defied cultivation but there appeared to be a rise and he moved his position to neutralise the fore-shortening.

From his new station he could see that his eyes had not deceived him. The ground lifted gently, swelling into a small foothill of the Downs proper, about fifty feet high. It would certainly overlook the house and make a less obvious observation point than the hill where he stood, but the problem was its proximity to the farm – three hundred yards at the most. It would be difficult to watch from there without the occupants' knowledge. Conversely its very nearness and lack of cover would rule it out as a vantage point from most people's minds, so attention was more likely to be concentrated on the towering mass of the Downs proper. Until a professional viewed the situation.

But he had to begin somewhere. Pool's house was already guarded and Praeger's home did not lend itself to easy invasion. You did not attack men like Praeger head-on, anyway, unless it was unavoidable or a perfect opportunity arose.

Bellman turned back and headed for the car.

He drove slowly over the crest of the hill, away from the lower land which had interested him.

He was worried about the Ford. If it was discovered in the area by Praeger's men it would be natural for them to associate a vehicle hired by means of a stolen driving licence with himself. To take it to a town where it would go unnoticed meant a long walk back. That did not matter so much as the fact that it would be out of reach.

There were several tracks leading off the road, unsurfaced incursions pushing into the bordering woods. He tried one but it ended a few yards from the highway, opening out into a circular, litter-covered picnic spot.

He was luckier the second time. The track was more heavily defined, straight, except where it met large trees which it skirted before continuing on line.

After five minutes of jolting progress a building appeared

on the right. It was stone, nearly circular, with a dilapidated roof consisting mainly of beams and laths, the few remaining tiles clinging tenuously to the apex.

Bellman left the Ford and inspected the ruin. It was empty apart from fallen timber and a pile of rubbish in one corner.

It was difficult to force the car through the bushes surrounding the building to the entrance on the far side, but he managed it, disregarding the paintwork as he pushed by the clawing branches then revving furiously to reverse into the narrow opening.

The passage through the undergrowth had left a trail of crushed and bruised bushes. He spent ten minutes lifting the broken branches into a semblance of their original position. The result was not very satisfying, but there was no more he could do.

After removing the frame-pack from the car he rooted among the rubbish in the corner, finding two serviceable sacks and pushing them between the straps of the pack, then returning to search for an old spade or similar instrument. There was nothing but an ancient bill-hook, a blunted tool whose wooden handle had rotted away leaving a skeleton of metal where the original covering had been. He stowed it in the pack, censuring himself for not foreseeing the possible need for an entrenching instrument.

The pack settled comfortably enough on his shoulders but the polythene water container bumped against his hip and the pressure of the straps forced the Webley hard against his ribs. But at least that was a reasuring presence.

He set out through the woods, attempting to steer a course parallel to the road which led to the north feature of the Downs. The going was rough and several times he broke through the trees to find the road beneath his feet. He gave up and settled for the tarmacadam.

Only one car passed him before he came to the bend that overlooked the Mansley home, a mile away from where the Ford was hidden.

He left the road and made his way over the rough ground until he was in a position to see all of the holding, then he sank into the bracken and waited.

There had been no movement below so Bellman was surprised when lights appeared in the farmhouse with the onset of dark.

He waited for two hours then moved downwards, guided by the lighted windows.

At the bottom he found it strange to be on level ground again after his ankles had become attuned to the gradient.

The sky was bright with stars, the outline of the small hill before the house a faint silhouette. Bellman walked to the mound then covered it comprehensively. He was not enthusiastic. There was one large outcrop which would make cover for an observation point. But an obvious one. The few slight folds in the otherwise smooth sweep would conceal him from the house, but not from the hill he had just left. Or a ground hunt.

Forced to make a decision he chose a spot some twenty feet from the hilltop and thirty yards from the craggy outcrop which drew the eye.

He lowered the pack to the ground and pulled the sacks free from the straps, then removed the bill-hook.

He examined the slight fault on the surface of the hill with his hands. It was little more than a crack in the chalky soil but it did create a small overhang.

The bill-hook was not an ideal tool but he used it to cut at the soil, scooping the excavated earth into one of the sacks. It took him half an hour to part-fill the bag which he carried some distance from the scene of his burrowing before scattering the contents over a wide area.

He returned carefully, avoiding the stringy grass which reared before the hole he was making. It was difficult work making the cut while lying on his side, but he was forced to work from that angle if the entrance was not to be trampled and damaged.

The space he was hacking into the hillside was more of a slot than a hole in the accepted sense, a diagonal cut-out reaching into the earth, which, when finished, would accommodate his body, with a little to spare.

As he worked he remembered the other hillside. A green one, covered with tropical vegetation. He had dug there with little difficulty, the soil moist and pliable.

They had drawn lots, three of them, for different ambush points. And he had drawn the one where the Wounded Tiger had appeared, the slight man with the shrunken arm and dramatic name who held hundreds of square miles of steaming country in a grip of terror.

Of the dozens of guerilla leaders, the Wounded Tiger was not the biggest. Neither was he the most influential. But he was the most cunning, and therefore likely to survive and become a major political issue.

Bellman had waited for six days in the slot. Six days of bugs and leeches, prickly heat and devastating mental illusions in the blackness of the night, and rotting flesh, his own.

But most of all the heat. The sweltering, watery, jungle heat which threatened to drown you if it did not first unhinge the mind.

And he had let bandits pass. Encased in the stinking pit he had admired the advance guard, not one but two men, then, after a pause, a third. Then the compact, tempting bunch of four together. Then a long gap. *Then* the Tiger.

Bellman had been sure the first time because of the formation of the party and the crimped carriage of the damaged arm, but the light had been fading and he had been told to be certain of a kill.

He had been worried that they would not use the path again for a long time, but the Tiger had been sure of his advance sacrifices. And Bellman had killed him.

The thought of what followed the killing made him pause in his work.

For three hours he had watched as the Tiger's men had searched for his executioner. They had refused to panic, realising the single shot was from a specialist and not part of a full scale ambush.

He had sent the 'killed' message immediately after firing the shot but there had been no way of knowing if it had been received; his radio was a damp and crawling box.

The bandits themselves revealed the fact that his own group was nearby when they filtered away like shadows.

He had emerged from the slot a living part of the saturated hillside.

Bellman bent again and reached far in to hack savagely at the soil, chalk-dust filling his nostrils. He could at least have used that sympathetic, watery earth.

After three journeys with the sack he wriggled into the slot to try it for size. More work was necessary before he was satisfied.

He left some soil in the sack and ensured there was enough space in the side cavity he had made in the slot to accommodate both it and the frame-pack which rested on the hillside.

He walked a little way down the hill to view the entrance of his hiding place but the darkness and angle defeated him. He could just see the spiky grass which shielded the opening but how effective it would be in daylight he could only guess.

With the perspiration drying on his skin he sat down to clean the Webley with a small piece of cloth, then reloaded it and fitted it back inside the holster.

After a final cast around he unpacked the sleeping bag and eased himself into it then slipped feet first over the lip of the slot. Inside, he pressed and punched the pack and bag of soil into the space of the recess at his shoulder.

He was still warm from his exertions and the insulated satchet trapped the heat before it escaped. It had been his intention to watch the house until the lights were extinguished but the warmth made him drowsy.

The last thing to strike him before he slept was the hope that the bloody hillside would not cave in on him.

It was light when he woke and struggled a hand free to look at his watch. Six-thirty. His body was warm but his face told him that the air outside had a definite bite.

This was the worst time. Early morning gumminess and no hot drink to disperse the fur. And the agony of a needed cigarette.

He gave a grunt of disgust and groped for the piece of sacking he had torn to approximate size. It had worked itself beneath his body during the night and he twisted until it came free, then threaded the sticks he had cut during the afternoon through each end of the material.

The miniature banner he draped across the opening before his face, securing it in place by pushing the sticks into the soil at each corner of the entrance. It effectively curtained off the outside world and concealed his movements as well as sheltering the binocular lenses, cutting out the possibility of give-away reflections.

He lifted the glasses and focused them on the house. The hessian of the sacking only partially obscured his view. The house was dead.

At eleven o'clock a woman appeared at the side of the building, pottering in a stretch of garden which looked as though it might contain herbs.

And that was the total of the day's activities. Or all that was visible. The ridged track leading to the house fed into a larger one which ran along the base of the Downs and during the afternoon Bellman heard a tractor nearby which he thought was on the bumpy roadway but it failed to enter his field of vision.

When it was dark he emerged from the slot like a giant chrysalis, the sleeping bag peeling away from his body in lumpy rolls. He stuffed the bag into the opening then stood and stretched luxuriously.

The urge to urinate was pressing him but he waited until

he had walked behind the hill before emptying his bladder. He had provided himself with plastic bags to contain body functions but hoped he would not be forced to use them in the slot.

During the day he had eaten very little of his provisions and sipped only twice from the water container, but he knew if the observation was to continue he would need to eat and drink more and be prepared to endure the uncomfortable method of relieving himself.

Sheltered by the hill he used his jacket to cover the glare from his lighter as he lit a cigarette. It was a beautiful moment. He dragged deeply at the tobacco, cupping his hand to conceal the fire-fly speck.

There was a tug at his stomach for the drink that usually went with the cigarette but it was not urgent. He decided he had been unnecessarily hard on himself by failing to include a small bottle of whisky in his provisions.

What the hell.

He lit a second cigarette from the stub of the first. When it was finished he buried both carcasses in the same, scraped grave.

Moving to the house side of the hill he looked at the gleaming windows and thought of going nearer, deciding against it at once. The woman he had seen could only be some sort of servant. The Mansleys were obviously away. Or they had turned into recluses.

It struck him that possibly they were – temporarily. If Praeger had warned Mansley. . . . He must not start on the 'ifs' again. Mansley was a Member of Parliament. It was hardly likely that he could confine himself without raising awkward questions. And where was his wife? No. They were away but would return shortly. The conviction was short-lived. Supposing they had moved out until . . .

He returned to the rear of the hill and lit another cigarette, shivering slightly, missing the clinging warmth of the sleeping bag.

After exercising for an hour, an activity confined to the

vicinity of the hill, he returned to the slot and crawled into the earth.

The second day was almost as uneventful as the first. The woman servant appeared again, stooping to gather something from the garden only yards away from the spot where she had been the day before.

For the want of something else to do, Bellman studied her through the binoculars. She looked fiftyish and had a flat, unintelligent face.

In the afternoon a white estate-car stopped in front of the house. The woman who got out wore a sheepskin coat and had her hair covered by a scarf. She knocked on the door of the house with commanding authority. Bellman could see the servant woman's outline when the door opened. The conversation was short, terminated by the caller with an abrupt turn and steady retreat to the car. When she had gone the house returned to its former, deserted aspect.

Bellman grew bored. The quietly-tuned radio was no help. Briller's murder had lost news-appeal. The bulletins concentrated on international happenings.

He left the slot as soon as it was dark, venturing further afield this time, but still staying clear of the house. During the day he had eaten from a tin of meat, following it with an apple and an orange. His stomach now protested so he made for the ditch by the side of the track and used it for a lavatory.

He stayed out for three hours, walking to exercise his muscles.

Back in the slot he watched the lights in the house go out. Whatever the woman was she did not appear to be afraid of the dark. Or an empty house.

Sleep came to him only fitfully. The fact that nothing had happened troubled him. It was no consolation that he did not know what *could* happen.

Mansley arrived the following day.

Bellman had lapsed into a fixed stare of boredom. It was movement on his right which jerked him back to reality, hands fumbling for the binoculars.

The Range Rover turned off the track and stopped in front of the house. The driver was Mansley. He was easy to identify, as was his wife, dressed in tweeds which could well have been the clothes she wore when photographed for the newspaper article.

The Labrador was there too, lolloping to the ground in his mistress' wake. He was followed by a black mongrel. Bellman thought that the cur was probably kept out of range when photographers were present.

The door of the house opened and the woman servant appeared with outstretched arms, waiting to receive the bundle of parcels and clothing Mrs Mansley had gathered from the vehicle.

Then Bellman saw the man beside the politician's wife. He must have been seated low down in the rear when the Range Rover arrived. Now he was standing watching the unloading, making no move to help. He was young but looked about with the confident air of one who was sure of his capabilities. Bellman had never seen him before but was in no doubt as to his profession.

Mansley had vacated the driving seat to hover near the scene of activity, making the useless, forward darts and withdrawals which go with offers to help that are tersely refused by womenfolk. He was finally trusted with a suit-case which he carried to the door.

Bellman had a good view of Mansley as he returned to the vehicle. He did not look a happy man. The round face appeared unnaturally taut; his movements were hurried and jerky. But his appearance was not necessarily indicative of any special stress he was under; politicians cultivated the concerned outlook to show they were continually in the fray.

The younger man climbed into the Range Rover beside Mansley before it moved off with an abrupt jump, kangarooing to the corner of the building where it turned and disappeared.

The women entered the house by the front door, leaving the dogs to cast around, sniffing at cornerstones for messages of strange canine visits.

Bellman eased the glasses slightly, releasing the skin which had been pinched by the eye-pieces. The newcomer could be an ordinary detective. It would only need a report of a threatening telephone call for the police authorities to provide a temporary body-guard, but he thought not. The man had the assured look of an agency-trained man, someone who was not afraid to use extreme methods to fulfil his duty.

Bellman was sure that Praeger had detailed the guard for Mansley. The excuse for such an action would be easy to invent.

After the brief burst of activity there was no more movement until three o'clock when a green mini appeared from behind the house. It stopped at the side, the door swinging quickly open to let Mrs Mansley out who strode determinedly to the rear of the premises.

Bellman trained the glasses on the car. The stolid figure of the servant sat in the passenger seat, staring fixedly forward.

The Mansley woman returned within minutes, seating herself in the driving seat of the car, talking to someone out of sight through the space of the still-open door.

Edward Mansley came round the corner of the house, stooped, talking pleadingly to his wife, hands working feverishly.

Praeger's man stood just to his rear.

It was not necessary to hear the words to realise that some sort of altercation was taking place. Mansley's actions looked like those of someone trying to explain something to an irate wife.

The stranger bent towards the car to add to the politician's argument and Mrs Mansley's parting shot must have been directed at him. His head reared suddenly as the door of the mini slammed shut and the car moved off, gravel spurting from below the toy wheels : a retreat of two penned females, feathers bristling with indignation.

Mansley watched the car out of sight, the mute appeal of the hands clearly visible to Bellman. The two men turned and slowly made their way to the house.

With the scene quiet once again, Bellman considered the position. He wanted to get to Mansley – badly. The bodyguard did not worry him, but was the situation as simple as it appeared? The reluctant departure of Mansley's wife nagged at him. Why had she arrived only to leave again shortly afterwards? And why did she take the other woman?

He attempted to look at the position from the opposing side's viewpoint. After a few minutes' mental calculation he thought he knew the answer.

The night hours dragged by in a series of sounds, most of them imagined. He could not sleep. The tension brought thirst. The water he drank demanded immediate exit. Bellman swore silently as he used a plastic bag. When he had finished and the bag was knotted he experienced a momentary sense of triumph. If they were out there, he had not been forced to emerge.

And they were.

The first light was diffused by a thin mist, the moisture clinging to Bellman's eyebrows. Gradually the outline of the house firmed through the white curtaining and the mass of the hill on the right loomed clear.

The last, twisting skeins of mist dissipated quickly, leaving the countryside stark and bare with no soft shadows.

Bellman saw the first movement high up on the eastern shoulder of the Downs. He focused the glasses and searched the crest. Even from the restriction of the slot he could see six men. They were strung out, searching the bracken as they moved down the hill. Every fifty feet or so each individual would turn and scan the slope behind him. Bellman observed this with a grudging admiration. Whoever had briefed the men was no beginner.

The realisation spurred Bellman into action. He fought the earth-filled sack from the recess and pushed it into the opening of the slot after tearing away the sacking curtain. When it was in place he tore a slit in the material and began to squeeze and pummel the contents until he could feel the soil spewing out. When the bag was nearly empty he eased it back until he was sure it would not be visible from the outside.

The spill of earth had left only an uneven, two-inch gap at the roof of the entrance. He was happy with that.

The footsteps, when they came, seemed to be directly over his head. In fact they were made by a man ten yards to his right. Bellman kept absolutely still until the man moved forward and he could watch his progress. Like the searchers on the Downs he turned at intervals to review his route, the professional check to prevent overshoot. But the eyes believed the featureless ground.

Once, the tinny sound of a radio came clearly to Bellman's ears.

As the search drew away towards the house, four more men came into Bellman's view, walking in line abreast, searching, but without the diligence of the men on the better-covered, large hill.

Five men to cover a seemingly bare feature. Bellman admired the thoroughness again.

But the bastards had failed.

They had been trained properly. But you never believed – until you actually found someone hidden as he was. And that could sometimes be fatal for the successful searcher.

The gathering at the front of the house was like the coming together of men after a day's hunting. Bellman grunted as he watched. That is what it was.

He tentatively crumbled away another few inches of soil

from the bulkwark at the entrance and refitted the hessian screen.

He noted each man as he appeared, through glasses growing caked with soil. Most drifted forward from the foot of the large hill but some from the country behind the house, the remnants of a sparse line which he had not noticed until late. His attempt to add up their numbers was defeated by the figures themselves as they meshed and broke up again, individuals moving from one small group to another, talking of their fruitless efforts.

Cars began to arrive. One was driven by the bubble-man. He was the only one that Bellman recognised. The faces were similar, keen, confident, hard and he wondered where Praeger had recruited them from. They could not all be directly connected with Decimate L – if Kitholm was to be believed.

Then Swingler walked forward.

Bellman twitched involuntarily. He had studied each man with particular attention to Swingler's proportions, but the light-haired, sadistic bastard must have entered the house when he was concerned with the men tramping over his head.

Swingler was with Mansley, walking slowly towards the assembled men. The MP's attitude was noticeably more relaxed. He touched Swingler's elbow confidentially and smiled. Swingler nodded in reply, but he was far from happy and making no effort to conceal it.

The men turned expectantly as Mansley approached. He spoke to them with the tips of his fingers resting lightly in his pockets. The listeners seemed unimpressed, growing progressively more restless until the thank-you speech was ended.

When Mansley finally turned away with a practised lift of his hand, the group dispersed to the cars which moved off as soon as they were filled.

Two of the searchers stayed behind with Swingler and Mansley. Swingler instructed them with emphatic chops of his hand before climbing into the one remaining car and disappearing. Mansley led the two men to the house.

Bellman could see that one of the men was the one who had arrived in the Range Rover the day before.

When the three were out of sight, he felt as if the whole scene had been a figment of his imagination. Only the scattered soil before his eyes and the drying perspiration beneath his arms told him that it had really happened.

He would have liked to move in directly after the search had ended, while the guards were lulled by the recent action, but there were still several hours of daylight remaining and he could not cover the foreground unseen.

He comforted himself with the thought that he had been right to stay put the night before. The operation had been classic; undoubtedly men would have been positioned to prevent escape before the search began. The inward progress of the hunt carried the expert touch, making sure that an intruder was not flushed away.

Which reminded him of the Ford.

Had the start-point of the hunt encompassed the area where the Ford was hidden? He thought not. If the car had been discovered it was hardly likely that the men would have been withdrawn.

He moved himself into a more comfortable position and tried to rest until darkness.

Chapter Twenty-four

Bellman moved before it was completely dark. The farm-house was obscured and he wanted to reach it before those inside grew night-alert.

After removing the envelopes containing the reports from the pack he pushed it into the slot, following it with the sleeping bag.

As he crossed the open ground between the hill and the farm the claustrophobia of the last few days evaporated, to be replaced immediately by fury with Mansley.

There had been occasions in the past when he had known of crooked dealings by men of power and he had experienced the frustration of being unable to prove his certainty. Now he found himself a tool of such men.

The appearance of Praeger's men had confirmed his reasoning.

If the original version of his part in Decimate L had been true, there would have been some justification for the operation. The thought produced an image of Kitholm and the pious explanations.

Kitholm?

He shook his head. Praeger, yes. Mansley, yes. But Kitholm? Cynicism there must be but that Kitholm knew what was really going on, he was not prepared to accept.

Further thoughts were harried from his mind by the pain in his knee as he collided with the wall surrounding the spread. He rubbed the injured bone and carefully climbed the rough stonework.

A dog began to bark as he neared the house.

He stopped at the corner of the building and waited. The

noise subsided as a shaft of light lanced from a doorway at the rear. A massive, distorted, human shadow briefly visited the ground outside the door, then vanished as the strip of light narrowed and disappeared.

Bellman stood perfectly still. A full minute passed before he heard footsteps. He could hardly believe that the guards had split forces. The Webley was in his hand as he crouched, apparently in the path of the approaching man.

Even as the footsteps drew nearer, Bellman analysed the pause outside the door. If it had been to accustom eyes to the darkness, or to listen for sounds of an intruder, or both – then it had not been long enough. Which surprised him when he considered the professional demeanour of the men he had watched from the confines of the slot.

The guard showed no poor judgment when he rounded the corner of the house, standing well away, secure from an attack by anyone pressed close to the wall.

But Bellman was not beside the wall.

The ground betrayed him as he launched himself at the shadowy figure, small stones and gravel crunching under his feet. The man spun to face him when he was still eight feet away.

Ignoring further noise, Bellman dropped the Webley and charged, a bull-rush of desperation, aiming to reach the man before he could cry out.

They closed in a flurry of tangled arms. Feet scrabbled for purchase on the shifting surface when they were not kicking and gouging. Bellman concentrated on the other's throat, mouth, anything to stop a call for help. His adversary fought back with the growing strength of conquered surprise. He caught Bellman with a straight-handed chop, the blow missing the intended target but slicing down on his collar-bone in a flare of pain.

Bellman bent his knees, then straightened them, butting with his head at the indistinct face. The connection missed the paralysing area of nose and chin, landing on the cheekbone, but the cry of pain was sharp, followed by courageous retaliation, a swinging kick at Bellman's genitals.

He swayed aside but the foot caught him on the inside of the thigh, a numbing blow which made him buckle.

Then the guard reached into his armpit for a gun and Bellman knew that he would win. A man who had recovered so well from a surprise attack should not have wasted precious seconds on drawing a weapon, but concentrated on delivering a crippling blow – and shouting for assistance.

Bellman's flying kick landed in the other's exposed stomach. The collapse was sudden and total, followed only by the movement of twitching limbs and fingers which clawed among the loose stones.

He bent over the unconscious man and pulled the automatic free of the holster inside the coat, sending it spinning into the darkness. He could not be sure in the poor light, but the man on the ground appeared to be Mansley's companion of the previous day.

He lifted the head and rammed it to the floor. After that there was no movement of any sort.

When he had recovered the Webley he stood upright, drawing in great, greedy mouthfuls of air while he tried to tune his hearing to the comparative quiet that had fallen.

It was the telephone that worried him – more than the second guard or Mansley himself. He had noticed the wire joining the house to the poles beside the track. If those inside had heard the scuffle they could already have called for help.

He swore quietly at his decision to leave the wire untouched because of its prospective usefulness to himself.

Once his breathing had quietened, Bellman followed what he thought was the intended route of the man he had disabled, circumnavigating the house, pitching up by the rear entrance.

The door was fitted with an old-fashioned lift-latch which gave a metallic screech as he levered it up and pushed against the woodwork. The door opened.

Inside was a small, poorly-lit room, an old scullery which appeared to be used for the shedding of outdoor clothes and footwear.

Opposite the outer door was another, part open, giving a limited view of the furnishings of a sitting-room; the dark wood of a sideboard, heavy chairs and, in the background, crimson curtains. A soft, yellow light played over the scene.

Bellman paused for a moment. The silence was unnatural. There were no sniffing, investigating dogs; no enquiring calls. His respect for the man left with Mansley grew. He took a few strides around the room, whistling softly, then he returned to the door and banged it loudly before standing to face the light flowing in from the other room.

This time there was a call: 'John?'

Bellman grunted and shuffled his feet.

When the shadow appeared in the doorway of the facing room, Bellman knew he had miscalculated. It was blurred and without sharp outline, emphasising that he presented as good a target as the man approaching.

To confirm his realisation a gun blasted with deafening resonance, the bullet screaming hideously as it tried to escape the confines of the room.

Bellman fired twice from his position on the floor, the two explosions combining to make a vortex of sound which threatened to shake his body apart.

The doorway was empty again. Bellman got to his feet and fired into the opening, following the bullet with his own headlong charge into the room. He twisted as he threw himself down, raising the Webley in search of a target.

He saw the flash of the explosion from behind the chair before his abused ears registered the sound. The whuffle of the passing bullet sounded far more menacing than the charge which had propelled it.

His own shot hardly made a mark, perforating the centre

of the seat-back, but a resulting cry brought him to his knees only to launch sideways again as a figure rose from behind the chair, gun outstretched.

Bellman fired on reflex, punching the man backwards with outflung arms.

He remained prone, nerves raw, eyes desperately seeking the one man remaining.

A sound slowed down the spinning interior of his brain. Whimpering. A frightened plea.

Bellman raised himself cautiously, automatically kicking the gun away from where it had fallen when the man had collapsed behind the chair.

Mansley was sitting, wide-eyed, on a couch at the end of the room. One hand still remained clamped round the muzzle of the Labrador which was desperately trying to hide behind his back.

The other dog was already cowering in a corner, the frightened whines now mixed with sharp yaps of fear.

'Gun-dogs have to be trained or they're as frightened of explosions as any other animal, Mansley,' Bellman said, raising the gun and aiming at the wavering head.

The politician made two movements, one voluntary, the other completely without control. He released the dog and raised both hands in a pathetic gesture of supplication; at the same time his body deflated. The movement was not simply the expulsion of penned air but a general shrinkage, accompanied by clumped shoulders and drooping head.

If ever a man believed he was about to die it was Edward Mansley, Member of Parliament for Orsly West.

'Stand up,' Bellman ordered.

Mansley shakily complied, the Labrador bolting to the corner to join its companion.

Bellman said, 'You armed?'

Mansley shook his head vigorously as though the vehemence of the denial would spare his life. A strangled sob rattled in his throat.

Bellman patted him down then pushed him roughly back on to the couch. 'Put your fucking hands down. You look ridiculous.'

Mansley did as he was told. Tentatively.

Bellman recovered the automatic from the floor before checking the body of the man sprawled out. He was dead. Two stains spread through the white shirt. One exactly over the heart.

'Did either of you use that phone before I got in?' Bellman said, indicating the instrument on a small table behind the door. He accompanied the question with a jab from the revolver.

Mansley shook his head again, fear pouring from his eyes.

Bellman believed him. He hooked an upright chair forward and set it to face Mansley.

'You know who I am?'

'Bell ... Bellman.'

Bellman lit a much-needed cigarette. 'That's right. I'm here to kill you.'

Mansley slumped forwards, hands over his face. 'For God's sake.' The appeal was muffled by the twisting fingers.

'It's a bit late to call on him,' Bellman said, enjoying the moment.

Mansley's head jerked up, eyes appearing over the hands like a frightened child. 'Why must I die. Surely there's been enough killing.'

'There has indeed,' Bellman said, pointing to the dead man. 'He died protecting you, and I don't suppose he knew the real reason. I would much prefer to see you lying there, Mansley.'

'But ...'

'Why?' Bellman drew deeply on the cigarette. 'It would take too long to tell you all the reasons. You're a bastard, Mansley. A creeping shit. A man who ... no, you're not a man. You're one of those apologies for humanity who suck the lifeblood...' He stood up. 'Christ Almighty! Use all the clichés about immorality and then begin.... GET UP FUCK-PIG!' The agony of finding no adequate words changed the command to a scream.

Mansley shot upright, hands held out pleadingly. 'Look can't we talk? Perhaps ...'

'*Talk?*' Bellman screamed. 'Oh, yes, you could talk, Mansley. That's your one asset – talk. The great persuader. Reams of verbal shit which you don't believe yourself, aimed at digging a way out of another situation.' He lowered his voice. 'You won't talk your way out of this one, buddy-boy. Now – outside and pick up the other bloke who tried to save your cringing guts.'

Mansley tottered towards the door, followed by the dogs who turned on their backs when Bellman neared them, legs spread wide in the ritual of submission, tiny jets of yellow urine spattering to the carpet.

Outside, Bellman made Mansley lift the unconscious man and carry him inside. Under the light the man looked as lifeless as his contemporary, but Bellman found the pulse was faintly discernible.

'Put him on the couch.'

Mansley showed the strength of fear as he manœuvred the body-guard as Bellman ordered.

'Now,' Bellman said, 'tell me all.'

Mansley stood beside the couch, the first touch of colour returning to his cheeks. 'What do you mean?'

Bellman holstered the Webley, took one step forward and hit Mansley on the nose. A massive, crunching blow. The bone snapped audibly.

Mansley fell to the floor screaming.

Bellman occupied himself in reloading the Webley while he waited for Mansley's cries to diminish.

He used the gun as a pointer when the noise had subsided to agonised sobs. 'Up again.'

Mansley stood up unsteadily. 'What do you want to know?' The blood from his nose had coursed into his mouth, filling the gaps between his teeth making him look grotesque, clownish.

'That's better,' Bellman said. 'Everything that concerns your connection with Praeger – or Rolland as you know him – and Pool.'

Mansley's head drooped. 'It seems you know everything already.'

'Not everything. I'll stop you when you get to the bits I know.'

Mansley dropped his head even lower. The words came out in a dull monologue. 'I was a member of a committee investigating criminal trends and possible future effects. It was a far-reaching enquiry. Not to put too fine a point on it – the position was hopeless. It became obvious that there would always be people who would benefit from crime – detached people, I mean.'

'By detached you mean the hierarchy – those who benefit without taking the physical risks.'

'Yes.'

'And?'

'Well, with that in view it was decided that we might as well be the beneficiaries.'

'As simple as that?'

Mansley shook his head. 'Not exactly. I am not proud of my actions, but you must understand. I am not a rich man. The temptation was too . . .' He broke off as Bellman gave a growl of contempt.

'Spare me the excuses. Who was the instigator?'

Mansley looked down at his feet. 'No-one, really.'

Bellman lifted the gun again.

'It's true,' Mansley pleaded.

'Someone must have taken the first step.'

'Well, Warwick Pool and I were talking . . . after he had pointed me towards a directorship. In retrospect I know the reason he cultivated me was because he already had the intention in mind, but our views coincided so don't think I'm transferring the blame to him.'

'Very laudable.'

Mansley merely shrugged. 'I contacted Rolland. I knew him slightly. He had just been given the position of a new type of crime controller. Previously he had been engaged on ... security.'

'Was it difficult to coerce him?'

Mansley laughed dryly. 'No. In fact our suggestion was heaven-sent. By coincidence Rolland had arrived at the same conclusion as myself. You must understand, although we didn't know it at the time we approached him and had to tread very carefully, he was a very disillusioned man. He has been around for a long time. In the past he has found himself warning of possible security risks to superiors who themselves were part of the problem. ... Philby and others before and since.

'He is beyond cynicism. Once the initial fencing was over he made it plain that he believed the country to be run by weaklings and self-seekers. He felt justified in climbing on the wagon.'

Mansley broke off to laugh bitterly, the movement starting the blood flowing again, soaking through the handkerchief he held to his nose. 'It was his suggestion to employ someone like you – Decimate L was his child. It came as a complete surprise when the strategy was approved. Our own plans were advanced by then so the plan was adapted to suit us. It was quite easy. Rolland is very influential – on criminal matters, at least. Even the HS is guided by him and consequently the ...' He put a hand to his head and winced. 'I must sit down.'

When Bellman nodded permission he perched himself on the part of the couch not occupied by the injured man.

'Do you know something? Perhaps it's the usual thing to say but, well, I'm glad it's all over.'

'It's not – yet,' Bellman said shortly.

Mansley managed a tired smile. 'I think it is. The signs are only too obvious. If I had known what was going to happen I would never have got involved.'

261

Bellman snorted loudly, contemptuously. 'It's amazing. Stupid or clever. Thugs or gentry. They all say the same thing. "I'm glad it's over" and "I wouldn't have got involved if I'd known". Of *course* you bloody wouldn't, you prat.'

'Yes. You were a policeman once, weren't you? I suppose you've often heard it said.'

'That's right. Now. Tell about the activity earlier on. What was all that about?'

'If you saw it you must know – they were looking for you. Rolland is desperate. Pool too. Rolland thought you would stay in London. When he couldn't find you he turned to the spots where he thought you might appear.'

'Spots?'

'The grounds of Pool's home were searched yesterday.'

'Those men weren't all from his department, surely.'

'No. He has very few outside operatives on Decimate L but he can call on many more – courtesy of his previous spell with the national security set-up. They weren't told much about the reasons – only that you must be found. Even his own men know very little about the operation. It would be too dangerous – lead to inspired guesses.'

Mansley's voice had firmed, the tremors were diminishing as though the confession was bracing him. 'I realised it was all over when Kitholm was killed.'

'*Kitholm? Killed?*' Bellman shouted incredulously.

'Didn't you know?' Mansley said dully. 'He was killed last night. You will be held responsible.'

The transfer of blame was no surprise to Bellman, the calm manner of Mansley's explanation was.

'How did he die?'

'He was shot – somewhere in the West End.'

'And the police believe I did it?'

'They haven't been given your name yet – but they will be soon. For the moment Rolland is concealing it.'

'He wants me dead so there can be no denials?'

'Yes.'

'Why did he kill Kitholm?'

'Because he confronted Rolland with your report. The facts you assembled were very ... damaging.'

'I assembled assumptions. Facts I was short of.'

Bellman thought of Kitholm. Dull, pedantic, rule-book Kitholm, who had strayed from his comfortable world of regulations just once – and been betrayed. Kitholm, with the hint of northern fiords in the name he had been so proud of.

'I suppose Kitholm would have been eliminated eventually in any case?' Bellman said. 'Together with me.'

'Yes. When everything was ... finalised. When Pool's organisation was in an unassailable position.'

There was no comfort in the fact that Kitholm's fate was already sealed.

'For some days Rolland has been assuring us – Pool and myself – that everything was under control,' Mansley said. 'We had to trust him, even though it has been obvious for some time that a major catastrophe wasn't far away. We tried to persuade him to cut our losses; lower our heads and attempt to ride out the storm. Something could have been salvaged.'

'He wouldn't do it?'

'No. It seems to have become something personal – between him and you, I mean.'

'Where is Praeger right now?'

'In London. He is still convinced you are there, even though he sanctioned today's search.'

'You made your wife leave,' Bellman said, deliberately changing the course of the conversation.

'Yes,' Mansley said, lowering his eyes. 'She was reluctant to go. She doesn't know anything. I invented an anonymous threat as the reason for the search.'

'At least she won't have to face the agony of a long-drawn-out trial. You'll be dead, I mean.'

Mansley disintegrated at once. 'For God's sake, Bellman. What is the point in killing me?'

'Why not? You're not fit to live.'

'Look, I can help ... surely. I'll do ...'

'Anything?'

'Yes, yes.'

Bellman let his gaze travel round the room. This would have been one for Kitholm. How to obtain complete co-operation: enter shooting, kill a man, leave the body lying around, threaten ...

When he said, 'Maybe. Just maybe,' he saw the hope flare in Mansley's eyes.

He crossed the room and returned with the telephone, paying out the flex as he walked. When he was before Mansley again, he said, 'I am going to ring a journalist. You will tell him everything you have told me.'

Mansley blinked, opened his mouth then shook his head before any words could come.

Bellman dialled the number and asked for Peter Say. There was a long delay before the operator said, 'I'm sorry, Mr Say isn't here at the moment. Can anyone else help you.'

'No. Can you find him?'

'Is it urgent?' The voice sounded dubious.

'Yes. I will ring back in ten minutes. If Say isn't on the other end of the line your paper will miss the biggest exclusive it's ever had the chance of.'

'Who's speak ...?'

Bellman cut the voice off.

'I'm not sure I can ...' Mansley began.

Bellman stopped him by indicating the dead man then pointing the gun at his head.

Mansley drooped, defeated.

There was a long silence, the imminent telephone call raising a barrier between them. Bellman acknowledged it as strange that he should think of Jo in the moment of tension. During the time in the slot she had never been far from his thoughts but that was in idle moments when nothing was happening – or about to. He wondered if she had found the village and the smallholding as welcoming as she had thought it would be. He hoped so.

'If it's money ...' Mansley said.

'What?'

'Money. Would you accept money. I'm not rich but I could probably ...'

'Mansley,' Bellman said heavily. 'You're beginning to make me feel more nauseous than before. Don't imagine I see myself as a champion of contemporary society's morals, or a man about to rescue the country from a terrible fate – I've seen and done too much towards what has happened for that. But don't think you can buy me off. My only chance for survival is to somehow neutralise Praeger. It's a very slim chance. Your offer of money is just the sort of thing which could make me pull the trigger of this gun. Don't repeat it.'

Mansley kept his eyes downcast, 'Right, right ...' but he would have continued unless Bellman had waved the Webley to silence him.

Say was there when Bellman rang again after the ten minutes was up, but he sounded annoyed. 'Who is this?'

'Mike Bellman. I'm returning a favour.'

'Now look ...'

'Shut up, Say. I haven't much time. Can you tape this call?'

'Yes. That's automatic under these circumstances but ...'

'Tape it. Tomorrow you will receive a report from me. It will give an outline of something important. This call confirms what I have written. What you will hear will be said under duress, but it will be true. I appreciate that you will have to check it out and even then I don't know how much of it you will be able to use, but that's your problem. There will be other events in the near future which will tie in with what you hear. Sorry that I cannot be more specific at the moment. I think you'll soon understand. I give you Mr Edward Mansley MP.'

'*Whaaaat!*'

The voice was still squawking when Bellman placed the telephone on Mansley's lap.

Mansley lifted the receiver timidly. 'What do I say?' he pleaded.

'Tell him everything – just leave my name out for now.'

'Hello ...' Mansley held the instrument to his ear as though it was hot. '... yes, that's right, well ...'

'You do the talking,' Bellman said.

Mansley gulped, opened his mouth several times then turned to Bellman shaking his head. 'I can't....'

Bellman lifted the Webley and blasted a shot past his ear.

Mansley screamed, hands lifting to his face in futile protection, the receiver falling to the floor.

Bellman picked it up and thrust it back into the quivering hands. '*Talk!* The next one ...' He lifted the gun.

Mansley almost shouted into the mouthpiece. 'This is Edward Mansley. I have a confession. I have conspired with ...'

The self-condemnation took four minutes. Bellman used the time to replace the spent bullet.

When Mansley's words petered out and he said 'Yes' several times, Bellman took the telephone away from him and disconnected the call.

'He was asking where you were?'

Mansley waved his hands in desperation. 'Yes. I had to say something...'

'It doesn't matter. I expected it. They will send the police now.'

'I couldn't help but ...'

'I've already said – it doesn't matter. We must move, that's all.'

'We? Can't I stay ...?'

'No. You're coming with me.'

'Do you still intend to kill me?'

'Not if you do exactly as I say. If you don't I will shoot you without a moment's hesitation.'

266

'All right, all right.' Mansley's relief was almost tangible.

'Where's the Range Rover?' Bellman asked.

'In the garage – the old stables at the rear.'

Bellman checked the man on the couch before leaving. He was still alive, gaining strength, in fact. He ushered Mansley to the door.

When they reached the garage Bellman opened the doors wide then got into the rear of the Range Rover. 'You drive.'

Mansley obediently got behind the wheel and started the engine. 'Where to?'

'There's a road which goes over the Downs,' Bellman pointed in the general direction.

Mansley said, 'I know,' and moved the vehicle off.

They were forced to travel towards the village before turning off. Bellman watched for the first sign of a police emergency light but none appeared and they were soon climbing the hill.

Bellman mistook the turning and Mansley clumsily reversed from the tree-lined track before finding the road again and Bellman directed him to the opening which led to where the Ford was parked.

Mansley transferred to the car willingly enough but wrestled amateurishly with the controls before finally extricating the car from the narrow entrance.

Bellman again sat in the rear, directing Mansley to follow the route which had brought him to the Downs, south towards the coast, then east and towards the area of London which sprawled below the Thames.

Once, far away, they heard the hee-haw note of a police siren, then they were among a thin line of vehicles travelling steadily towards the city.

Bellman told Mansley to stop just once, compelling him to post the three remaining reports which told of the conspiracy.

Chapter Twenty-five

The telephone box was one of those English oddities, standing alone at a cross junction in the country where, without the other scraps of civilisation, the illuminated kiosk looked like an alien intrusion.

'Do you remember what I said?' Bellman asked as Mansley stopped the Ford. 'The slightest hint to Praeger and I'll kill you.'

Mansley nodded worriedly. 'I know. I'll do the best I can to convince him.'

'If your best isn't good enough – pray.'

Bellman stood with one foot wedged against the door of the kiosk, leaning close to Mansley as he dialled the Selgo number.

The coin clattered into the container when the rapid pips sounded.

'Mr Rolland, please. Tell him it's Teddy.' Mansley covered the mouthpiece. 'He's there,' he said to Bellman. 'They're connecting . . . hello.' The telephone was to his ear again. 'Vincent? – it's Teddy.'

Mansley grimaced at Bellman as the metallic voice came stridently over the line. Finally he broke in. 'I know, I know. Now wait, Vincent, this is important. I must meet you. Bellman has visited us . . . yes . . . no – Gardener fought him off. The other boy's dead. . . . No, we got out soon afterwards. Gardener and I are now on our way to London. We must meet . . . yes . . . it will take us about another hour and a half. How about the Music Wheel? What? . . . yes, all right, in the bar. Goodbye.'

Bellman was only slightly uneasy as they walked to the

car. He had not been able to hear what Praeger was saying but Mansley seemed to have played it straight enough.

'Now pray that Praeger doesn't hear of the call to the newspaper,' Bellman said as they entered the Ford.

Mansley was as inept at direction-finding as he was at driving, needing constant directions from Bellman.

When they had been travelling for ten minutes Mansley said, 'Once Rolland ... Praeger ... Once he appears, I go free, is that right?'

'That's right,' Bellman said. He let the silence stretch before adding, 'Unless ...'

'Unless what?' Mansley chipped in nervously.

'Well, if Praeger appears with a posse of men – or even if he appears alone and I think he's been warned by something you said – I'll kill you.'

Mansley drove silently for a time, then, 'My life hangs on your judgment, then?'

'That's right,' Bellman said, watching Mansley's face in the interior mirror. 'You did somehow warn him, didn't you?'

'No, no.' The denial was too quick. Too emphatic.

'Mansley,' Bellman said heavily. 'You must realise by now that I am desperate. I do what I say. It is now my belief that you are lying and I'm going to shoot you in the back of the head. The subsequent crash holds no fears for me. You have been given too many chances ...'

The car swerved violently. 'Bellman – please!' Mansley's head was turned, the whites of his eyes visible.

Bellman said, 'The truth, then. The truth within ten seconds or I kill you. There will be nothing so dramatic as a verbal count – you'll have to do your own estimation of time. Beginning ... now!'

Mansley capitulated in the first three seconds. 'All right ... It's one of Rolland's gimmicks. If, during any of our conversations no reference is made to the share index it means that the talk is being overheard or influenced in some way.'

'So Praeger knows I'm with you?'

'Yes. He guessed.' Mansley's voice rose. 'He would have learned what had happened in any case. He's very well organised. The action of the local police being called to the house would have been relayed to him.'

Bellman sat back in the seat again. 'You've just saved your skin, Mansley ...' He mused for a time. 'At least the result will be the same – Praeger will turn up at the Music Wheel. I presume you were telling the truth when you said you'd met there before? He knows the lay-out?'

'Yes. It's quite a ... gaudy place, but very "in", you know – particularly with the young folk, and I have to mix with them too.'

'I'm sure,' Bellman said, still thinking.

'What happens to me now?' Mansley put the question without a tremor and Bellman knew that the continuous tension had not only worn off, but was now working in reverse, arming Mansley with a mental adrenalin which could lead to him making a suicidal gesture.

'You're meeting in the bar?' Bellman said, more to gain time than anything.

'Yes. It's ... do you know the set-up there? It's ...'

'I've been there a couple of times,' Bellman said, remembering how he had purposely avoided the club when showing Jo around.

'Then you'll know ...'

Mansley broke off startled when Bellman said, 'Stop the car. You'll have to walk from here.'

Mansley drew the Ford to a halt, the relief showing in his controlled actions.

'Leave the keys and get out,' Bellman ordered, opening the rear door.

As Mansley exited backwards, Bellman struck him on the head with the Webley. Mansley collapsed with a loud sigh.

It could have been mistaken for a sound of relief.

'It ain't your lucky day, Mansley. A busted nose and a sore head.' Bellman was clucking sympathetically as he levered Mansley into the foot-space in the rear of the Ford.

Bellman drove on, stopping once, by a collection of farm vehicles parked in a roadside field where he hunted for and found a rope which he threw into the car on top of Mansley's prone form.

He checked Mansley's condition before entering London proper. The politician was breathing stertorously, far from consciousness.

Bellman took the Ford over Westminster Bridge from south to north. The illuminated dial of Big Ben showed that it was eleven-thirty.

He stopped the car when he had passed the centre of the bridge, the vehicle nose-down on the slope, pointing to the Houses of Parliament on the north bank.

Bellman knew he only had a short time to do what he wanted before the halted vehicle would be noticed and investigated by the police.

He opened the rear door and feverishly struggled to tie the rope beneath Mansley's arms. It was difficult to secure the knots in the confined space but he eventually succeeded, giving the last one a vicious tug of resentment.

Outside the car again, he waited for a strolling couple on the opposite pavement to pass. Central London at any time proved an inconvenient attraction to lovers and visitors alike. There was more movement near the traffic lights where the bridge joined the embankment. It was possible to make out the white blur of uplifted faces as the curious stared up at the towering clock.

There was also a flash of silver light which could have been the reflection from a helmet badge.

Bellman towed the rope from the car to the balustrade, securing it with looping turns. Then he pulled Mansley from the car, dragging him across the pavement until he was able to support the sagging body against the rails of the bridge.

When he tried to lift the politician up the dead weight defeated him, the body sliding to the ground, limbs asprawl like a rag-doll.

Bellman paused for breath and glanced around. There were no pedestrians in the immediate vicinity and the occupants of the vehicles which crossed the bridge appeared to notice nothing unusual.

Until the bus passed.

The conductor who stood on the rear platform, one hand grasping the vertical hand-rail, viewed the outstretched body with alarmed eyes, his head turning with the passage of the bus.

Bellman bent desperately to his task, the knowledge that he had been seen providing extra strength. He levered the recumbent figure to the top of the balustrade.

Below, the river was a path of churning light.

Bellman grasped the rope trailing from Mansley's armpits, took the strain, and pushed the body over the edge. For the first few feet of Mansley's descent he managed a steady control but as the weight gained momentum the rope burned his palms and he released it, hearing the creaking protest of the strained fibres.

When he peered over the rail, Mansley was swinging like a pendulum, turning simultaneously so that sometimes he faced the building where his voice had so often been raised in righteous indignation then, when the rope's torque came to bear, traversing the water and south-bank buildings.

Bellman slid back. It was a pity he did not have enough time to call Say and request the attendance of a photographer. Still. Talk your way out of that, Edward Mansley.

Crossing the pavement he could see that the bus had halted near the traffic lights. The conductor was gesticulating to someone by the roadside.

Bellman started the Ford and swung it in a screeching turn across the wide road, accelerating away, heading back towards the south.

Behind him there was the sound of a whistle, a single blast at first, followed by another, merging into almost continuous alarm.

He pushed through the gears, careering through the one-way system by County Hall, leaning heavily on the wheel to keep the car tight in, following the road that ran beside the river.

When he was half a mile from the Music Wheel he slowed and slid into the side streets, stopping the Ford on a small piece of waste-ground.

Chapter Twenty-six

Bellman sat in the car pondering the internal complexity of the Music Wheel and its approaches.

He had visited the club twice before – long ago. He remembered it as a confusing inferno. Understandably.

The success of the night-spot was one of the entertainment world's greatest enigmas. Especially as it was the brain child of Harry Fenner.

Fenner was the son of a doting father who had thieved all his life – with some success. He had spoilt his child when he was alive and left a substantial sum of money to him when he died.

Harry Fenner took the money and rid himself of the dust of East London, settling instead in Chelsea where he believed he could make his mark in the stratum of society he longed to join. As a man of means he was welcomed by the black-sheep dandies of the area who proceeded to milk him and treat him as something of a joke at the same time.

Fenner, while not exactly vulgar, had a tendency to do or say the wrong thing at the wrong time. King of the *faux pas* his mistakes were never an embarrassment to himself and because of this he was regarded, particularly by females, as a lovable necessity at any gathering. Fenner found this agreeable, but longed for recognition in his own right as a genius. He envied the smooth and sometimes contemptuous attitude of restaurateurs and club owners towards their patrons.

When the Thames dockland trade declined and much of the riverside property fell into disuse, Harry Fenner's prayers were answered. Hearing that a large warehouse only yards from the waterfront had fallen vacant, Fenner leased it and the Music Wheel was born.

Only Fenner could explain why he designed what he did; no-one with a normal amount of acumen would understand. After applying for and getting the various licences needed for opening a night-club, he set about building his dream.

His plans were a hotch-potch of borrowed ideas, copied examples, misunderstood successes, and a minimum of originality. The warehouse was cleaned from top to bottom, then given a coat of white emulsion. A bar running the whole length of the building was equipped with every drink that Fenner knew of. The giant doors were retained – in the summer they would stay wide open.

Service rooms were opulently fitted-up and a dance-floor was laid at staggering cost. The space available for anyone wishing to cavort to music was approximately the size of an aircraft hangar.

With an enthusiasm verging on the manic, Fenner designed and had built a wheel, thirty feet high, which was set in the rear wall and rotated by hidden machinery. The wheel, decorated with hundreds of coloured lights, carried a honky-tonk piano set on gimbals on the outer face. The music, amplified so that it pulsed in massive waves through the monstrous cavern, would be made acoustically perfect by the press of humanity on the floor, Fenner said.

With the intention of employing individual artistes, Fenner designed a rostrum as high as the apex of the wheel. A spotlight would transfix the performer on his daring perch, once he or she had mounted the steps leading to the top.

Fenner worked hard glad-handing everyone he wished to attend the opening night.

And attend they did. In their hundreds.

The Music Wheel opened at eight pm on a spring evening. An hour later it was full to capacity, the patrons treated to a unique sight.

The wheel turned, transporting a pork-chop-whiskered pianist. A female singer hollered from the rostrum – inevitably labelled 'the pulpit' – while high above the floor a glass ball speckled the walls and dancers with spots of reflected colour from its angled facets.

Everyone was dumbstruck – an achievement in London.

At ten-thirty the pianist fell from the piano when his seat was at the highest point, and the singer, in sympathy, lost her nerve and demanded rescue from the pulpit, something she would not allow, however, until a safety line was fitted to her waist.

Even in the early hours the first-nighters were still weak. Fenner presided over all with an air of triumph.

It was said afterwards that the opening week was peopled by the same customers over and over again who returned because they refused to believe their own memories.

The Music Wheel was a brash, vulgar, ill-conceived, pandemoniac night-spot. But it was original. And it succeeded.

Pianists not subject to sickness and singers not affected by vertigo had to be found, but Harry Fenner did that and subsequently became a legend. Just as he knew he would.

Certain concessions had to be made: the introduction of taped pop music to appease the young set was one, and the admittance of youngsters who merely wished to sample the music and dancing without patronising the expensive bar or restaurant another, but that was acceptable to Fenner. He was lord of his own domain and suddenly the roles were reversed; everyone wanted to know the man whose father had been a thief.

Bellman climbed from the Ford, slowly shaking his head. His recollections of the history of the Music Wheel and the geography of its environs had decided him that there could be no set plan in locating Praeger.

The only thing that was certain was that he would *not* be at the bar where he had told Mansley to meet him.

There was little doubt in Bellman's mind that men would be posted to intercept him before he reached the club, but he also appreciated the difficulties such men would encounter. The location of the club did not lend itself to easy surveillance of its approaches, the area being a myriad of dockside roads, alleys and cut-throughs. A virtual army would be needed to cover it comprehensively.

Praeger, he was sure, would concentrate on the entrances. And he would expect to see Mansley too. Bellman gave a satisfied grunt at the thought. Other than that there was little he could anticipate. Praeger might possibly expect an unorthodox approach so it was his intention to make a simple and direct one; through the main entrance.

He leaned for a moment on the side of the car, weary from the recent events.

He had a moment of doubt as he stared across the metal of the roof. Was he doing the right thing? Was it necessary? The reports would be publicised, or at least Pool and Cliveson would be dealt with; and Mansley.

But it was possible that Praeger would be able to ride the storm. Just. And if he did, well, his own life was ...

Praeger must be killed. And Swingler. Swingler of the leather strap.

Bellman set off towards the Music Wheel, rubbing the stubble of his chin. It was heavy and he knew he must look dirty and unkempt, the heavy chalk-streaked boots creating the impression of a builder's labourer, but he was not particularly concerned with that. The Music Wheel catered for all types, among them the strangely-dressed 'young set'. His own outfit could be taken for eccentric wear. Just. Money was the key. He had plenty of that.

He gave a reassuring pat to the Webley beneath his arm, wondering if he should have brought the captured automatic too. Shit! Let's get on with it.

When he came to where the road joined the dockside causeway, the club was two hundred yards away. Already he could hear the blare of noise. He could see couples and small groups heading towards the sound. Few were leaving.

Of those who were leaving, the West Indian and his girl had almost passed Bellman before the idea struck him.

He called, 'Hey!' and the coloured boy with the outrageous hat turned his head from the girl at his side.

'You talking to me, Man?'

Bellman said, 'Yeah,' and retraced his steps. 'How much for the lid?'

'Huh?'

'The hat – how much?'

The long, thin fingers reached up and removed the monstrous, wide-brimmed hat. 'Hey, baby, the dude wants to buy mah cover.'

The girl giggled.

'You know what these things cost, man?' He turned away, a hand on the girl's shoulder, replacing the hat.

'A score – twenty,' Bellman called.

'What?' The brown face looked back at Bellman suspiciously.

'Thirty,' Bellman bid.

'Man, show me the money an' you gotta deal.'

Bellman crinkled the notes.

The owner whisked the hat from his head and placed it on Bellman's, removing the notes as his hand swept down. He held the money to catch the street light. 'Whatdya know about that.' He ushered the girl before him, afraid Bellman would change his mind, then, 'Hey, honky!'

Bellman turned.

'You wanna buy a pair of strides?' The laughter was high, joined by the girl's.

Bellman laughed quietly. 'Don't tempt me, chocolate.'

Beneath the hat Bellman caught the whiff of paraffin, the heating of the sunny isles.

He had the impression of walking beneath a great canopy. But it was ideal.

Twice he saw men 'walking to nowhere', the aimless

stroll of the observer. Praeger's men. But they gave him only a cursory glance. He had thought of somehow attaching himself to a small party until remembering that Praeger expected Mansley too. A lone man was less suspicious.

The Music Wheel was jumping. As a concession to the heat generated by the horde of bodies, the large doors had been left two-thirds open. Just inside, standing like a reef before the colourful, heaving sea of dancers was the reception desk. All business concerned with gaining entry was conducted by the two men positioned behind the solitary compromise to normality.

Bellman adopted the foot-tapping, shoulder-twitching movement of the dancing mass as he completed the formalities.

His dress failed to raise even an eyebrow.

He studiously ignored the two other men, standing in a quieter spot behind the desk. They were trendily dressed but betrayed themselves by watching all newcomers, especially, Bellman noticed, those arriving in pairs.

The dance-floor was flanked on two sides by islands of chairs and tables. On the right, running the length of the interior, was the bar. On the opposite side, doors led to the utility rooms. The internal entrance to the restaurant was also there, tucked away in the corner.

In Bellman's rough estimation, between two and three hundred people were present. The activity and noise gave the impression of twice that number.

Three-quarters of the total were on the floor, moving in various interpretations of the music from the clanking piano.

Of those not dancing a few sprawled, straight-legged on the chairs by the tables, but most were in constant transit between the bar and the fringes of the broiling mass of dancers.

The colours were exotic; the noise deafening.

Bellman filtered on to the edge of the floor, the area of

neutrality between committed movement and prospective respite. From the shelter of the crowd he looked at the men by the desk. They were still inspecting the arrivals.

Nearer the bar, wearing a conventional suit, was a tall man whose eyes roved continuously over the faces before him. Two more, similarly dressed, lounged by the opposite wall, one directly outside the men's room.

Praeger was nowhere in sight.

Bellman knew that the length of time he could wander around without apparent purpose was limited so he moved into the throng of pulsating dancers. His lack of a partner was no problem. The free-for-all mood concealed who was dancing with whom.

He caught sight of Praeger as he was lifting his hands and eyes in response to a female raver's entreaties.

The pulpit was not lit by the normal spot-light and Praeger occupied the place where the singer usually stood. He was standing at one side of the platform, a hand clasping the protective handrail. His head moved constantly, eyes flitting over the scene below, the thin face reflecting the rainbow colours of the revolving wheel beside him.

Bellman almost stopped moving.

The sight of Praeger standing imperiously above the throng gave a convulsive jerk to his stomach that was almost like a physical blow.

He edged towards the wheel, moving back into the dancers. The floor of the pulpit looked solid enough to deprive a bullet of lethality, if not actually capable of stopping it. The rails supporting the wood where Praeger's hand rested might also deflect a shot, but those he could not angle away from.

By the time Bellman had arrived at what he considered to be the ideal position he found he had somehow become attached to a tall, thin female who confronted him with eye-rolling, arm-waving exhortations for him to follow her lead.

When he drew the Webley from beneath his arm, the

girl's smile froze while her movements slowed like an unwinding toy.

'*Praeger!*' Bellman's hoarse bellow was dwarfed by the surrounding noise. But Praeger heard.

Bellman raised the gun in a two-fisted aim, arching his body to counter the intruding hat. Praeger identified and acted instantly, one hand pointing downwards, the other gesturing to the men at the edge of the room.

Bellman controlled his technique and fired a single, ringing shot instead of the usual two. The bullet struck the handrail beside Praeger, stripping away a long splinter which spun through the air like a small propeller.

Praeger ducked involuntarily and backed away, showing his desperation by quickly returning to the same position, hand groping beneath his coat.

Several screams followed the explosion and those near Bellman backed away, leaving him like an island in a retreating sea.

He aimed again and fired a double volley, the detonations merging.

The first bullet took Praeger on the point of the chin, smashing through the bone, then spreading to tear away the roof of the mouth before scrambling the brain.

The second shot went inches wide.

Praeger moved backwards until he met the rail at the rear then, as though his senses still functioned, gently rebounded from the contact. His legs began to buckle as the trunk moved forward, folding over the handrail above Bellman. The weight of the upper body bore down, flipping the legs over the bending woodwork, allowing it to fall clear.

The piano, rising and swaying on its gimbals, received Praeger like an unopened coffin, the pianist recoiling as the body poured on to the lid, coming to rest with the exploded head overhanging the keyboard.

The movement of the crowd, slowing at the second fusillade, stopped altogether with the cessation of the music. Screams and shouts began as the full horror dawned.

Bellman charged towards the door, cleaving a swathe in the press of bodies. Some were slow with shock and he cannoned off them before reaching the outer edge of the crowd.

The men who hovered near the desk faced him with drawn guns, the barrels wavering nervously in face of the tumult at his rear.

The man covering the bar was more positive, his position not prejudiced by the crowd. He fired as Bellman gained the open space by the door.

Bellman felt the bullet strike his hip, a numbing blow which buckled his knees, thrusting him forward. He kept his feet and fired a single shot above the two who were attempting to cut off his retreat, rushing past them as they crouched in reaction.

The pain in his hip developed as he ran along the dockside. There was a shout from behind as he drew level with an approaching couple, the shot that followed was pulled high in deference to the innocent pair.

Swingler stepped from the shadows as Bellman scittered round the corner in the direction of the waiting Ford.

It was too dark to see the face, but Bellman knew it was Swingler, appreciating the assured action of one who had patrolled off the point of contact to wait his chance.

Swingler dropped into the bent-leg stance of the trained gunman, arms out-thrust, a replica of Bellman's own technique, but his impetus prevented him from adopting a similar attitude.

Bellman fired one, snap-aimed shot which went wide before Swingler's crashing double reply.

A single bullet took Bellman beneath his left collar-bone, exiting through the shoulder blade at the rear. He was thrown down, his body spinning on a hip-bone pivot.

Bellman's revolving body scraped to a halt as Swingler loomed above him, pistol raised.

It was the deliberately slow, sadistic aim which got Swingler killed. Bellman wrist-raised the Webley and shot him in the stomach.

He got to his feet as Swingler doubled over, screaming.

Then he was running, his passage the blundering, desperate haste of the wounded. Even then his smell came to him; sweat; warm blood; fear.

Far back, a scrabble of feet slithered to a stop beside Swingler. Then nothing more.

He entered the Ford and started it with surprising co-ordination, checking the mirror several times as he pulled away. There was no-one near enough to identify the vehicle.

The journey over the river and into central London was automatic. A steady, instinctive passage with no conscious recognition of landmarks.

He headed north. He was clear of the West End before his thoughts regained cohesion, remembering and dismissing the room that awaited him at the Y.

But where did he want to be? He knew he must stop the car and think.

The pain in his hip was worse than the mutilated section of his upper body. The shoulder was numb. Only lower could he feel the blood flowing over his ribs.

Then the street lights jigged, a crazy jumbling of stars which gradually stilled through a hazy curtain. He pulled the Ford over and halted it where the road was quiet, then struggled to fold his handkerchief into a pad and push it between his shirt and the mush of flesh at his shoulder.

When he slid his fingers inside his trousers the flesh there was damp and tacky, but the blood was not flowing.

He started the car again, eyes searching for the fuel guage. It was nearly empty. He must fill up. Why? He wrestled mentally for the name. Duston? Dawston? Durston ... Yes.

Jo was there.

What had been her directions? – east, far up. The A1, then across country to the coast. He hunched his body to keep the pad in position, swearing at the pain that flooded over him each time he changed gear.

Then the mist descended. The lights stayed still, but the haze made them less effective. He swore again at the round-about, the gearstick eluding his fingers. He thought it was the nerves in his arm, the lever had never been slippery before.

To save lifting his hand he rested it on the chromed shift.

The tunnel before him was long and straight, illuminated by soft anaesthetic light.

Bellman grunted a laugh at the thought and pressed down on the accelerator. Below his hand the metal gave way to a fast-creeping tide of red.